Alaska Fish Wars

Nobody Wins

Ron Walden
Alaskan True to Life Crime Writer

ISBN Number: 978-1-95-726332-8
eBook ISBN Number: 978-1-95-726330-4

Library of Congress Number: 2019936738

Copyright by Ron Walden
2019 - First Edition
2022 - Second Edition

Cover photo by Brian Montalbo

Manufactured in the United States of America

⮞ Acknowledgements ⮜

The theme of this book, hopefully, will be controversial enough to make everyone reading it angry about some part of it. As you will find while reading, I believe there are no innocent parties in this argument. I'm a sport fisherman and have fished king salmon on the Kenai River for forty-five years. I tell my friends I am the person who wrecked the fishing in Alaska. It was pretty good when I arrived.

I have commercial fishermen as friends. I have sport fishermen as friends. I have many personal use fishermen as friends. It was not my intent to leave anyone out of the equation in the blame game. Some of the issues and efforts are real, some are not. This book is fiction. The problem is real. Everyone looks out for pocketbooks and few look out for the fish.

I have been associated with the Kenai River Sportfishing Association over the years and find them to be the most accurate voice for the fish. Their director, Ricky Gease, has been a friend for many years and I value his expertise and experience. He is a very intelligent individual and I thank him for the advice and information I was able to get from him while writing *Alaska Fish Wars: Nobody Wins*.

I thank all my enforcement friends as well as all my biologist friends for their help. I admire those commercial fishermen who urge change and give suggestions to make them. We must all do our part to succeed. I blame no one as individuals. I have done my share to destroy the resource and hope I have contributed something toward saving it.

⇒ Prologue ⇐

After the bombing of Pearl Harbor on December 7, 1941 President Franklin Delano Roosevelt declared in a speech before the U.S. Congress that this act of war would forever LIVE IN INFAMY. News reels showed pictures of dead and wounded sailors and other military personnel. They showed sunken ships and sinking and burning ships. This heinous act of barbarism united the American people like nothing seen since the American Revolutionary War in the 18th century. Even World War I didn't generate the singlemindedness to be seen in the United States during the last weeks of 1941. Young Americans were lining up at recruiting offices to join the military and serve this wounded country.

Historians debate, even today, the reasoning behind the attack. Many theories have emerged, but one possibility remains a leader. There is one school of thought that the Japanese used the Pearl Harbor, Hawaii bombing as a cover and a distraction while they sent a force to the island of Adak in Alaska. The goal was to secure a victory that would ensure Japan gained control of all far north fishing grounds, thus guaranteeing unrestricted fish supplies for the island country. This was a realistic quest when realizing Adak is closer by many miles to Japan than to Anchorage, Alaska.

History relates how the war progressed and how it ended. The battles fought in the territory of Alaska were called the *Thousand-Mile War*. The Japanese plan was to systematically move up the Alaska Peninsula to the main body of the U.S. Territory. The United States military built an impressive array of gun emplacements and defenses in a very short period of time. The Japanese military was defeated as much by harsh Alaska weather as by the U.S. military might. Few people understand the hardships endured by both sides and how, in the end, the Japanese military, using the cover of the darkness and the stormy weather, evacuated their soldiers from the small Alaska island.

The Japanese had been in conflict with American fishermen in Alaska waters for decades. It has been said that Alaska fishermen mounted guns on the bow of their boats to shoot at Japanese fishermen. Though unconfirmed the statement is probably true. In the years since World War II there has been an invasion of boats from almost every country in the world: Japan, Poland, Russia, Korea and the list goes on. Each fleet is here to catch fish, kill whales, harvest crab, net scallops and in modern times they have added pollock to the list of fishes being harvested.

Over the past three quarters of a century there have been hundreds of international commissions, panels, forums, delegations, and regulatory commissions regulating the fishing in international waters. For all the carefully crafted words there is only one driving force: Not feeding the multitude nor protecting the resources, but the quest for dollars. In all this time none of the commissions or delegations have protected the fish, but have carefully seen it necessary to impose quotas to ensure the even distribution among the fleets of all the catches on all the seas.

In the 1950s an Alaska Native by the name of Johnny Rock gave a passionate speech before the U.S. Congress begging them to stop the use of commercial fish traps in Alaska rivers and estuaries. His words were heard and the fish traps were removed. It took some rivers more than 25 years to recover.

Commercial fish representatives lobbied for changes in regulations to make net fishing more efficient. The size of the Alaska waters fishing fleets as well as the set net fisheries increased by leaps and bounds. With monofilament nets and electronic fish detection equipment the fleets became more efficient thereby devastating the same spawning stocks rescued by the removal of the fish traps.

After World War II and the building of the Alaska Highway, along with the prosperity afforded by the ending of the war and the return of soldiers and sailors to the work force, tourism became a driving force for Alaska. By the time of Statehood in 1959 there were travel trailers and passenger ships bringing tourists and sport fishermen to the abundant waters of the new state. River guides were available, but not common in those early days. Hunters came from all over the world to experience the bounty of Alaska, and hunting guides flourished and prospered from the notoriety of their hunts.

Commercial fishing became more and more competitive and dangerous—boats ramming boats, boats cutting fishing nets and "corking off" competitors on the fishing grounds. (Corking is the act of setting a net immediately ahead of another net to catch the oncoming fish before the competitor's net could be reached by the returning schools of salmon.) Fistfights, shootings, and other conflicts were common.

Many of the fishermen in the Bristol Bay Fishery were from out of state and were ruthless and greedy. When the season was over they left Alaska taking the money they had made, which in some cases was millions of dollars, back to the places they called home in California, Oregon, Washington, etc.

To some extent this free-for-all continues today, though not as challenging and robust as was once the case. The process of canning fish has diminished and is nearly gone from the market in favor of freezing and shipping fresh fish to other countries for sale on their markets. The numbers of canneries and processing plants has dropped dramatically. Ownership has also changed from large food processing companies to foreign owners, mostly Japanese companies.

In the early days when fisheries managers tried to close a fishing period to save the salmon stocks they were met with strong opposition by the cannery operators claiming they needed to keep fish coming into the cannery to keep the processing crews busy. They claimed if the fish stopped, even for a short period of time the migratory workers would leave to return home and the companies could not afford to pay for their return and would not have enough local help to handle the processing. Local fisheries managers argued it would devastate the returning salmon stocks, but they were overridden by their bosses in Juneau. The fishing lobby was, and is today, a very powerful political force.

All these same elements of conflict are still in play today. Today as it was before World War II the war for fish goes on; still managed for dollars as opposed to managing fish. And the situation is not unique to Alaska; it is worldwide. The same management for greed prevails in the Atlantic tuna fishery, in the Mexican billfish and albacore industry, and in every fishery in the world with the fisheries managers blaming global warming, pollution, naval training procedures and UFO's for the decline of fish stocks in the oceans of the world.

This is not meant to be a condemnation of the commercial fishing industry, but of the motivation of those tasked to manage and protect the FISH by balancing fish stocks and fishing practices. Johnny Rock had a wish to protect the fish and delivered a passionate and emotional speech on their behalf. It appears he was only able to change the methods of abuse; but greed is a formidable adversary. It is not all doom and gloom. There are many factions in this fishing industry who wish to correct the problems by better regulating the commercial fishing industry as well as the other users of fishing stocks: sport fishermen, fishing guides, subsistence users and land owners.

Sport fishing guides have existed in Alaska waters since territorial days, but until the early to mid-1970s there were only a few scattered guides for either salmon or halibut. The need for guided fishing grew with tourism when inexperienced boatmen were hurting each other accidentally. During this period a young school teacher and avid fisherman, Spencer DeVito came to Alaska and settled in Soldotna. He didn't invent guided fishing, but was the individual who showed the locals how to make money at it. The guide industry grew until it was regulated by a state agency. At one point there were more than 500 licensed guides operating mostly in the lower portion of the Kenai River. Sport fishermen became a hated group for disrupting the one-sided use of the resource. The guides were not a courteous group, giving the impression that any boater not a licensed guide was a menace, and some were. Commercial fishing interests claimed the guides were destroying the spawning salmon by fishing on the spawning grounds, a claim not entirely unfounded, but greatly exaggerated.

With all these factions feuding with one and another, care of the fish stocks began to fall. The Alaska Department of Fish and Game set minimum escapement numbers for the spawning fish, but when the returns failed to meet the minimum numbers the agency lowered the numbers. This enraged every user group and caused the Department to lose credibility. In the ensuing years escapement numbers have continued to fall, harvest numbers have continued to fall, and fishermen in all user groups are angry. One king salmon (Chinook) fisherman looked at the problem philosophically and said, "Don't worry. When the fish are gone and no one can make a living from them any longer the problem will take care of itself."

A very studious outlook, indeed.

⇒• Chapter 1 •⇐

Several miles upstream from the Soldotna highway bridge on the Kenai River, guide Lenny Durham was drifting downstream with four out of state clients. Lenny was one of the few guides fishing this stretch of water because of the large boulders in the area. He used a power boat, a flat bottom boat with a fifty horsepower Yamaha motor, in his guide business. The boat was old, but the motor was only a year old. He was a good guide with a good catch average. Fishing Chinook salmon on the Kenai River with a proven guide is an experience of a lifetime. The Kenai River boasts the world record sport-caught Chinook salmon, caught May 17, 1985 by Les Anderson, a local Soldotna, Alaska resident and businessman. The fish weighed 97.4 pounds. News of this catch fueled the "salmon fever" on the Kenai River and caused a flood of guide applications.

Lenny was watchful as he drifted down stream with his clients. He saw the big new power boat coming up-river at full speed. The river is one hundred fifty yards wide at this point with plenty of room for boats to pass. At first it appeared the shiny red power boat was going to pass on the shore side of the drifting boat, but as it got close it veered directly across the stern of the older boat. It crossed close enough for the wake of the speeding boat to severely rock Lenny's drifting boat. He immediately added full power to pull away from the peril, but the wake from the other boat poured a large wave over the transom of his craft and the back of the boat where Lenny was seated, causing it to be filled with large amounts of water.

Lenny shook his head and wiped the water from his eyes and could now see his clients were still in the boat and mostly, except for their feet, dry but frightened. Lenny turned to shake his fist at the driver of the other craft and screamed, "What do you think you're doing you S.O.B.?"

In addition to presenting a great danger to his clients, the passing boat had cut all four of the lines of his fishermen. Lenny could see the other guide laughing and giving him an obscene gesture as he motored on up the river without stopping to see if he had caused any injury.

Once the danger passed he turned to his clients: "Are you all OK?" he asked.

The client from Oregon, sitting closest to Lenny and obviously frightened, asked, "What was that all about? That guy could have killed us all. If that's the way this place is I want to get off the river now."

Lenny only nodded. "How about the rest of you? do you want to keep fishing or go back to the landing?"

"I agree with Fred; if this is the way it is here I don't think I want any more of it," was the answer from one of the other fishermen. The remaining two said nothing, but nodded agreement.

Lenny couldn't blame them for feeling this way and began to gather the rods to put them in the rod locker built into the side of the boat. He turned the nose of the boat downstream and added enough power to control the boat before reaching for his cell phone to call 911 and ask for an Alaska State Trooper to meet him at the landing when he arrived.

At the landing Lenny told each client how sorry he was for the bad experience and wished they would come again for a more enjoyable trip. He said he would refund the fees they each had paid and asked them to wait at the landing until the state trooper arrived to take a statement.

The four clients stepped aside while he secured his boat and held a small conference. When Lenny had finished tying up his boat the four men approached to speak with him. The spokesman, the one who demanded to return to shore, did the talking. "We know none of this was your fault. I apologize for my attitude in the boat. We were scared to death. We're still frightened. But we talked it over and want you to keep the fees we paid. We took up a little collection for a tip, perhaps enough to pay for the gear you lost. We realize this day was as bad for you as it was for us. We would like to buy you lunch after the trooper is finished."

"Thank you, fellas. I was scared too. That guy has a reputation for such behavior. He likes to think he owns the river and I hope they arrest him. I'll take you up on the lunch offer. I'm going to load my boat on the trailer while we wait for the trooper to get here."

He had just finished loading and securing his boat on the trailer when the trooper arrived. "Are you the party who called about being assaulted by another boat?"

"Yes, I own this boat and these are the clients I had out there when Dean tried to swamp us."

"You say the other guide was Dean? Do you know him?" asked Trooper Gleason.

"Yeah, all the guides know him. He's a real renegade. If you checked his engine I bet you would find he has more horsepower than the law allows. He's always bullying other boats and wrecking gear. This time he endangered my clients and nearly swamped my boat. I want him stopped and off the river forever." Lenny spoke in an angry tone.

"Can you give me his guide number?"

"Yes," Lenny quoted the number, "It's a new red Willy Boat, 22-footer; one of the new wide beams."

"Do you think he's still up-river?"

"Probably. He was on his way upstream when he attacked us. He usually fishes just below the closure buoy at Funny River. He had four clients in the boat. I'd bet he's up there fishing."

Trooper Gleason reached for his radio. "Dispatch, would you have Alaska State Parks contact a red boat downstream from the Funny River closure buoy in regard to an assault on another boat?" He furnished the guide number and boat description. After the radio call the trooper interviewed each of the four fishermen, asking them to meet him at the trooper building to furnish a written statement.

After the interview the four met at Froso's Family Restaurant for lunch. Sitting at a large table the men ordered, sipping iced tea while they waited. "Does this sort of thing happen often?" asked one of the clients.

"Not often, but it does happen. The river is so crowded during king salmon fishing season that sometimes it is impossible to fish a given hole because of the number of boats. Every guide will tell you that there are fewer fish each year and the size of the fish is dropping drastically. Some guides, like Dean, attempt to intimidate other guides and cause dangerous situations in the process. We have a guide association, but we have no authority to really do anything. Today, Dean went over the line. What he did today is a criminal act and with luck he'll be arrested for it. If he's charged the guide association can recommend revoking his license."

"I'm sorry the day turned out the way it has, but we four fish all over the world and won't be back to this river because of the danger. We don't hold you personally responsible, but we have to think of our own safety. We're lucky; we can afford to fish anywhere and we have scratched this river off our list." The speaker was the number two man to speak in the boat.

"I was born and raised here. I went to school here and have been a Kenai River guide since I got out of high school. Guiding is my trade and profession. I hate to see the river this way. I personally think the river lacks adequate enforcement and regulation.

"Alaska State Parks claims ownership of the river, but it supplies little management of user resources within the state designated management unit. State Wildlife troopers do a pretty good job of enforcing the laws, but can't patrol the entire river and the volume of boats and fishermen on the entire length of the river. Thousands of clients fish five days a week, twelve hours a day. I really don't know how the river can stand the pressure. I know I'm part of the problem, but it's my livelihood."

"I understand commercial fishing is out of control in the entire Cook Inlet region. Isn't there any restriction on that fishery?" Fred, the leader of the fishermen, asked.

"The state imposed a limited entry system to control the numbers of fishermen in the state's fisheries industry, but I think the system has failed. Of course, I'm biased." Lenny Durham was smiling as he spoke. "When we finish lunch I'll take you over to the trooper office to make your statements. Trooper Gleason asked me to stop by too. I hope they arrested Dean."

Trooper Gleason had been in contact with the Alaska State Parks ranger as he met with the river guide, Dean. He ordered the guide to take his clients back to the landing in Soldotna.

"I can't do that, I have clients on board and they paid for a day of fishing," shouted Dean.

"That's why I am asking you to take them to the landing. I can arrest you here, if you like, but it would be better for all involved to have you take your customers to the landing and meet with the trooper there. It's a matter of safety. I'll follow you down river to the landing."

Dean was unable to think of a good argument to the ultimatum. "OK folks," he said to his passengers, "the ranger wants us to go to shore. Reel up and we'll go to the landing. Once this is cleared up we'll come back out and finish our trip. I have no idea what this is all about, but we'll find out at the landing. I'm sorry for the interruption. I'll make it up to you later today."

Dean stowed the rods on his boat and began the motor trip back to the landing with the park ranger following in his boat. The ranger called Alaska

Trooper Gleason on the radio to report he and the other boat were headed his way and would arrive in ten or fifteen minutes. The landing in this case was at Centennial Park in the city of Soldotna. Gleason was waiting when Dean beached his boat at the boat landing to unload his passengers.

An angry Dean climbed from his boat to confront the trooper.

"You're under arrest for the dangerous assault on another boat and the passengers on that boat. Please turn around and place your hands behind your back." Trooper Gleason wanted to handcuff the very large and very healthy river guide.

With the handcuffs in place he turned to speak with the fishermen who had been with Dean during the incident. "I'm sorry to wreck your fishing trip, but a complaint has been made on a very serious charge against your guide. I'll need to speak with each of you and have you come to the office to make a statement."

"What are you going to do with my boat? I don't want to just leave it here unprotected," demanded Dean.

"Where is your trailer?" asked Gleason.

"In the parking lot hooked to my truck," barked Dean.

"I am going to impound the boat and trailer as evidence. I'll have them taken to the trooper office for safe keeping."

Hours later, after statements had been taken from all those involved in the incident, Dean was taken to the jail where he was booked on felony assault charges. He immediately called a lawyer to arrange bail. Though conflicts were fairly common on the river most were verbal and seldom involved physical confrontations. Trooper Gleason returned to the office where he and the Parks ranger prepared a report to be submitted to the District Attorney for prosecution. This task took the two men the remainder of the day to complete and deliver the report to the DA's office in Kenai. Lenny and his clients had been to the office to submit their statements and then left.

Chapter 2

There are five varieties of salmon to be commercially caught in Cook Inlet; chinook, the largest, the largest, coho (silver), sockeye, the most plentiful and lucrative, pink salmon, plentiful, but low price, and chum salmon, large and plentiful, but low priced and not a basic catch in the upper Cook Inlet. Most commercial fishermen in the Inlet target sockeye salmon. The price is good and the fish plentiful. The Alaska commercial fishing industry generates about two billion dollars annually. This number is the basis for all the enthusiasm, labor, struggle, heartbreak and success of commercial fishermen. It is what keeps them fishing and struggling in bad years and bragging about their profession in the good years. Commercial fishermen are a proud lot and rightfully so. A lucky fisherman in a good district can make a fortune in a good season while a fisherman with bad luck can go bankrupt in an off season or in a poor district. An annual income can be generated in a few weeks or a boat can fail and cost an annual income amount to repair.

Don Webber was born in Alaska and is a commercial drift fisherman as was his father before him. When his father retired Don bought his boat and kept his crew. He is a young skipper, but has been working the fishery since he was a teen. Don worked his boat out of Homer Harbor, but fished on the west side, as a rule. Many of the west side fishermen owned property on that side of the Inlet. Some considered Don an interloper and open feuds existed among the drifters.

This season had begun slowly with low numbers of fish caught. Tempers were beginning to flare. Willie Hickson owned property on the north side of Chinitna Bay. He operated a set net site at his home-site in addition to the drift boat he personally operated with two deck hands. He resented the boats from the east side of the Inlet fishing in his area. He had threatened many of those drifters in the past. Among those was Don Webber as well as his father in early days. The feud had escalated to violence on several occasions. Hickson had rammed the Senior Webber's boat on more than one instance and had corked him off at least once each season. The intensity of the battle had not diminished with the father's retirement.

On this day Don had arrived in his area, just south of Chisik Island before full daylight and an hour before the opening of the fishing period. He and his crew were in the cabin drinking coffee and planning the pattern of the set when out of the semi-darkness came glaring lights running at a fast speed in their direction. The crew scrambled for a hand hold knowing the oncoming boat was going to strike them. At the last second the lights veered to their left, but the boat struck the port side of Webber's boat, (the *Chilkoot*), with such force one of the deckhands fell backwards into the cabin table. The second deckhand fell to the deck, but was unhurt. Don, seated in the captain's chair, was able to hang on and stay seated. The impact was enough to cause items on the table and in a locker to fly about the cabin. The attacking boat did not stop, but sounded its horn as it motored away from the scene.

Don stepped from his chair to check on the unconscious crewman lying on the deck. He wasn't bleeding but was moaning loudly. He covered the man with a wool blanket that had spilled from the locker to keep him warm and minimize possible shock. The second crewman had stepped to the back deck to check for damage to the boat and equipment. He returned a moment later.

"Hey, Skipper, we got problems. The collision broke the net reel loose and it's hanging loose on one side. I don't think we can fish without repairs."

"Did you see the numbers on the other boat?" asked Webber.

"No, but I think it was that goofy guy from Chinitna Bay, that Hickson guy."

"Keep an eye on Freddie while I call it in to the troopers." Don picked up the marine radio and asked the operator to contact the Alaska State Troopers and report the incident and inform them he had an injured crew member.

"How badly is your crewman hurt?" asked the voice on the radio.

"I'm not sure, but he's still unconscious and groaning a lot. The crash has caused us to suffer equipment damage, though. We're not taking on water, but we won't be able to fish this period until we come back to Homer for repairs. I'm going to head back now and I'll call when I get close to have an ambulance meet us to take our man to the hospital. I would appreciate it if the trooper would meet us at the dock."

"Affirmative, Chilkoot. I'll relay that information. Do you have an ETA?"

"It depends on the water and how badly the bumping affects my crewman. I would guess a little less than two hours."

"Call back if there are any changes in your situation," said the voice on the marine radio.

Calling back to the crewman on the rear deck, Webber ordered, "Hey Lou, try to chain down the net reel and secure it for a rough ride. I'm heading to Homer and getting Freddie to the doctor."

"Gotcha, Cap," was the reply.

Moments later Don started the big diesel engine on the 32-foot drift boat. They had not set an anchor and immediately began to idle in the direction of the Homer Harbor on the other side of Cook Inlet. Within minutes Lou was inside the cabin tending to the injured Freddie. Don inched the throttles ahead until he noted the pounding of the boat on the waves caused Freddie to moan in pain and backed the speed down until it didn't seem to hurt his crewman lying on the cabin deck. Two hours later, as they approached the channel marker he called on the radio to notify the marine radio operator of his location and contact the ambulance and the trooper.

EMTs were waiting on the dock and helped secure the boat. Two medics climbed aboard to check on Freddie. After some examination they decided to use a backboard to transport the injured fisherman.

While two medics secured the man the third spoke to Don. "It appears your man has a possible broken spine. We've given him some medications to ease the pain, but he's still unconscious. We'll get him to the hospital and taken care of. I know you're meeting the trooper. He's waiting for us to get the patient off the boat. Come to the hospital as soon as you finish."

"I'll do that. Thanks for being so helpful. The trooper will have the report if you need specifics on your report. Thanks again," said Don.

The trooper stopped to speak with the EMTs as they carried Freddie up the ramp from the docks before walking on down to the slip where the *Chilkoot* was moored. Don was on the rear deck waiting when he arrived.

"Captain Webber?" inquired the trooper.

"Yes, that's me. I own the boat and the permit. The man on the bow is my other deck hand, Lou."

"I'm Trooper Biggs. Andy Biggs. May I come aboard?"

"Certainly," said Don. "Let's go inside the cabin where we can sit to talk."

Inside the cabin the trooper took a seat at the crew table while Don sat in his pilot chair. It was a comfortable setting, a workman's area, without frills. He took a notebook from his pocket and began to write, checking the time as he did so. "Can you give me a brief description of the incident?"

"Sure; we were on the other side near Chisik Island preparing to make a morning set when the fishing period opened. The three of us were in the cabin, here, having a cup of coffee and waiting for the light to get better. We were going over details of the way we were going to make our set this morning when the other boat turned on all his overhead lights and came right at us. He was so close I thought he was going to ram us straight on, but at the last second he turned toward the stern, but he was going too fast and was too close. His boat threw water completely over the wheelhouse on our boat and struck us broadside. The impact caused Freddie to fall backward against that table where you're sitting. Lou was knocked to the floor of the cabin, but wasn't hurt. When he hit us he just kept going, sounding his horn all the way.

"Lou went to the rear deck to check for damage while I tried to see what was wrong with Freddie. I couldn't wake him up. A few minutes later Lou came back and said the hull was OK, but dented, and the net reel was broken loose and we wouldn't be able to fish until we had repairs. If you look back there you can see we chained the port side of the reel in place to make the run to Homer."

"Could you identify the boat if you saw it again?" asked Trooper Biggs.

"With the lights shining in our eyes and the suddenness of the event I didn't get the numbers, but I swear it was Willie Hickson from Chinitna Bay. He doesn't like us fishing on his side of Cook Inlet. At any rate, he must have scrapes and damage on his port side. If you find him soon you will know it was him. He's probably fishing just south of Chisik Island today. The boat is aluminum and the cabin is painted green. It's 32 feet with a net reel on the back deck like mine." Don paused to think.

"Hold on a minute, Captain. I'm going to call to see if Wildlife troopers have a plane in the area. If they do, I'll have them check the boats in the area." Don nodded agreement.

Biggs learned there was an airplane, a state Super Cub, a few miles north near Kalgin Island and asked to have the pilot check the area south of Chisik Island for a damaged fishing boat. The pilot would be able to report directly to Biggs by radio.

"I hope they find whoever did this. I think Freddie is hurt pretty bad. When we finish here I'm going to the hospital to check on him."

"The EMTs said they thought he had a fractured spine and possibly a concussion. I asked them to call me when they have a diagnosis of his injuries."

"Thanks," said Don.

"This fella, Hickson, you mentioned, have you had trouble with him previously?"

"Yeah, a lot over the years, but never anything like this. He lives in Chinitna Bay and resents any of us from the east side coming over here to fish. My dad had confrontations with him when he owned this boat before me. He's a cranky old geek and doesn't even get along with the neighbors over in the Bay. You know how fishing is; we are all competitive, but we respect each other." Don was shaking his head with disgust.

"The Wildlife trooper should be able to locate the boat within a few minutes. If you don't mind I'll wait here until he lets us know if he found it." Trooper Biggs was writing in his notebook while he spoke.

"Fine, I'll use the time to contact a marine mechanic to come down and check on what repairs we need to make." Captain Webber reached for his cell phone and dialed the number he had taken from the pages of a large notebook on his console. The mechanic answered and Don explained what had taken place. He told Don he would come right down to the harbor and survey the damages.

Minutes later Trooper Biggs received a call on his official radio. The pilot relayed a short report including the registration numbers of a boat matching the description and with the described possible hull damage. "That boat belongs to Willie Hickson. He lives over in Chinitna Bay. Do you want me to have one of the enforcement boats contact him?"

"If he's close to the area have him check Hickson out. The enforcement boat can contact me directly on the trooper frequency." Biggs was smiling and turned to Webber, "They located the boat and you were right about the owner. The pilot said he could get an enforcement boat to check it out and interview the skipper. Once you speak with your mechanic you can go on up to the hospital to check on your deckhand." Biggs gave Don Webber a business card. "You can call me at this number when you finish. We probably won't stop him from fishing but will contact him when he brings his catch to the cannery. It looks, at this time, like this is a deliberate assault. We may arrest Hickson when he gets to the dock. I'll let you know what is taking place."

"My mechanic should be here in a minute. I need to be here when he assesses the damages. I know he can fix most of it, but we may need to order parts for the net reel. Once we have a plan for repairs Lou can take over while I go to the hospital. I'll stop by your office when I finish there."

Trooper Biggs gathered his notebook, shook the hand of the skipper and left the boat. Don walked to the back deck to begin noting the exact damages in preparation for the arrival of the mechanic.

Chapter 3

When the mechanic arrived it took almost an hour to evaluate the exact extent of the damages. The mechanic made a list of tools and parts he would need to complete the repairs. "That sprocket and gear mechanism is broken. It'll take new parts to fix it. I can order them right now and have them shipped by air, but it will still take two days to get them here. I can give you a cost of the parts, but I don't know what the freight cost will be."

"Get it sent by air. We can't fish until it's fixed," said Captain Webber.

"If you'll let your deckhand help me, I'll move the boat to dry-dock to do the work. I should have the welding and fixable repairs made by the time the parts arrive. They should be here the day after tomorrow."

Don was nodding agreement. "Hey Lou, stay with the boat and help him move it to dry-dock. I'm going to the hospital to see Freddie. Call me if you need anything."

"Sure thing, Cap," replied Lou.

Turning back to the mechanic Don spoke again, "OK, I'm leaving things in your hands. Call me if you need anything at all."

"My helper is on his way down here now and will meet us at the dry-dock. You go and see your man. I'll call if I need anything else."

By the time Don reached the Emergency Room at the hospital Freddie had been X-rayed and examined by the orthopedic doctor. The ER doc and the orthopedic surgeon were in a conference when he arrived. The nurse gave Don an explanation of Freddie's injuries and asked him to wait to talk with the doctors about what treatment to expect. He went back to the small exam room and sat next to the injured patient, waiting. The waiting would continue until very late in the night while the surgeon applied his skills. Finally, at 1:00 a.m. the doctors told him he should go home and wait for a call. The patient would be kept sedated for two more days until the healing began.

The mechanic and his two helpers, including Lou, had worked long hours completing the repairs to the hull, rail and net reel. Long hours of welding, pounding and pulling, and bending were needed to complete the repair. Don spent his time running for parts and assisting where he could. He was pleased the repairs were completed by the end of the second day, but the new hydraulic parts for the reel had not yet arrived. Frustrated, Don took the four of them to dinner as a reward for a job well done. They sat in Fat Olive's Restaurant in Homer eating calzone and pizza with a glass of Merlot to wash it all down. The dinner was delicious and the crew relaxed for the first time since the incident occurred.

"The troopers called to tell me they're still investigating, but they have evidence Willie Hickson was responsible and told me there has been several other incidents around Cook Inlet and on the Kenai River. They say it has been a violent season up until now. They want to meet with me this week to discuss what to do about these aggressive attacks. If the parts aren't here in the morning I am going to go to the hospital and see Freddie and then on to the trooper office to meet with Trooper Biggs. If the parts arrive after I leave just go ahead and install them and adjust the reel so we can go fishing."

"I'll check the mail first thing in the morning and if the parts haven't arrived I'll call the company to get a delivery date. Sorry about the delay, Don, but some things are out of my hands." Wesley Beason was the mechanic and had been steadfast in his attempt to repair the boat in time for the next fishing period.

"I don't blame you, Wes. I think we all need a good night sleep and start fresh tomorrow. Just keep me posted on the parts and let me know if you need anything else." It was true that all the men were tired and edgy. Each went home for the prescribed sleep.

Don Webber was up early the next morning to have breakfast at home. After breakfast and a shower he read the newspaper and left the house to go to the hospital where he hoped to meet the doctor on his morning rounds.

In the hospital Captain Don Webber was directed to the room of his deckhand, Freddie Deeks. He entered the room quietly, but Freddie was sitting up in bed eating his breakfast and smiled when Don entered.

"Mornin' Cap," he muttered through a mouthful of scrambled eggs.

"You seem cheerful this morning," greeted the captain.

"That's 'cause their feeding me. I just woke up last night and man, was I ever hungry." Freddie took another forkful of egg.

"What did the doctor say about your surgery?" asked Don.

"Nothing yet, he said he would be in this morning to see me and explain it all, but I still can't get up to go to the bathroom."

"You've been out of it for four days. We've been worried about you, Freddie." The two men chatted a few minutes while Freddie finished his meal and until the doctor made his appearance.

"Good morning, Fredrick," greeted the doctor.

"Mornin' Doc," he replied.

The doctor turned to Don, "Good morning to you also, Captain Webber. I'm glad you're here. With Fredrick's permission we will discuss his condition and prognosis."

"Sure, Doc, the Cap is the closest thing to family I have in Alaska," replied Freddie. "Hey, but don't call me Frederick. My mom don't even call me that. Call me Freddie."

The doctor smiled, "OK, Freddie, let's talk about your condition." He studied a file he was holding. "You have a crushed vertebrae in your lower back. We repaired it as well as possible and put a stabilizing plate on either side of it with two screws on each side to hold it in place. You're going to be uncomfortable for a while, but once it has healed you will be as strong as ever, though you may have some limitations on your agility. It is in the lower lumbar area, L4 vertebrae to be exact, but you will recover. With therapy you should be able to return to work in about two months' time."

"Hey, Doc, fishing season will be over by that time. I have to get back to work." Freddie was genuinely concerned about his livelihood.

"Don't worry about it, Freddie," said Webber. "I have insurance that will cover the hospital and a policy to cover your wages until you get well. Your job right now is to get well and strong for next season. I'll try to find someone to take your place for the rest of this season."

The doctor listened patiently, but now continued, "I am sending a therapist to get you out of bed this morning. He'll help you get up and start you walking." He turned to Don, "Captain, I would like to speak with you out at the desk, if you don't mind."

"Of course, Doc," replied the Captain.

When the doctor finished, Don followed him to the nurses' station in the hall. "I didn't want to have this conversation in the room with the patient, Captain. The truth is that he may not be able to return to work next year. It depends on how well he recovers from the surgery and how well he responds to therapy. He has had a catastrophic injury. We repaired it, but how well he heals is an unknown at this point. I don't mean to be pessimistic about his recovery, but I rate his ability to return to fishing at about 50 percent. Only time will tell how it turns out. We were hesitant to do surgery in the first place because of the concussion he suffered, but decided the injured spine had priority. He suffered some very serious injuries."

Captain Webber stared at the floor for a long moment. "I'm sorry to hear that, Doc. Freddie has worked for me for a long time and is a good hand as well as a good friend. I want him to have all the care possible. What the insurance won't cover I will. If I have to sue Hickson to recover the damages, I will." Don paused again, "Thanks for being honest with me, Doctor."

"I understand your concern. If there is anything we at the hospital can do to help, please let me know. I just thought you should be aware of the possible outcome."

Don nodded, saddened as he returned to Freddie's room.

"What was that all about?" asked Freddie.

"He was just asking about insurance stuff," Don lied.

"Oh," grunted Freddie.

"Sorry, Freddie, but I have to go. I have to see the trooper this morning. He said they have evidence that Hickson was the one who rammed us. I'll keep you in the loop about the investigation." Don stood to leave.

"Cap?" inquired Freddie.

"Yes, Freddie."

"I just want to know, Cap, am I really going to be all right again?"

"I'm counting on it, Freddie, I'm counting on it."

Don had just seated himself in the driver seat of his pickup when his cell phone rang. It was Lou telling him the parts had arrived and the repairs should be completed by the end of the day.

"That's good news, Lou. Freddie has a lot of healing to do and probably won't be back this season. We need to find another deckhand to take his place for the rest of the season. See if you can find someone you can work with, will you?"

"Sure thing, Cap, I might know someone, as a matter of fact."

Don started his truck and drove to the trooper office to meet with Trooper Biggs.

"We've sent a report to the District Attorney for review, but we're filing assault charges against Willie Hickson. You should feel free to file a separate civil case against him for damages. By the way, how is your deckhand?"

"I just came from the hospital and he's awake and eating. The doctor said he won't be able to come back to work this season. When I leave here I have to contact my insurance company to file a claim for the repairs being made to the boat and another to take care of Freddie's hospital stay and loss of wages. I'll ask them what to do about filing a civil suit. They may want to do that to recover what they will have to pay."

"For what it's worth, I am going to meet with our legislator this afternoon. We have had several violent incidents, both in Cook Inlet and on the Kenai River. We have to find a way to stop this behavior. Tempers are getting out of hand. Fish stocks are dwindling and fishermen's numbers are still growing. It can only get worse if we don't put a stop to it now. Limited entry was supposed to keep this from happening, but as fish stocks decline and the competition increases it is destined to increase. The same is true for the guided fishing on the Kenai River. Conflicts are increasing there also. I'm hoping our local senator will do something about it before it becomes a full-fledged war."

"You have my vote, Trooper. It's not easy getting a flotation device on over my body armor." Don was being facetious, but made his point.

Trooper Andy Biggs had consulted the Wildlife trooper captain. It seemed no one wanted to volunteer to do anything to improve the situation. No one wanted to be responsible for what was happening in the fishing industry. Perhaps a legislator from this area would want to attempt at making this industry more civilized. When the limited entry and commercial fish regulations were formulated there were too many commercial fishing boat owners who were in the legislature; too many set net owners in the legislature; too much lobbying money directed at saving the owners of the local fisheries, many of whom were non-resident fishermen from Seattle and elsewhere. This same group had poured millions into an attempt to stop the federal government from outlawing the fish traps in the mouth of many rivers in the state. One of the largest was the trap at the mouth of the Kenai River. It was owned by the local cannery and had bought a lot of legislative clout. Things were different now, but lobbyists still bought votes in the state legislature. It was time someone did something.

Trooper Biggs had an appointment with a local legislator, Dalton Price, this afternoon in his Homer office. The front office was vacant when he arrived, but Price was expecting him and his office door was open in order to hear him enter.

"Come on back to the office," called Price.

Andy Biggs walked to the open office door and peered inside.

"Come on in, Trooper. My receptionist has gone out to run some errands. Would you like a cup of coffee?" Price remained seated behind the desk.

Biggs entered the office and took a seat in front of the desk. "No thanks Mr. Price. I won't take a lot of your time, but I think what I have to say is important and you may be able to help resolve an on-going problem."

Dalton Price closed the file he had been working with and looked up. "Now, what can I do to help the troopers?" he asked.

"Being from Homer you must be familiar with the escalating fishing problems in the Cook Inlet and on the Kenai River. I'm referring to the increase in the number of violent incidents occurring this season. There was a near collision on the Kenai River the other day when one guide attempted to intimidate another, endangering his clients in the process. And, I am investigating a case right now of a commercial fishing boat attacking another one over near Chisik Island. One of the crew members was seriously injured in that incident. These incidents have been on a steady increase for the past several years. Someone is going to be killed and I would like to find a way to stop this kind of behavior before that happens. I don't believe I'm the first to bring this up." Biggs paused a moment.

"Yes," began Dalton Price, "I have concerns just like you. This all dates back before the Limited Entry laws were passed. The fishing used to be the largest industry in the State of Alaska and only moved to second when oil was discovered and later when the pipeline opened it fell further behind. Back then the state was poor and fishermen controlled the largest voting bloc in both houses in the legislature. Powerful men manipulated the tax structure to exclude fish from the non-renewable resource taxes, some called them depletion taxes. This is a fifty-year-old fight that has never been won except by the fishing lobby. So, how do you propose I go about changing all that now?"

"That is precisely why I came to you. I don't have an answer, but I'm convinced it has to change or people are going to die. It nearly happened this week." Biggs had a stern look on his face and resolve in his voice.

Dalton Price gave a huge sigh, "OK, you must have some definition of the problem and some idea of how to go about fixing it. Let's start there and see if there is a way to change it.

⇶ Chapter 4 ⇠

Willie Hickson had not come to the cannery since the incident with the *Chilkoot*. He and his deckhand, his son-in-law Burt Calhoun, had sold their catch to the fish tender in the Inlet and returned to the family property in Chinitna Bay. Troopers had flown to the property twice to interview them, but had not arrested the pair.

"What we gonna do if the cops come over here and arrest you?" asked Burt.

"I thought o' that," replied Willie. "I want you to keep fishing. Get that crazy neighbor kid down the beach to work with you. I know you don't like him, but he'll get you by until I get back here. I don't think they have any evidence to prove it was us that bumped Webber's boat or they would have already taken me away. Webber can't identify us or we would be in jail now. Tomorrow we clean the boat and fuel up. We fix the nets and get ready for the next period. We ain't got nothin' to worry about. I been fishing this side of the Inlet for all these years and ain't nobody goin' to get in on my fishing grounds. We done good this period. We're goin' to keep fishin' 'til the end of the season. You and Sarah come over for dinner tonight and we'll have a drink. OK?"

"Sounds good, Pop," said Burt.

That evening at the family dinner table the conversation was about domestic problems— the water pump needed work and the clothes line out back needed new wire. After dinner the ladies, Ma Hickson and her daughter, Sarah, were doing dishes in the kitchen while Willie and Burt poured themselves a tall whiskey and stepped out to sit on the porch to sip the drink and smoke a cigarette. Ma didn't like them to smoke in the house.

"I talked to the neighbor kid and he said he wasn't working this summer and would be able to come in and work for me if we needed him," said Burt after taking a long slug of whiskey.

Willie sucked down half his glass before answering. "That's good, Burt. We may not need him, but at least if they take me to jail you can keep fishing. You know you have to set two miles north when we go out again, right?"

"Yeah, Pop. You taught me how to fish this side. I can handle it. Me and Sarah are going home early tonight. I'm really tired. Seems like we work harder and harder for the same money each year."

"I know what you mean, Son. I been doin' this for a lot of years and it gets tougher each year. Maybe I'm just getting old." Willie reached for the bottle to fill the two glasses again. "I remember when some of us old boys would sneak up the mouth of some of the rivers on this side at night and drop a net in on the incoming tide. Boy, we caught a lot of fish. Nobody ever paid us much attention 'cause there was always a lot of fish. Then the sportfish guides on the Big Su and Deshka Rivers started to complain about no fish in the rivers. Fish cops got really picky then. They arrested anyone anywhere near the mouth of a river. It kept gitin' worse and Alaska Fish and Game shut down the whole upper region; no commercial fishing. They moved all the set netters to the east side and gave them sites outside of the existing nets. That made everybody over there mad. River guides claimed the set net sites cut off all the fish in the Inlet bound for the Kasilof and Kenai Rivers. Fish and Game didn't do nothing to help out the drift fishermen like you and me. We just try to find the fish and make a catch, that's all. And they wonder why I don't like those guys from the east side fishing over here. I'll run 'em off if I can."

"I don't like fighting the other fishermen, though," remarked Burt while sipping his fresh drink.

"I don't either, son, but we have to protect what's ours. We have to keep those boats from the other side out of our fishing area. Only way to do that is to scare them out like we did with the *Chilkoot*. By damn, we showed 'em." Hickson raised his glass in salute. "We better finish up for the night. We have a lot of work to do on the boat tomorrow. We need to check one more time to see if there are any scratches on the hull that they might find."

"OK, Pop. Sarah and me will be back in the morning. Have a good night." With that he tipped up his glass and drained the last drop and stood to leave.

At the Homer Harbor the following day Don Webber checked his stock of supplies on the boat while the three-man crew worked on the net reel hydraulic system. It was nearly noon when the mechanic came to the wheelhouse to tell the captain the job was finished and the new power system on the net reel was working properly. Don stepped out onto the back deck to make a test of the hydraulics and found them to be as good as new.

"I'll have to figure out how much you owe me. It will take the bookkeeper a couple of days to get all the bills together for a total. I'm thinking you're going to fish tomorrow and won't be in town. Just cut me a check when you get back into port." The mechanic was wiping the oil off his hands on a red shop towel while he spoke. "You should take the boat out and lay out the net for a dry run sometime this afternoon. Just to make sure it all works like it did before."

"We can do that right now, if you want to go out with us in case it needs fine-tuning."

"That would be a good idea, Don."

Webber told the deckhand, Lou, to make ready for a test run with the boat. He started the engine to warm it up then reached for his cell phone to call the trooper and let him know what was happening. Dropping a net in the Inlet outside of an official fishing period could cost him his permit. By the time the captain finished speaking with the Fish and Wildlife trooper Lou had the boat untied and gear stowed for the test run.

They ran out past the channel marker a short way before dropping the net over the stern of the *Chilkoot*. They ran the net out and retrieved it three times before agreeing it was trouble free. It was now late afternoon and Webber had some shopping to do before quitting time. He offered to buy dinner for the mechanic as a bonus for his efforts, but the man turned down the offer.

"My daughter has a soccer game this evening and I can't miss that." The men shook hands and parted.

Don had never married and lived alone in a small house near the beach on the East End Road. Lou, too, was single and rented a cabin on the other end of Homer. Lou assisted with the shopping and helped load the purchases into the truck before the two men went to dinner, again at Fat Olive's. At dinner the two men discussed the strategy to be used for fishing the day after tomorrow.

"I think we should leave the harbor this evening on the tide. Evening high tide is at 7:16. That would give us plenty of time to make sure the boat is running correctly and the gear is ready. I plan to fish just north of where we were when Hickson hit us. You know the place; we have to move east because of the depth in that area. Willie fishes that area, so we need to be on the lookout for him and his boat. I've met his deckhand. He's Willie's son-in-law. He isn't as aggressive as Willie, but he does what his papa tells him to do. There are usually only two men on the boat, but they work hard and are good at what they do."

"Do you think he'll try to ram us again?" asked Lou.

"I doubt it, but you can never tell what a crazy person will do. This time we'll be on the cautious side. When we get ready to drop the net and are waiting for opening time, I want someone on the back deck at all times. We need to keep a lookout for Hickson and his boat. We'll be ready for him this time. Trooper Biggs said Fish and Wildlife troopers were going to have a boat in the area for the opener, but they can't see the entire district no matter where they are. We will have to look out for ourselves. He just wants to chase all the East side fishermen from fishing the West side. Well, I'm not quitting. Our boat is faster and more maneuverable, so we can get away from him if it becomes necessary, but we have to see him coming.

"Once we get over there me and Eddie will take turns watching. Once the sun comes up and the fishing starts Willie will be too busy to worry about us, but he might try to cork us off or run over our nets. I don't trust the guy. Above all, I don't want to have another crew-member hurt." Don Webber had deep concerns for his boat and crew. "I plan to give Freddie his share of the catch, so each of us will be a little short. We will have to catch more fish to make up for it."

"I wondered about that, Cap. Thanks for thinking of Freddie." Lou and Freddie had been longtime friends both on the boat and on shore.

The two men joked and laughed the rest of the dinner hour. Don planned a late start for tomorrow and was looking forward to a good rest tonight.

In the morning the captain was on the boat re-checking the repairs and new hydraulic system when Trooper Biggs came down the dock and asked to come aboard.

"How about some coffee?" asked Webber.

"I'd like that," said Biggs as he climbed aboard the *Chilkoot*.

Inside the cabin Don poured two cups of hot, fresh coffee. "Have you arrested Willie yet?" he asked the trooper.

"No, the DA is still sitting on the paperwork. You know how busy his office is these days. If you could have identified the boat or the skipper we could have arrested him on your ID, but without that we have to wait for the DA to decide if we have enough evidence, which I think we do." Biggs picked up his cup of coffee and tested it.

"I'm ready to go fishing and we're leaving this evening on the tide. I plan to be ready to lay net when the fishing period opens in the morning. I've already told my crew to be vigilant when we get to the fishing grounds."

"I have to warn you, Don. You can't pick a fight with Hickson. I don't want to have to arrest you or any of your crew."

"I had a discussion with my crewman last night about that. I plan to avoid Willie and keep a watch for his boat. My plan is to run from a fight, but that means we have to see him coming. I don't want another crewman injured. The doctors say Freddie will be out of work for the rest of the season."

Biggs sipped his hot coffee, "Have you contacted your lawyer about a civil suit?"

"No, I've been too busy with the repairs, but after this period I plan to do just that." There was resolve in Captain Webber's statement.

Trooper Biggs finished the last of his coffee and stood to leave the cabin. "I just wanted to come by and see if you were ready to go fishing. Have a good fishing trip and call me when you get back to Homer."

"Thanks for the visit, Andy. I'll try to avoid any more damage or injuries on this trip."

"I've told the Wildlife trooper to keep an eye out for Hickson and his boat, but they have a big area of patrol and someone is always calling for help. Be careful and good luck." Biggs was a very large man and had to duck to exit the cabin.

Late in the afternoon Lou boarded the *Chilkoot* accompanied by the new deckhand, Eddie. Don briefed the two men on his plan for the trip and asked them to re-check everything on the boat to be certain they were ready to go fishing. Lines were checked, fluid levels were checked, fuel quantity was checked and equipment was checked with everything seemingly in order. By high tide they were ready to leave the harbor.

Chapter 5

Andy Biggs had been a state trooper for a very long time. In his seventeen years of service he had been stationed in urban as well as remote places. He had worked city streets of Fairbanks and Anchorage as well as the coastal villages of western Alaska. Andy had learned that the changes he had seen over the years had less to do with the law than how much money the State of Alaska cared to spend. In recent times laws had been changed to keep criminals out of jail because it cost too much to house them. Offenses that only a few years ago would have resulted in arrest are now only a citation, like a traffic ticket. Drug offenses were the worst. It seemed to Biggs that the cost had now shifted from the state to the honest citizen whose greatest concern was to provide a decent and safe environment for his family. These changes were not the doing or wishes of Alaska citizens, but Alaska politicians protecting their budget. They had always spent more money than was generated, but now with oil revenues in decline it seemed the folks had been forgotten. They now had three responsibilities; education, transportation and public safety. Monuments had become more important than the three priorities named in the state constitution.

These thoughts were on his mind as he drove to the Legislative Information Office (LIO) to meet with Representative Dalton Price. The receptionist was at her desk when he arrived.

"Good morning, Trooper Biggs. Representative Dalton is waiting for you. Would you like a cup of coffee or something else to drink?" The petite young blond was pleasant and friendly.

"No thanks, Ma'am," said Biggs. "I just finished breakfast."

"Go right on in then, he's waiting for you." She smiled as he nodded and turned to enter the representative's office.

"Good morning, Trooper Biggs, please close the door. I think this conversation should remain between you and me."

Biggs closed the office door before taking a seat in front of the large wood desk. "Were you able to make any progress in solving this violence problem among fishermen?"

"I didn't realize what a can of worms you were opening when you came to my office." Dalton Price was shaking his head. "The further I dug into your suggestions the more insane it got. I found the entire history of these fishing regulations, and the laws for participation have been biased in favor of the commercial fishing industry since their inception back in the 1950s. I only researched back to the time of the congressional hearings on fish traps, but from the beginning there has only been one goal; protecting the commercial fishing industry. The intent of the federal law changes back then was to protect and ensure the survival of the resource. Since that time the fish populations have decreased dramatically. I understand how it got this way. In those days the commercial fishing industry was the largest employer and greatest revenue generator in the State of Alaska. Quite honestly, Trooper Biggs, I don't know if we can resolve the problem."

Andy Biggs was beginning to show his frustration. "What do we do, then? Just let it all go on until someone gets killed?"

"I'm not saying that, Andy. I'm just saying it won't be easy. The fishing industry has the best financed lobbyists in Juneau. I know you're right about preventing the escalation of conflicts, but I'm not sure I have enough influence in the legislature to resolve the problem. I may be able to chip away at it, but I don't see an immediate solution."

"You've lived here as long as I have and have seen the regulators ignore all logic in setting fish quotas. They set fish minimum escapement goals and when they aren't met they lower the minimum number rather than stop the fishing. The commercial fishermen hate the river guides because they catch fish when the numbers are low. The fishing guides hate the commercial fishermen because they set out nets and stop entire runs of fish from reaching the rivers. Individually they are each only trying to make a living, but collectively they are destroying the resource for all areas and all species. I believe there is room for a commercial as well as a guided fishing industry, but not an unlimited raping of the resource in the form it is being practiced today. I see big trouble coming and it will cost lives." Again, Trooper Biggs was airing his frustrations.

"Don't give up, Andy. I think together we can come up with a plan of attack and begin to change things. Help me make a list of what we see as problem areas and suggestions on how to eliminate the problem." Dalton

Price wanted to ease Biggs' frustration and formulate a plan of action. "Where do you think we should begin?"

"Perhaps we can start with the perpetrator of the problem. The Department of Fish and Game is amazing and accurate at predicting and forecasting the size of approaching salmon runs. They have done a miserable job at regulating all fishing to protect the run. Everyone seems dedicated to protecting fishermen without regard to the well-being of the fish. I'm not a biologist, but a fourth-grade kid can tell you if you kill off all the adults there will never be any babies. I don't see that as a science, I see it as lunacy." Biggs was glad the door to the office was closed.

"OK, you have a theory, identified a problem, and put forth a solution. That is something I can work with. Let's keep going." Price was writing on a yellow legal pad and smiling at Trooper Biggs.

For two more hours the two men worked to define problems and devise solutions that should subdue the tensions between the factions competing for a share of the resource. The list on the yellow legal pad was long and detailed. Finally, Trooper Biggs checked the time.

"I'm sorry Dalton, but I have to get back on patrol. There are more crimes out there than you can imagine. It's up to me to prevent as much of that as possible. I think if we accomplish half of what we have on that list and change the management strategy from managing dollars to managing fish it will be a giant step in the right direction. I apologize for some of my attitude, some, but not all." He was chuckling as he stood to leave the office.

"You don't have to apologize to me. I understand how you feel. Most folks and legislators, for that matter, only complain. I admire your willingness to take some kind of action to correct a very real problem. The legislature won't be back in session until January, but I will take these notes and hold some public hearings to see what other citizens think of your proposals. It has been a pleasure working with you today, Andy."

Andy opened the door. "Just keep me in the loop. I will be interested to learn what the rest of the public thinks. See ya later."

On the west side of Cook Inlet the fishing period was in full swing. So far there had been no violent episodes, but Hickson had found Webber and the *Chilkoot* and twice corked off his set forcing Webber to move in order to avoid confrontation. Hickson took the lack of personal response as a sign of personal victory. It was nearly noon when Hickson moved toward the Big River mouth to make a set outside the legal fishing limits. There were nearly

150 seals basking in the sun at the mouth of the river and began to stir as the fishing vessel moved closer to where they were resting.

Don Webber had detected a sizable number of fish moving north but further off-shore. As he maneuvered to drop his net he recognized Hickson's fishing boat moving toward the mouth of the river and reached for his cell phone to report the illegal positioning of the boat. He had been busy minding his own fishing business and doing well on this set when he saw the state Super Cub flying toward the mouth of the Big River. Minutes later Webber noticed the Wildlife trooper enforcement boat moving in the direction of Hickson's vessel. He was too busy with his catch to watch what was taking place two miles away.

By the end of the fishing period the fish hold was filled and Captain Webber was happy. The crew cleaned up the equipment and hosed down the net and deck as the captain pointed the *Chilkoot* toward Homer and the cannery. It had been a very successful day indeed. It was unusual to find the fish running this far off-shore, but, as sometimes happens, he was able find the fish and to net his share. It had been a profitable day in spite of Hickson and his antics.

Willie Hickson and his son-in-law, Burt, were so busy in the shallow waters of Big River they failed to see the approaching Wildlife enforcement boat. They had noted the state Super Cub that had been spying on them was now gone. The incoming tide was causing navigational problems for Hickson requiring him to work the wheel constantly to stay in the center of the river channel. Burt was only able to deploy half the net on the reel in the confined fishing corridor, but it filled quickly and he retrieved the net, picking the fish expertly as the net wound up on the large aluminum reel. He had picked and re-deployed the net, now for the fourth time, when a siren whelped, startling both Burt and Hickson. The skipper was so surprised by the sound he nearly jumped out of his seat. Hickson watched as the trooper boat dropped a large rubber raft into the water and saw two troopers jump into the Zodiac.

As they approached Hickson's fishing vessel they shouted, "Captain Hickson, we are coming aboard. Reel in your nets and move out of the river area."

Stunned, Hickson had no choice but to comply. Burt retrieved the net while Willie slowly moved his boat out of the mouth of the river. When he stopped the engines the Zodiac raft came alongside and tied up to the fishing boat. Both Wildlife troopers stepped up onto the deck.

The taller of the troopers, the one with sergeant stripes on his sleeve, spoke to Willie as he came out of the cabin. "Mr. Hickson, we observed you fishing illegally in the mouth of the river. We have video of you resetting the net and harvesting salmon while in the estuary. I will need to see your vessel registration papers and yours and your crewman's fishing permits."

"You ain't got no right to come aboard my boat," shouted a shaken Hickson.

"We observed you repeatedly and deliberately violating commercial fishing regulations. I intend to seize your boat and your catch. It will be up to the judge to say what becomes of these assets. Please get your papers for me, sir."

"What's your name, Sergeant?" demanded Willie.

"I am Sergeant Wilczeski and the trooper with me is Wildlife Trooper Bill Buttons."

Thinking of nothing else to say, Willie Hickson went into the cabin to get the requested paperwork. When he returned he handed the packet to the trooper. "What's going to happen to us," he asked.

"As long as you don't make trouble I'll allow you to stay on the boat until we reach the cannery and unload the boat. You will be given an accounting of the fish taken from your boat. Again, dispensation of this asset will be up to the judge. Since you are this far up the Inlet in this district I intend to file the charges in the Kenai District Court. Do you understand what I have explained to you?"

"Yeah, you're busting me for illegal fishing," snarled Willie.

"Trooper Buttons and I will remain on the boat until we reach the cannery in Kenai. If you don't cause me any grief on the trip back, I'll release you at the dock once you have a copy of the fish count. I will impound your vessel pending your court appearance. I must warn you that there is a warrant issued for your arrest on the charge of assault. That means your deckhand will be allowed to go home, but you will be held on the warrant until your court appearance which will be tomorrow in Kenai."

"You're going to throw me in jail?" shouted Willie.

"Sorry, Mr. Hickson, but that is what I am required to do. Now, are you going to be nice and drive your boat to the Kenai Cannery dock or am I going to arrest you here and let Mr. Calhoun deliver the boat to the cannery?"

"I'll take the boat to Kenai, but I want to contact my lawyer as soon as we reach the dock."

"Agreed. Now let's head across. It's getting late." The sergeant was now in full charge of the vessel.

At the dock the fish were unloaded and a copy of the fish ticket was given to Hickson. A local trooper was waiting to take Willie to the local booking facility, but Sergeant Wilczeski and Trooper Buttons stayed with the boat to see it safely moored and secured before returning to their own offices.

Chapter 6

The following morning Don Webber had finished breakfast and read the local newspaper by 7:00 a.m. Two hours later he had finished his bookkeeping chores and showered to meet the day. His first duty for this morning was to stop at his insurance company office. The owner and chief agent at the office was a woman he had grown up with and attended school with her in Homer. After graduation Don had begun his career as a commercial fisherman while Lucile Hardy had gone to college in Fairbanks for four years to achieve a degree in business administration. With her credentials under her arm she returned to Homer and purchased a bankrupt insurance agency. It took her a couple of years to turn the business around, but it was now very successful.

Don entered the office and was greeted by the receptionist, a young woman named Tammy. "Good morning Mr. Webber," she greeted him.

"Good morning. Is Lucy in yet?"

"Yes, sir, I'll tell her you're here." She dialed the intercom and spoke with her boss. "Go right in Mr. Webber. She's waiting for you."

Don walked back to the office where he found the door open and Lucy seated at her desk. "Good morning, Don. I thought you might be in today. I heard about your incident last week. How is Freddie doing?"

"He can't fish any more this season. I hate to lose him. He's a really good fisherman."

"What can I do for you today," she asked.

"I have a list," joked Webber. "First of all I want to file a claim for my boat repairs. I have to warn you it cost a lot. I also need to know if I can sue Willie Hickson for ramming my boat and injuring my crewman? I need to know if Freddie's wages are covered during his recovery time."

Lucy went to a file cabinet and pulled the insurance file for Don Webber and the boat *Chilkoot.* She opened the file and sat, reading the policy. She was silent for several minutes before answering. "Yes, the damages to your boat are covered. Bring me documentation of the costs and I'll have Tammy prepare the estimate for the company. Freddie's wages will also be covered, but I'm afraid they will not be as much as he would make if he were fishing, sorry. Thirdly, I am going to have to speak with the company about a lawsuit. I'm sure you can recover, assuming you win and can collect from Hickson, all wages and damages plus whatever compensation the lawyers dream up, but the company is going to want to be reimbursed for what they paid out in damages."

"That's the first good news I've had this week. I had a call last night, late, to tell me Willie had been arrested and his boat seized over at Big River. He was fishing in the river and the Wildlife troopers arrested him and took his catch and boat. Couldn't have happened to a nicer guy. The trooper said he'll go to court in Kenai today on all the charges including the assault he committed on my boat. I'll be anxious to hear how that turns out." Don seemed pleased with all of the news.

"I'll start all the paperwork today. I will need to have copies of the repair billing as soon as you can get them to me." Lucy was making notes on her calendar.

"Except for the circumstances, it's good to see you again, Lucy. I'm planning to grill a steak for dinner tonight at my place. Can I put another steak on the grill for you?"

"It will be late, almost seven before I can get there. Is that too late?"

"That will be great. Do you want wine with your steak?" he asked.

"No thanks, it's a work night, but thanks for asking. See you around seven."
Don stood to leave, "Good. See you tonight."

"Have Tammy come back to my office when you go by there, will you Don?"

Don Webber had spent the majority of the day on the boat cleaning and checking the gear. Everything seemed to be in order. He took the boat to the fuel dock and filled the tanks in readiness for the next fishing period which was two days away. Just as he returned home, his phone rang. It was Trooper Biggs.

"Hello, Don, it's Andy. I just had a call from post headquarters to let me know Willie Hickson went to court today. He pleaded out to illegal fishing and got a hefty fine and forfeited his catch. They gave him his boat back, though. They also arraigned him on the assault charge for ramming your boat and injuring your crew-member. He pleaded not guilty to that charge, but he posted bail and was released. He'll be back out on the water next fishing period. I'm telling you this so that you will be watchful on your next trip out."

"I'm sorry they didn't throw him in jail, but I guess I should have expected it. Thanks for calling me. I appreciate it. Just so you know, Freddie came through the surgery just fine, but he isn't going to be able to fish for the rest of the season. I was in contact with the insurance company this morning and I hope they will give him some kind of compensation on his time off."

Andy Biggs gave out a huge sigh, "I know how frustrating this is for you as a victim, but I can't tell the courts what to do. I've been talking with Dalton Price and we have proposed some things to change the laws, and hopefully, make your profession a little safer. The violence is increasing at an alarming rate. I want to do something to stop it."

"I wish you luck with that, Andy. You probably realize this war is affecting all areas of fishing—sport fishing, subsistence fishing, personal use, and commercial fishing. It has to stop somewhere."

"Is there anything I can do for you, Don?" asked the Alaska trooper.

"No, but thanks anyway. My crew and I will be out there in a couple of days. We have to keep fishing or starve this winter. See ya, Andy," said Don Webber as he hung up the telephone.

Webber showered, changed his clothing and began preparing the potatoes for baking and fixing a green salad before lighting the barbeque grill. He was looking forward to seeing Lucy. They had dated from time to time in the past and he enjoyed her company. It was exactly seven o'clock when there was a knock on the front door. When he opened the door she was standing there with a bottle of red wine in her hands.

"I changed my mind about the wine with dinner," she said.

"Come in and we'll see if it tastes good." He kissed her on the cheek and took the bottle from her hand.

Lucy helped Don clean up the table after dinner which was excellent. Don poured the last of the wine into their empty glasses and the pair stepped out onto the rear deck to enjoy the magnificent view of Kachemak Bay.

"You and I have been seeing each other off and on for a long, long time and for my part I would like to continue to see you. I could never let my personal life take priority until this year. It looks like I'll have a good season, in spite of the way it has started," began Don.

"I'm happy to hear that, Don. You deserve it. I think a lot of you, always have, and I think it would be wonderful if you could begin to enjoy life for a change. I've seen how hard you worked over the years and have always admired you."

"I'm glad to hear you say that, Lucy, because I have something to say, and don't really know how to go about it."

"Just say what you have on your mind, Don. We always have."

Don paused and took a deep breath as well as a sip of his wine. "We've known each other since high school. I think we get along as well as any two people can. Because of my debt load I could never ask this before, but do you think you could dare to make our friendship a relationship? And if that works out perhaps we could make it permanent?" Don sipped again on his wine glass.

Now it was Lucy's turn to pause and sip wine. "There have been times when I wondered if we would make a good couple. I have admired you since high school and I think we might just make things work. You know how crazy my work schedule is and I understand yours. We would undoubtedly have some things to work out, but yyeeess, I think it would work wonderfully. When would you like this new relationship to begin?" she asked, smiling.

He put his wine glass on a small table and stood, walked the two steps to where she sat and bent to kiss her passionately. "How about now?" he said when their lips parted.

Later, as she slipped on her sweater to leave for home she turned to kiss him once again. "I'm so happy, Don. I'll see you tomorrow."

Don stood in the doorway and watched as she drove out of his front yard. He was smiling as he returned to the kitchen to clean up the dinner dishes. He had never considered sharing his life with anyone until now, but this seemed like a natural thing to do; he felt happy.

He was in the engine compartment the following morning when Lou and Eddie, the new deckhand, came aboard. "Whatcha doin', Cap?" asked Lou.

"Oh, hi there Lou, not much. I noticed the main battery cable was corroded and decided to change it out. Give me a minute to tighten the clamp and I'll be up to visit." Only a minute later he came out onto the rear deck and onto the sunshine. "What brings you to the dock on a day off?"

"Eddie and me just came to see if there was anything needing to be done before we go out tomorrow. It looks like you took care of it. Have you seen Freddie?"

"Yes, he's doing fine. They had him up and walking yesterday. He has a plastic back brace he wears when they get him up. He's pretty weak, but he is getting up and around. You should go by and see him." Don was wiping the oil from his hands.

"Yeah, I think I'll do that today." Lou was looking at the net reel. "The new bearings and hydraulics sure made the net reel work nice," he commented.

Don chuckled, "I guess I should thank Willie for getting it fixed for me. By the way, Trooper Biggs called to say Willie is still in jail. He pleaded out on illegal fishing charges, but he is still in jail on the assault charge. He got his boat returned to him, so I expect his lawyer will get him bailed out and he will be back to fishing tomorrow when the fishing period opens. I talked to the biologists and they told me to expect a nice run to occur just off Johnson River and outside of Chisik Island. I think that's where we'll make our first set in the morning. We will try to find the fish on the fish finder and get ahead of them. I want the two of you to keep a watch for Willie and Burt. We can't afford to lose another period for repairs."

"We'll be ready, Skipper. Old Eddie, here, he's going to work out just fine. He just needs to get used to how we do business." Lou slapped Eddie on the shoulder.

"OK, guys, get rested up. We have a long day tomorrow."

Don watched them as they walked back up the dock to shore. While he watched he called the local flower shop and ordered a large bouquet of roses to be delivered to the insurance office with a card addressed to Lucy Hardy. An hour later he was on his way to her office to ask her to go to lunch.

Chapter 7

The following morning Webber and his crew left Homer Harbor very early. There was a light breeze blowing and clouds rolling from the south. The weather forecast was for a three-foot chop on the waters in the area near Chisik Island. Captain Webber motored at half throttle toward the area he had chosen to fish today because of the building waves. They arrived in the area they had chosen to make the first set of the day, but had to wait until the fishing period to open at six a.m. Lou and Eddie were inside the cabin drinking coffee with the captain and talking strategy. He ordered them to wear flotation devices today because of the choppy sea.

"I came across a lot of fish on the way over. All headed north, of course, and I want to make the first set outside the island. It worked the other day and we may get lucky again. Eddie, I want both of you to use extra caution today. The deck will be wet and the boat will be rocking. I can't afford to lose another crewman. The fish finder says there are fish beginning to show, so when the clock strikes six we start laying net." Webber gave instructions and caution warnings to his crew.

"Hey, Cap," asked Lou, "Have you seen any sign of Willie or his boat?"

"No, and I hope we don't. I don't want to play games in these waters," said Don. "Try to keep an eye out for any other boats today, just as a precaution."

Eddie wasn't much of a conversationalist, but a good fisherman. He only nodded and put on his flotation device. Don had practiced emergency procedures with his crew early in the week, hoping they would never need them.

As time neared he told the crewmen to get ready and he would blow his horn when the time was right. "Don't go by what other boats are doing," he cautioned. Minutes later he blasted the horn and gunned the engine to pull the net from the reel on the rear deck. It was difficult to see the white floats because of the wave action, but they saw fish in the net from time to time. Webber had been correct. The deck was wet and the boat was bouncing and pitching insanely. He had no trouble laying out the net but had trouble keeping a heading while taking the net back aboard. The net was far from loaded, but there were fish to be wrenched from the mesh. With the fish in the hold and the net back on the reel he decided to move to the inside of the island to find calmer water. Both crewmen came inside the cabin while he made the move. Once on the inside of the island near the mouth of Tuxedni Bay the water was somewhat calmer. Webber maneuvered in the channel until he found the fish and told the men to get ready to make a new set.

They fought the rough waters all day, but had not seen Hickson or his boat. By the end of the fishing period they were tired and ready to go to shore. The catch had been light, but enough to make expenses for the day. Don was disappointed and exhausted. Both crewmen slept on the trip back to the cannery to unload fish.

It was very late when Don Webber made his way to his home on East End Road. His phone recorder was blinking when he went into the kitchen. He pressed the play button to hear Andy Biggs' voice.

"Hello, Don, this is Andy Biggs. I have an appointment with Dalton Price at nine in the morning. If you don't fish tomorrow I would appreciate it if you would come to that meeting. He has a plan to change the administrative directives for fisheries management. I don't know specifically what his proposals are going to be, but since you are part of the reason these changes are being proposed, I thought you should be in on the discussion. Come to the LIO office at nine a.m. and sit in on the briefing. Hope to see you there."

Don checked the time and decided it was too late to return the call but planned to attend the meeting. In the morning he was out of bed early and drove into town to have breakfast at Duncan House. The café owner came to his table to say good morning and to ask how fishing was going so far this season.

"We had one accident that cost us a couple of days, but the rest of the season has been fine. The weather was a little nasty yesterday, but we fished and did OK, not great, but OK."

"Yeah, several of the skippers quit early yesterday because of the rough water, but next week is predicted to be good," said the owner of the café.

"We got beat up pretty bad yesterday. I hope we get a few good days. It gets pretty hard on my crew when they have to work in that kind of sea."

"Well," said the café owner, "Good luck," as he turned to tend to a customer at the front counter.

Andy Biggs was standing in the sunshine, waiting, when he arrived at the LIO office. "Mornin'," he greeted as Don stepped out of his pickup truck.

"Morning to you, too," he replied. "What's this meeting about?" he asked.

Trooper Briggs commented, "As you know, violent incidents are increasing at an alarming rate throughout the entire fishing industry. You were a victim of one of the incidents. Well, they're happening everywhere, including among the sportfish guides on the Kenai River. We have to send a rescue team to the mouth of the river at least twice a week to rescue some dip-netter who got washed out to the salt water. The subsistence fishermen are fighting with each other on the beaches. It's becoming dangerous to go fishing. I talked with Dalton and asked him to help solve the problem and gave him a short list of suggestions.

"He has put a list together and intends to hold public hearings all over the state to discuss the problem and to gather information to draw up proposals for changes in the laws, management objectives, seasons, catch limits, priorities for closures, and on and on. The objective is to save the fish. It will take a lot of work and I expect the biologists to argue that science takes precedence over legislation while commercial fishermen will argue they have already given up a lot. The federal government will argue subsistence fishing has the highest priority. I think every competing faction is going to argue they're right and all the others are wrong. There has to be some fair reasoning in this argument, but since the fish have no voice in the matter they are suffering the consequences. Dalton seems to think like me and wants to hold public hearings on the subject."

"It all sounds quite noble and righteous, and I'll try to be objective, but I don't know how much more I can give away and still survive."

"I understand, Don. Let's go inside and see what Dalton has for proposals." Biggs held the door of the office open for the commercial fisherman.

Four hours later the two men exited the office. "Well, my friend, what do you think now?" asked Biggs as they stood in the parking lot ready to leave.

"I'm impressed, Andy. I have to admit I was skeptical at first, but after listening to Dalton I think he's on the right track. I agree with him that something has to be done and no one is going to be totally satisfied or happy with the adjustments, but if nothing is done we will all lose everything. It will be difficult to get the so-called scientists at Alaska Fish and Game to admit they have been wrong for the last fifty years. I would like to attend some of these seminars or public forums to hear how the general public views the problem."

"I know I don't have the answer, but there are a lot of people out there with more knowledge and insight than me." Andy was scratching his head and thinking, "There will be a lot of opposition to any public hearing. Sportfish will claim they are being left out of the equation, commercial fishermen will claim loss of their fishing rights and livelihood. Subsistence fishermen will drag the federal government into the argument, claiming it is their God given right and cultural heritage to set personal nets. Everyone will be angry and argue against what should be done, but somewhere in all this there has to be a real, legitimate and fair solution. I don't want to investigate any more injuries or any deaths before it's changed."

"I think I'll have a beer," joked Don Webber.

Andy Biggs smiled as he opened the door to his patrol car. "I'm going to work or I would join you."

Don drove to the hospital to visit Freddie. The crewman had been up and walking with a walker for much of the day. He was in his bed sipping ice water when Don arrived.

"Hey Cap," he said as Webber entered the room.

"How are you doing, Freddie?"

"The pain pills are working really well," confessed Freddie.

"You should try to get off those things as soon as you can," commented the captain. "Can I bring you some magazines or books to read?"

"No, I'm doing fine. I'm starting to like soap operas on the TV."

"Have they told you when you can go home?"

"Yeah, they said when I can walk around without the walker I can go home, but I'm going to need a nurse or someone to help at home for a while."

"I'll look for someone for the job if you want me to," said Captain Webber.

"I want someone young, pretty and pleasant to be around," Freddie said.

"A Marine Corps drill sergeant would be my choice."

"I'll get my own nurse. I'll start interviewing tomorrow." Freddie laughed with Don.

After the visit Don drove to the insurance office of Lucy Hardy.

"Lucy said I was to let you come to her office anytime, so go on back, Mr. Webber." The receptionist was smiling broadly as if she knew a deep secret.

Don smiled, too. "Thanks," he said and walked back to her office.

Lucy had heard the exchange in the outer office and was grinning when he entered. "I wondered if you were going to stop by here today."

"I had an appointment with Dalton Price and Andy Biggs this morning or I would have been here earlier. Did you miss me?"

"I sure did," she confessed. "I was thinking about taking part of the day off and wondered if you wanted to kill a couple of hours with me?"

"What did you have in mind?" he asked.

"I'm not bribing you. You have to spend the morning with me because I'm so wonderful."

"If that's the case, I agree. Your place or mine?" he quipped.

"Oh no, I need to go to Soldotna to deliver some papers and wondered if you wanted to go with me?"

"Aw shucks, ma'am. I'll drive." The two of them laughed together. The close relationship was beginning to take on new meaning, a strong meaning.

Minutes later they were driving up Baycrest Hill toward Soldotna, eighty miles north. Don was driving while she held his hand near the gear shift lever. "You know, Don," she commented, "I can never remember being this relaxed and content with life as I have been since we agreed to see each other. Do you still feel like it's the right thing?"

"Yes, I do. Yesterday we were in heavy water all day and I was pre-occupied, but as soon as the boat was moored I began wishing I was able to spend time with you. It was almost midnight when I got home, so I didn't call, but I wanted to. I feel as silly as a school kid again." He looked into her eyes and smiled.

She squeezed his hand gently.

Four hours later they were driving down Baycrest Hill returning to Homer. "I have some ribs in the slow cooker at the house," said Lucy. "How about I get the cooker and take it to your place and we can have ribs for dinner?" She leaned close and placed her cheek against his shoulder.

"Good idea, but I should go by the dock and check the boat on the way home. We don't fish tomorrow, so we can stay up late and watch a movie, if you like." Don didn't want to admit just how much he was looking forward to spending the evening with Lucy.

It became a very wonderful evening indeed.

Chapter 8

I t was that same sunny Saturday morning in the lower Kenai River in a narrow stretch of river just above The Pillars boat launch site where guide Justin Gabriel and his four clients were back trolling for king salmon. Two clients were old hands at fishing the Kenai River, here for a few weeks to fish for Chinook salmon (king salmon). The other couple was newlyweds from Virginia and fishing novices. The fishing trip was a gift from the bride's wealthy parents.

"OK folks, reel up and we'll go back up and try this stretch again," said Justin. The four clients began to reel in their lines and lures.

Justin didn't pay any attention to the boat being launched at the Pillars and watched his clients take in their rods for the short trip upstream. Suddenly he heard a loud, fifty horse, Yamaha outboard approaching. The twenty-foot river boat was coming full speed in an arc across the river directly toward his boat.

"Hang on, he's going to hit us!" yelled Justin just as the front of the approaching boat slammed up and over the left side of Gabriel's boat as it faced upstream in back troll mode. Justin hit the throttle in a vain effort to avoid the collision, but it was too late. Justin knocked his engine out of gear as the other boat roared up and over the side of his, knocking two of his clients into the water and falling atop the other two. Justin was horrified, unable to maneuver his boat to aid the two men in the water. There were fishermen on the dock at the boat launch and he called to them to help the men in the water. The men on the dock were seasoned river users and one picked up a long handle fishing net from the dock while the other found a mooring rope and began to untie it for a line to toss into the path of one of the men floating down the river. Another man, one of the men who assisted in launching the boat that struck Justin, was using his cell phone to call 911 for assistance.

As the two men in the water were floating past the dock one was near enough and conscious enough to reach out and put his arm through the metal hoop of the fishing net. He was grabbed by the man on the other end of the net and a bystander and pulled onto the dock. The other man was too far out and unconscious, therefore not able to reach the rope thrown by the second of the rescuers. He was quickly passing the dock when the second rescuer hooked a loop on the end of the rope to a boat cleat on the floating dock. Holding the other end of the rope and without a second thought he jumped into the icy, fast flowing river to reach the floating fisherman. He easily caught the man's fishing vest and held on while two more bystanders pulled and tugged on the rope to bring the two up to the lower end of the dock. Hands reached out to take the unconscious man and pull him from the water before helping the now shivering rescuer up on the dock.

Justin had managed to use his engine power to move his boat, with the other vessel atop it, toward the dock. He had no idea about the condition of the two people trapped under the fishing boat. At the dock, with his boat tied securely, he climbed up to see what condition the pilot of the boat that had struck him was in. He was lying on the floor of the boat, injured and bleeding, but conscious.

"Get this guy off my boat before I kill him," he called to onlookers on the dock. Two men climbed aboard and lifted the injured man over the side onto the dock.

With superhuman strength Justin put his back under the front of the boat crossways of his and pushed with all his strength. He was able to lift and push it enough that the boat began to slide backward into the current of the river. He pushed again and again until the boat slid off and he was able to see the two injured fishermen beneath it. It had only been a matter of minutes since the incident but he now heard sirens approaching and breathed a sigh of relief. He and onlookers gently lifted the injured man out of the boat and laid him on the floating dock.

Three men stepped back into the boat to attend, what they now saw, was a lady. Justin and his four helpers gently lifted the young woman out of the boat to lay her beside the other fishermen. Her husband had been one of the men knocked out of the boat in the collision. He was now semiconscious and realized who was lying beside him. With great effort he rolled to his side and placed a hand on her shoulder. "Lisa, Lisa," he said in a strained voice, "wake up Lisa." The effort was too much for him and he passed out again.

The EMTs arrived on the scene before the Alaska State troopers and moved all the rescuers away from the patients, but asked them to stay around to give statements to the troopers when they arrived. The medics immediately began to work on the injured patients. The most critical of the four fishermen was the man and the woman trapped under the boat. The man had been looking toward the shore and talking with his friend when they were struck and was knocked out of his seat and to the floor between two seat pedestals which protected him from the weight of the wreckage on top of him.

Lisa Wilson had heard the approaching boat and turned to see what was happening when the other boat struck her, pinning her in her seat, crushing her chest. This tragedy would leave her new husband, Kent, a widower on his honeymoon. The paramedic pronounced Lisa dead at the scene. Her new husband, now unconscious, was loaded into one of the two ambulances at the scene and taken to the hospital in Soldotna for treatment. He was in serious condition as were the other two men.

The driver of the boat was a sixteen-year-old boy going fishing with his father and brother. He had asked to run the boat during the launch. His father agreed and cautioned him. As the boat floated off the trailer with the engine running the lad put it into reverse to back out into the current. When safely away from the dock he put the motor into the forward gear and gave it throttle. He was standing near the motor giving it full throttle, toppling him from his feet to the floor leaving the boat to careen wildly across the current in an arc, striking Justin Gabriel's boat broadside. The impact further injured the young driver. The accident raised the nose of the twenty-foot boat high in the air and sunk the rear into the river, killing the engine. It was later determined the cause was the inexperienced driver of the boat that was being launched.

When the trooper arrived he saw that Justin was an angry man, worried about his clients and wanting revenge for the damages to his boat and his clients. State Trooper Beeson asked him to wait in his patrol car while he consulted with the medics on the condition of the injured patients. When he learned of the deceased patient he called for another trooper to assist him in the investigation.

By the time Trooper Beeson came back to his patrol car to speak with Justin he had calmed down somewhat. "How are my clients?" he asked.

"Three of them have been taken to the hospital for treatment. The fourth, the lady, was pronounced dead at the scene. I'm sorry." Beeson paused to give Justin time to digest the news.

"Oh, my God," said a shocked Justin. "How are her husband and the other two fishermen?"

"All three are badly injured, but in stable condition at this time. All the patients have been taken to CPGH for treatment. The young man driving the boat was also injured and taken to the hospital."

"Oh God, Oh God," sobbed Justin in grief. "I didn't see him coming. I was helping my clients and getting ready to move back upstream. I didn't see him."

"Just relax, Mr. Gabriel, and take it easy. I have to get some information from you and then I'll drive you to the hospital if you like. I will have to impound your boat here at the dock until the investigation is completed. The other trooper will stay here and safeguard the boat and your equipment for now. Did you bring your registration from the boat?"

The interview went on for nearly an hour with Trooper Beeson stepping out of the car to talk with the father of the boat driver twice during the interview. "The boy's father told me it was an accident. His son fell when the boat accelerated and was unable to prevent the collision. He has said his son was to blame for the accident and that he's sorry. He would like to speak with you when you get to the hospital. I think you should, but I don't want there to be any trouble." This was the word of caution from the trooper. "I'm going to speak with my partner over there. I'll be right back to take you to the hospital to check on your clients. Are you sure you don't have any injuries?"

"No, I'm OK. Just take me to town to see my clients. Oh God, Oh God," Justin was sobbing again.

On the way to the hospital with the trooper Justin called the private number of his attorney, Alan Cox, to explain what had happened and asked for him to meet with him in the emergency room of the hospital. Once there Justin and Beeson walked together into the waiting room. Beeson contacted the admitting nurse to see if Justin could see his three clients. Permission was granted and Beeson escorted the river guide into the treatment area.

His first visit was with Kent Wilson who was now fully awake and, though shaken, speaking clearly. His grief was understandable and Justin hugged the man, careful not to cause pain to the man's injuries—a broken left arm and multiple cuts and bruises.

"Is there someone I can call for you, Kent?" he asked.

"No, I had better do that myself, but my cell phone won't work because it fell in the river with me. I don't know how Lisa's parents will take this. I just don't know." Wilson was fighting the tears.

"Here, Mr. Wilson, take my phone while I go see the other clients. I'll be back in a few minutes. My lawyer is on his way down and will want to speak with you, if you're up to it." Justin handed his cell phone to the man.

"Thanks for the phone. I'll talk with the lawyer as soon as the doctors finish with me." Tears were flowing down his cheeks as he spoke.

Justin patted him on his leg as he left the room to see the other two men. The first man in the next room was knocked into the river with Kent Wilson. He was conscious with a dislocated shoulder and cuts and bruises from impact with the boat.

"How are you doing, Doug?" asked Justin.

"Pretty well, considering. I need to find out who those men were who pulled me out of the water. They saved my life. I'm very grateful. How is Lowell?" he asked.

"I haven't had a chance to see Lowell yet, but the report I got was he has a fractured skull and will need surgery. I don't think he's awake yet. If I learn more I'll let you know. The young woman in the seat behind him died in the accident. My lawyer is on his way down to see you and do what he can to help."

"How in the world did this happen, Justin?" asked Doug.

"I was helping you with your lines and rods and didn't see the boat coming. If I had I might have been able to get out of the way. The driver was just a young kid with no boating experience and hit the throttle too hard and fell down in the boat. It was a stupid accident and never should have happened. The damn law lets anyone drive a boat on the river." There was disgust in his voice. "If you're OK I'm going to check on Lowell. I'll be back in a little while."

In the hall between rooms someone called his name. He turned to see Alan Cox, his attorney walking behind him.

"Hold up a minute, Justin," asked Cox.

"Oh, hi Alan, you made it here quickly. No baseball game tonight?"

"Come on, Justin. You know I always come when you call. How bad is it?"

"One client dead, one still unconscious and two still being treated. Is that bad enough for you?" It was more than anger in his voice. It was rage and hostility.

"Let's go out to the waiting room and talk. We can't discuss this back here." Cox was trying to calm his client and friend down.

"Yeah, good idea. There's coffee out there?"

The two men walked back to the waiting room and found the thermos flasks with hot coffee.

"Listen Alan, I've never lost a client before. It wasn't my fault, but I have two regular customers in here, one with a fractured skull. I have a new customer here with a broken arm and a dead bride. You can talk with the clients if you like, but I think it would be better if you just contacted Trooper Beeson and get a copy of the report."

"My advice to you is to calm down. You aren't doing your clients nor yourself any favors with all this anger. The doctors will take care of the injured folks tonight. You need to go home and cool off. I'll call you later." Cox placed his arm around the shoulders of the river guide. "You can't make good decisions when you're angry."

Justin sipped his coffee, gave a huge sigh and said, "You're right, Alan. I apologize. Let's go check the clients one more time and then you can take me home. I can't fish tomorrow. The troopers have impounded my boat for evidence. We have to do something about safety on the river, Alan. We need to do it now."

⇛● Chapter 9 ◉⇚

The first order of business the following Monday morning was for Dalton Price to call Alaska Trooper Andy Biggs. "Hello, Andy, can you come down to my office for a meeting today? I think we have some new things to discuss in regard to the hearings my legislative aide is arranging. Can you make it this morning?"

"If I can come early, yes. I have court at one o'clock," replied Biggs.

"Good, Linda will be here in a few minutes and I want her to hear what we discuss and I want you to hear what she has learned as well. I'll make a fresh pot of coffee. See you in a little while." Price and his aide had been busy since Andy had last been in the office.

Minutes later Linda entered, walking directly to the coffee pot for a cup of the fresh brew.

"Andy will be here shortly. I want you to bring your notes on the proposed schedule for hearings around the state. Let's have this discussion in the conference room where we can spread out the paperwork." Dalton spoke as he took a file from his desk drawer. "I'm going to attempt to get Andy to come with us to all these hearings. If he agrees I'll call his captain and arrange for him to get the time with us."

Linda only nodded and sipped her cup of coffee as she went back to her own desk in the front office. She was digging out files from a metal cabinet when the front door opened and a uniformed trooper entered. He was a large man with an infectious smile.

"Is your boss in?" asked Biggs.

"Yes, sir. He wants to have this meeting in the conference room. Let me get the files and I'll take you there." She was silent for about a minute while looking at file labels. Finally, she pulled a stack of files from the drawer and turned to face the trooper. "I don't know if you remember me, I'm Linda; I work for Mr. Price."

"Yes, I remember. You make great coffee." Andy teased all the ladies this way.

"OK, I think I have everything. Let's go to the conference room and I'll bring you some coffee."

Andy followed the young lady down the hall with Dalton falling in line to enter the large meeting area. Linda dropped her stack of files on the table and left the room to get coffee for Andy.

Dalton sat at the head of the table, opening the file he had brought with him. "I had word there was another incident on the Kenai River over the weekend," he said.

"Yes, I read the report. Three fishermen injured and one killed. No criminal intent, but was caused by an inexperienced boatman; a teenager. Sad case, too, the one killed in the accident was a newlywed lady on her honeymoon. Her husband was injured pretty badly. The other two were fishermen in the same boat. One is just bruised up, but the other one suffered several broken bones, but will recover. The young man's father is taking responsibility for the incident."

"Sorry to hear about that one," said Dalton. "I have had Linda putting together a program for the public hearings we intend to conduct. The plan is to have these hearings in several places across the state beginning in mid-August. Fishing season should be ended about then and we thought it necessary to do them before all the fishermen left for the winter. I wanted you here this morning because your interest is less in fish than safety. Have a seat, Andy, and we will get started."

Linda began the formality of the meeting. "You realize, of course, these hearings are going to bring out a lot of hard feelings. Any time we mess with someone's paycheck there is a big furor. The press is going to slant the coverage in favor of commercial and personal use fishermen, leaving us to look like a tribe of headhunters. The fishermen's lobby will fight us all the way, and as you know the commercial fishermen pay a percentage of their catch for that purpose. The federal government has set subsistence fishing as a priority above all other and will defend that position with all the weight they can muster. I don't foresee that as a major problem since we don't have a subsistence issue in Cook Inlet. Personal use, however, will be another issue. You know how many fishermen take advantage of both the dipnet and setnet fisheries for personal use. The City of Kenai is invaded each summer by thousands of dipnet fishermen taking their quota of personal use fish. Kenai River guides are already mad at us for the poor fish allocations for sport fishermen. Alaska Fish and Game will defend their practices to the death and state their science is the only way to protect the fish. I am only relating these negatives to prepare you for the way I expect the hearings to go."

Dalton Price was the next to make a short statement. "Every user group in the state of Alaska will see us as wanting to take their privileges away. I doubt anyone will see this as a means of protecting the resource. Each group will see this as an attack on their kingdom." Price gave a huge grin. "Do you still want to be a part of this project?"

"I'm not so sure," admitted Andy. "Is there a positive side to any of this? And, do you see any chance of us winning any of our arguments? My goal is to end, or at least minimize tensions between groups. If we could get them to cooperate with each other we could make the entire fishing industry safer for every one of the factions."

Price chuckled, "I don't mean to discourage you, Andy. I'm only trying to show you what we're up against. Every user group will look at this panel as an enemy trying to stop them from making a living. Back in the early 1970s we thought the limited entry process would solve the problems, but it has only compounded them. When we attempt to limit the numbers of commercial fishermen there is an outcry from the entire industry about us attempting to take away the 'rights' of commercial fishermen to make a living at their traditional profession. Commercial fishermen are probably the largest lobbying group in the state.

"In light of all that cheerful news," began Andy, "does it make sense to even attempt to have these hearings? I'm not anxious to get into a fight I can't possibly win."

Dalton smiled, "We may not win the battle, but we'll put up a heck of a fight. The weight of my office will be behind us, and in the fishing industry I pack a little weight. It will be up to Linda and myself to assure the participants we have no intention of stopping any fishery. We'll be there to take testimony and, in the end, attempt to protect the fish stocks. It would be unfair to hold hearings to justify a pre-drawn conclusion. Every user group is aware the escapement goals are far from the numbers of those we saw only a few years ago. Alaska Fish and Game biologists are the same as fishermen; everyone is to blame for dwindling fish stocks except them. It's their job to protect the fish stocks. Their science is good, but their management skills are lacking. We must find a way to correct that without taking away the power they have to regulate and manage fish stocks."

"My goal," commented Andy, "is to protect the public. That includes visiting tourists, river guides, personal use fishermen, and commercial fishermen. Human behavior is human behavior and we will never stop all lawless acts entirely, but we can reduce the desire to commit them by reducing the intense competition for the available stocks. I'm not sure how to go about that task, but reducing the number of fishermen is an option."

Dalton was smiling again. "I think most of the user groups feel the same way, but no one wants the reductions to come from their group."

"May I interject something here?" asked Linda.

"Of course, Linda, I value your opinions."

"I just want to say my family has been commercial fishing since before I was born. We have had this discussion at the dinner table on many evenings. You're right about fishermen wanting it to change, but not for them. I think we should make sure they have a say in how the reallocation of fish stocks will be handled. Let them decide if permits should be taken away or brought back by the state in order to reduce the numbers of fishermen. Sport fishermen licenses are reissued each year, making them easier to regulate by quota. Personal use fishermen are issued permits on a one year basis and the same applies. I believe there are ways to regulate fishermen, but the big time operators will pour cash into the argument stating they have the most to lose. The corporations own fleets of boats and all the processing facilities. The seasons are short and therefore laborers are a major concern, but no matter what the argument the underlying fact remains: personal income. I think you will have lawyer upon lawyer representing every user group and all protesting the right of the state legislature to take away their clients' livelihood. I think it is entirely possible that some judge somewhere will rule this panel has no right to decide this question."

Andy was looking at the clock on the office wall. "I have to be back on duty in thirty minutes, so I'm leaving this argument for the two of you to work out. I want you to know I'm still in the fight. There is a need for change and for many reasons. I'll give you as much time as possible but I still have a job of keeping the peace and protecting the public." He stood to leave and turned back to the two at the conference table saying, "I think your job is more dangerous than mine." He left the room chuckling.

After Andy had gone Dalton turned to Linda. "OK, girl, let's try to set some priorities for the hearings. I would like to see them begin near the end of August, after fishing season, giving fishermen some time to put their boats to bed for the winter. We need to schedule public hearings in each major area of the state starting with Valdez. I want a clear agenda published for each meeting with ground rules to be followed. We can't let this turn into a free-for-all."

"Yes sir, I'll start on it right away." She paused a moment in deep thought. "You realize this could cost you the next election if it turns out badly?" making the comment as she walked from the room.

Dalton walked to the small coffee room for a fresh cup before returning to his office where he reached for the telephone. "Linda, see if you can reach my old friend Claude Bacus at his home over in Tutka Bay." Claude was a distant relative of Dalton Price and was once a ranking member of the state senate.

A minute later his desk phone jingled, "Good to hear from you, Dalton," said a friendly voice on the other end.

Dalton laughed aloud. "You know I never call you unless I have an unsolvable problem. How have you been, Uncle?"

"I'm doing fine, boy. There aren't any politicians over here on this side of the bay for me to fight with. I assume someone brought you a problem to solve and you don't know how so you called me. Right?"

The next half hour was spent giving all the details of the proposed hearings to Uncle Claude. Claude listened intently without replying the entire time. When Price had finished and paused a moment Claude answered.

"Wow, you've stepped on a hot one this time, Dalton. Everyone in the state is going to attempt to stop this fight. There is too much money at stake to let you change the accepted balance of power in this war, and it is a war. I think you're treading in dangerous territory and you could get hurt very easily. You're taking on a bunch of men who play rough."

"Do you really think it will be that bad?" asked Dalton.

"Yes, Dalton, I'm serious. You're in dangerous territory and these boys take it seriously. I've seen it before. If you plan to continue with these hearings you need protection. I suggest you ask the governor to give you a trooper for protection when you travel around the state."

Dalton blew out a huge sigh. "What are my chances of getting you to come over here and join the fight? I need your expertise and experience with this subject. I know some of the ins and outs of the fishing business, but you know all the tricks. What do you say, Uncle? You can stay with me and I'll pay your travel expenses."

There was a pause before he answered. "Can I call you back in an hour with an answer?"

"Of course," Dalton answered.

"By the way, Dalton, what have you heard about my old friend Willie Hickson over in Chinitna Bay? I read in the police report he was arrested for something, but it didn't say exactly what happened."

"Hickson rammed another boat over on the west side. That incident is one of the things setting these hearings in motion."

"Sounds like Willie. I'll call you in an hour."

<h1 style="text-align:center">➥• Chapter 10 •€</h1>

The month of July was about to end and commercial fishermen were beginning to complain about the price of fish for the season as well as the numbers of fish caught. The catch figures were down for set netters as well as drift fishermen across the entire Cook Inlet system. In years past when catch numbers were low the price per pound increased. Not this season. Prices for pounds of fish caught and sold to the processors were down by nearly 25 percent. Seasonal boat payments and fishing loans would take nearly all the revenues generated. Permit holders were beginning to worry about this year's paycheck.

Don Webber, too, was worried about the net profit for the season. He had not calculated the event of low catches in his formula to give a full share to the injured deck hand, but he had promised and would fulfill his debt to Freddie. With each opening of a fishing period he hoped for a bonanza that never materialized. Now with the end of the season approaching he was becoming worried about this season total. He and Lucy Hardy had made a list of plans for the off season, but there was no way for him to fulfill his part of the deal unless something very good happened here at the end of the season. The lost fishing days while his boat was being repaired and the added expense of the extra wages for Freddie would leave him very little income for the season. Unlike most of the fleet captains he had no boat payments to worry about. He began to consider the possibility of working in the oil fields this winter to earn money to live on.

Lucy had assured him she made enough in her insurance business to keep the wolf from the door, but he would hear none of it. It was his job to make the living and he would do it as long as he was able to do so.

These disturbing thoughts filled his head as he maneuvered his boat to make another set on a school of fish showing on his fish-finder. The skipper gave the signal and the crewmen began to deploy the gill net for the final set of the day. Commercial fishing is the only thing Don had ever wanted to do, but now he was unsure if he would survive the pressures of this season.

The stream of fish Don had seen on his fish finder was a huge one, probably the largest of the season. He was not alone in the sighting. There were five other boats maneuvering to lay out nets in the same area. These situations were always hazardous. Don had been lucky and the first on the school of fish. The nearest boat was dropping his net into the water to the west of Don's boat and net. Another boat, the *Durham,* a cannery owned vessel captained by a new 20-year-old skipper was running fast toward the two boats in an attempt to cork off the other two nets, but boat wakes in the area affected his turning ability and the boat rolled to starboard. It didn't capsize, but flooded the work deck in two feet of sea water. One man was washed overboard while the other deckhand clung to the net reel for security and was able to stay aboard, wet, but safe.

As the *Durham* righted itself and the water drained from the deck, the remaining deckhand reached for a safety flotation ring and tossed it to his partner in the water. The engine on the boat now began to sputter and pour white smoke from the stack. The seawater had reached the engine compartment and stopped the diesel engine. The young skipper came out of the cabin to help rescue the floating crewman and was immediately cursed by the crewman on the deck. The cursing was so loud it was heard by all the nearby boatmen. The man in the water was now being hauled safely aboard the *Durham.*

Don and his crew could see the man was wet, but otherwise unhurt. The crewman was still dripping wet when he called his skipper a very nasty name and punched him squarely in the mouth. Don and his crewmen watched the action and began to laugh at the scene, knowing this young man would no longer have a boat to run when the crew arrived back at the cannery dock.

This set was the best of the season and the crew took pleasure in picking the sockeye salmon from the net as it was reeled in over the stern. There was a great number of fish in the net and it took quite a while to care for the catch before turning the boat to make another set. Once the net was out the deckhands went inside to get coffee.

"That was a good set, Cap," commented Eddie the deckhand.

"Yeah, Eddie," replied Don, "I'm glad. We needed it. I'll try to stay on these fish as long as possible. I think we can make two more sets if the fish don't sneak off on us."

"Did you see that fiasco on the *Durham*?" asked Lou, the other deckhand.

"I made it out on deck in time to see the deckhand smack the skipper. The guy had it coming. I'm glad he couldn't cork us off like he was planning. I see they haven't moved. They must be having a discussion about who's going to be the boss. I'll bet they leave without making another set." Don was now chuckling with the other two men.

"That boat, the *Durham,* is a cannery boat out of Kenai. I'll bet the next time it fishes it will have a new skipper. I've seen that guy at work before and he's crazy," Eddie, the new deckhand commented..

"OK guys, enough fun for today. Let's keep working as long as we have fish," said Don. "Good job on the last set, by the way. Let's do it again."

Though the next two sets were not as good as the first, they were far better than they had seen all season. This fishing period wasn't going to make up for the bad season, but it was certainly going to help. Don was grateful for the good catch.

It was very late by the time the catch was off-loaded at the cannery in Homer and the boat secured for the night. Lou and Eddie said good night and left the dock while Don finished his fish reports and did the bookkeeping before entering the figures in his log book. He was about to turn off the lights and leave the boat when his cell phone rang. It was Lucy Hardy.

"Hi Lucy, isn't it past your bedtime?"

"Yes, it is, but I took a chance you were still working and called to see if you wanted to come by my place for a glass of wine before you go home."

"Only if you will make me a peanut butter sandwich for dinner," he said in a tired voice.

"I can do a little better than that for you. I have some wine here in the fridge. Just bring your tired self over here."

"I'm just leaving the boat and I can be there in about fifteen minutes."

"How was fishing today?" she inquired.

"Pretty good today. It won't save the season, but it will help a lot."

"I had a phone call asking for you today. I'll tell you about it when you get here."

"I'm on my way," he replied.

Minutes later he tapped on her front door and she let him inside before kissing him in greeting. "Welcome home Mister Webber."

"Had I known the reception would be this good I'd have been here earlier." He laughed and flopped into a recliner chair. "What was the phone call you had about me?" he asked.

"Oh, yes, it was from Senator Price's office. He wants to see you when you get some time. The girl said it was about some hearings they intend to conduct after fishing season. They want you to come to the office and help them with the agenda. She said Trooper Biggs recommended you. He's involved in it with the Senator." She returned from the kitchen with a glass of wine in each hand which she offered one to him.

"I wonder what they think I can contribute," he said, taking the wine glass from her outstretched hand.

"I don't know and she didn't say, but she said it was important. Now just sit still a minute while I finish your omelet." She walked away swinging her hips in an exaggerated manner.

A short time later she called him to come to the kitchen to eat. She had prepared a wonderful ham, cheese, and mushroom omelet with toasted homemade bread. It smelled delicious. He ate without speaking while she sat across the table and watched him. Finally, she spoke. "I like fixing dinner for you."

"And I like eating it. Maybe we should consider doing this on a daily basis."

"Perhaps we should," she commented. "Now finish up and go home. I don't want the neighbors to talk about you keeping late hours at my house." She was smiling a very seductive smile.

He finished his omelet and wine and helped her clear the table. "I hate to eat and run, but it's been a long day and I'm beat. I'll call you tomorrow."

"Good idea. Don't forget to call Senator Price's office and ask for Linda."

He hugged her tightly and kissed her forehead as he left the house. He slept late the next morning.

It was a bright and sunny morning in Homer. He had showered and shaved before deciding to have breakfast at the Duncan House Café. Hamburger steak and eggs satisfied his hunger along with his third cup of coffee. He was now ready to meet the day. He drove across town to the LIO to see a lady named Linda.

Inside the office he was met by a pleasant woman in her mid-forty's. "May I help you, sir?" she asked.

"Yes, I was asked to meet a person named Linda here. I'm Don Webber."

"Oh, yes, Mr. Webber. I'm Linda. The senator wants to talk with you. Just a moment and I'll tell him you're here." She picked up the telephone to speak with the senator in the back office. "The Senator will be right out," she said.

Senator Dalton Price was a tall, muscular man with graying hair and a winning smile. "Captain Webber, a pleasure to meet you. Come back to my office and we can talk."

Don followed the senator to the rear office and took a seat in front of his rather plain government desk. "I must be in a lot of trouble to get called to your office, Senator."

Dalton smiled, "Not at all, Don. May I call you Don?"

"Of course, sir. I was just curious to learn why you called me."

"I have been given a task to attempt to rectify the laws and regulations governing the fishing industry. It seems the violence in all areas of the fishing industry, commercial, sport and personal use, is escalating at an alarming rate. I am writing an agenda for a list of public hearings across the state with the intent of reducing the frictions among the various users and user groups. I understand you were a victim of a recent violent incident and I wanted input from someone at your interest level. I was given your name by Alaska Trooper Andy Biggs who recommended you as a commercial fisherman with a lot of common sense and good judgement. I was told you were a lifelong fisherman who loved the profession. I need advice from someone like you and I hope you will be willing to work with me and my office to see if we can fix some of the problems causing these tensions."

Don studied his feet a moment. "I can help you with identifying the causes of the frictions among fishermen, but I really don't know if they can be fixed. One of my deck hands was injured by another fisherman ramming my boat with his. That is not a rational act. I don't know if you can fix rage."

Dalton smiled. "I know I'm talking to the right man," he said.

The senator's desk phone rang. "My secretary says Trooper Biggs is on his way down here to join us. I think the three of us can come up with some ideas to take to these hearings and, of course, the attendees will add to the list of wants and wishes. I intend to hold the hearings across the state, beginning in Valdez, after the commercial fishing season has ended. Would you agree to become a part of my staff to give me professional advice? It will pay all expenses and per diem while traveling as well as a small salary for the duration of the panel."

Don paused several seconds before answering. "I have wished for a long time someone would do something about all the regulations and procedures that don't work. Everyone in the industry hates the way fish are allocated and complain when they get cut. It may not be possible to fix the problem and to make everyone happy at the same time, but there has to be some way to establish a sustainable fish stock and to regulate fishermen. There has been talk of buying out some permits to reduce the numbers of commercial fishermen. There has been talk of closing corridors to commercial fishing and a hundred other things, but just when we think a solution is at hand something happens, usually the cannery owners strong-arm the biologists into longer seasons, more openings, more permits and on and on. Someone has to take charge and actually enforce regulations that protect the fish. I'm a commercial fisherman, but I can see the system is broken. It needs to be fixed. I don't know if I'm the person to help you do this, but I'm willing to give it a try." He had just finished speaking when a large man filled the doorway. It was Andy Biggs.

"Come in, Andy. Don has just consented to join us and I agree with you. He seems to be the man for the job. Let's get some coffee and go to the conference room to do some brainstorming."

≫ **Chapter 11** ≪

The three men moved down the hall to the conference room where Linda was waiting. She had a stack of files in front of her and was studying a computer printout in the top file. When they entered she asked, "Can I get coffee for any of you?"

There were no takers. The three took seats at the table where Andy spoke to Don for the first time.

"I just came from the court. There was a hearing for Willie Hickson to set a trial date on your assault case. It's scheduled for the first week of September. I spoke with Willie's lawyer and she said she thought he was going to plead out, but was waiting for the trial date to do it. She thought he would get less jail time that way."

"I think he's crazy," said Webber. "My dad had trouble with him over the years, too. I don't know why he doesn't like me. I don't think I've spoken more than ten words to him in all the years I've known him."

"Wildlife troopers say he's nutty. They believe he's lived in Chinitna Bay too long and lost touch with reality. He just gets irrational if he sees a boat from the east side fishing the west side of the Inlet. I have no say in the matter, but I expect the judge to order him to pay restitution for your damages and for your deckhand's medical expenses."

"I hope you're right. It will keep my insurance rates from going through the roof."

"OK, folks," said Dalton, "let's get down to business. Linda, can you give us an outline of your plan so far?"

"Certainly, sir." She began to read from the computer printout she had been studying earlier. The meeting would go on for more than two hours. Linda had many pages of notes in front of her she would need to transcribe into her outline and meetings plan.

Dalton leaned back in his chair to stretch his back. "I think I've been sitting long enough," said the senator. "Welcome to the committee, Don. You made a great contribution to this meeting. I hope you choose to become a permanent member of these discussions. I can see you have great insight and knowledge. Linda will work on this new strategy and schedule another meeting in about a week. Are there any other comments?" A pause. "If not, we can adjourn. My thanks to both of you, Andy and Don," said Dalton, reaching to shake each man's hand.

"How is your deckhand?" asked Andy as the two men walked across the parking lot.

"I think he could go home if he had someone to care for him, but he lives alone. The doctor is trying to get some home health nurse or something, but Freddie is tough and says he feels good. He's weak and can't do much moving around. I hope the long-term effects aren't disabling for him. He's a really nice fella. I'm going up to visit him right now."

Andy nodded, "I have to go back to work, but please give him my best."

Don drove up the steep street to the hospital where he found Freddie sitting on the edge of his bed eating his lunch. A local news channel was on the television, playing very loudly.

"Good to see you sitting up, Freddie."

Freddie nodded and swallowed a mouthful of food. "It feels good too. They get me up every day to walk around the halls. I don't mind; the therapist is a good-looking gal." He took a last drink of cranberry juice.

"Do you need any magazines or anything?"

"No, I'm doing fine. How was fishing this week?"

"Pretty good, in fact the best day of the year so far," Don chuckled. "You would have gotten a kick out of what happened on one of the cannery boats from Kenai. The skipper, a really young guy, was trying to cork off our set and two other nets. He was turning tight and fast, nearly rolling the boat. One deckhand was washed overboard, but the other one got him out. It flooded the rear deck and killed the engine. When things leveled out the deckhand that had been in the water stepped up and smacked the skipper right in the teeth. Hit him a good one. Lou, Eddie, and I really laughed about that one."

Freddie was laughing. "Wish I had been there to see it," he said. "I'm glad you are finally catching some fish. I know it's been a slow season."

"Yeah, we need a few more days like that. By the way, Senator Price asked me to be on a committee to travel around the state holding hearings on changes to the fishing regulations. I was in a meeting with him and Trooper Biggs all morning. I think they are on the right track to get something done. I sure hope so."

"I hope so, too, Skipper. I am really tired of lying around and not being able to do anything."

"Speaking of which," said Don. "What is the doctor saying about sending you home?"

"He told me he's working on it and I may get to go home by the first of next week. He said everything is approved and the only thing left is to get the state to sign off on the paperwork."

"That's good news, Freddie." The two men sat silently several minutes. Finally Don said, "I guess I had better go to work. Call me if you need anything."

"Sure thing, Cap; thanks for coming." Freddie then picked up the TV remote control.

The next stop Don made was at the insurance office to see Lucy. He invited her to lunch at a local restaurant and she accepted. Over lunch he invited her to his place for a barbeque dinner of ribs and corn. She accepted this offer also.

After lunch he drove to the harbor to complete his chores on the boat before the next opening. It was always necessary to inspect the *Chilkoot* for wear and tear as well as unseen damages. He started the engine and moved the boat to the fuel dock where he loaded fuel and fresh water. He would get ice from the cannery tomorrow morning, early.

He spent the afternoon tending the boat, mostly cleaning decks, cabin floor and windows. Windows were always a problem from the salt spray making visibility poor and blurred. While working on the glass he noticed Willie Hickson strolling down the dock, walking directly toward his boat slip.

"Hey Webber," he shouted as he approached. "I want to talk to you."

Don stepped down to the rear deck, closer to the man on the dock.

"What can I do for you, Willie?" he asked.

"It ain't right you calling the troopers when we was just having a little fun over on the other side. My lawyer says I'll have to go to jail, but not 'till after fishin's done for the season. I'll settle with you then."

"You still don't understand, do you Willie? You hurt my deckhand. He may never be able to fish again. That is what's not right. Now get out of here. I don't want to talk to you."

"OK, but this ain't done. Stay off the west side and out of my fishing area. That is all the warning I'm goin' to give ya." With that comment he turned and walked back up the dock toward the shore.

Don watched him climb the ramp to the shore behind the Salty Dawg Saloon and go inside. He found his cell phone to dial the personal number for Trooper Andy Biggs to report the incident.

"I'll make a note and pass the information on to the DA. He may make this threat a part of his court case. I'll ask him what he wants to do about it and get back to you. Are you fishing tomorrow?" asked Biggs.

"Yes," answered Don. "I'm getting the boat ready now. I don't plan to fish that side of the rip tomorrow, so I shouldn't see old Willie out there." The rip is the fast moving tidal waters in the center portion of Cook Inlet where debris accumulates, and it is difficult to fish effectively.

"Just the same, keep your eyes open and watch out for him. I don't want to have another incident to investigate. Good luck tomorrow."

"Thanks, Andy. I'm through for the day and going home. I'm cooking ribs for Lucy tonight."

Don stopped at the local super market on his way home to pick up the ribs and fresh corn as well as a bottle of decent Muscato wine for Lucy.

It was nearly six when Lucy came from the office to Don's home. There was a long kiss at the door.

"Well!" said Lucy with a small gasp, "That was a nice greeting."

"Just in case you were missing me," replied Don.

"I have some good news for you, sir. I had word from the State of Alaska about Freddie's workman's comp claim. I gave them all the earning information and data they needed for the claim. They said they would process it right away and the first check should arrive in two weeks. I know you promised him you would give him a share from the boat, but this should help you and enable you to only pay the difference between his share and what the state is willing to pay." She chuckled, "After all we can't have him making a profit from his injury. If we do that, all the crew will want to get hurt."

Don chuckled, "Now you sound like an insurance agent," he said.

It was a nice Homer evening and the two decided to eat at the table in the back yard. Don had precooked the ribs in the oven and was finishing them with smoke in the barbeque along with several ears of fresh sweet corn. "I'll get the ribs and corn out of the barbeque if you will pour the wine."

There was much small talk during dinner. They talked about the off season, repairs to the boat, Don's appointment to the committee on changing fish allocations and other unimportant items. They had each consumed two glasses of the wine and were in a relaxed mood.

"You realize," he said, "I have to fish tomorrow. I'm going to have to sleep sometime tonight."

"I've been trying not to think about that," she commented. "Come on, I'll help with the dishes before I go home 'alone.'"

Lou and Eddie boarded the *Chilkoot* at 3:00 a.m. Both men, sleepy and groggy, set right to work with the chores of the day. Don had the engines idling when they arrived making it only minutes until they moved the boat to the cannery dock for some ice for the fish hold. It was 3:30 a.m. when they idled out of the harbor to turn west toward the open Inlet. There was a light wind and only eighteen-inch waves making it a pleasant journey to where Don began to watch the fish finder. He began to pick up fish and made his way to the front of the moving shoal. Ahead of the fish he took the boat out of gear, and he and the crew poured coffee to drink while they waited for the six a.m. time to drop the nets into the water. All three men were excited knowing they were about to drop nets on a good school of fish. Other boats began to gather in the same area as the *Chilkoot*, but only a few. They could see more boats to the west of the rip and slightly up the Inlet from their position.

"I'll bet old Willie Hickson is in that bunch of boats," said Don to no one in particular."

As the time got close he ordered the crew to take their positions and get ready to drop the net. Another boat, coming fast was aiming to cork off Don and his nets. Don sounded his horn in a long blast and slammed the throttles to spin the boat around and intercept the approaching boat. At the last second the other boat pulled back his throttles and turned back toward the west. Don had called the bluff and this time he won.

He quickly realigned the boat and with a toot on the horn ordered the crew to drop the net. The sun was shining and the breeze light when they began to reel in the net, loaded with fish. The first set was short of the huge one they had experienced days before, but nearly as good. Don began to relax about his financial plight and enjoy the satisfaction of commercial fishing as he had done for so many years in the past.

There were two more good sets made, both good net yield, when his oil pressure gauge began to fluctuate. He checked his engine oil level and found it full, but dark in color. This was to be a tough decision; run for Homer and safety or make another lucrative set? He decided to take a vote of the crew.

"Listen up, guys. Something is going wrong in my engine. I have to decide whether to make another set or run for the harbor. I don't want to shut down the engine for fear it may not start again. We can make a set, but you will have to do most of the work by hand without being able to use the engine to help retrieve the net. How do you want to play it?"

Lou and Eddie looked at each other only a second before nodding in agreement. "Keep her at idle, Cap. Lou and me can do one set the hard way. If the oil pressure starts going down let us know and we'll reel the fish and net onto the net reel and pick it later. Let's 'git er done.'"

Don accepted the advice and returned to the cabin to pilot the boat through one more set. The men worked hard and the set proved to be a good one. The fish hold now full, Don turned the boat toward Homer and the cannery. He motored at half throttle the entire distance back to port keeping an eye on the oil pressure and heat gauges. During the trip the oil pressure dropped a little and the engine temperature increased a little, but the trip was otherwise uneventful.

At the cannery dock he kept his engine idling while they unloaded, counted and weighed the catch. As soon as the cannery foreman handed him the fish ticket Don moved the boat, slowly, toward his mooring.

The crew had hosed down the deck and cleaned the equipment by the time they reached the landing.

"Thanks for a great day, guys. I appreciate both of you. Get some rest. We have one more period at the end of the week if the mechanic says the engine will take it. I'll call and let you know as soon as he inspects the engine."

It was early evening now, but Don knew the mechanic would still be in his shop. The mechanic answered on the second ring. "Marine Services," he answered.

"Hi, this is Don Webber on the *Chilkoot*. I have an oil pressure problem and wondered if you could take a look at it tonight."

"Sure, Don. I was just closing the shop. I'll be right down."

Half an hour later the mechanic came to the boat. "Start her up," he commanded as he stepped over the rail. When the engine was running he looked at the gauges and opened the engine compartment cover. A couple of minutes later he pulled his head out of the hole where the engine sat. "I think your filter is plugged. It must have sucked up some contaminated fuel or something. I don't know what caused it, but I have a new filter in the truck. I'll go get it."

When he returned with the filter and a bag of tools he poked his head inside the engine compartment again. Within minutes he came out with a dripping oil filter wrapped in a shop rag. "It was plugged all right," he said, showing the filter to Don.

Don had never seen a filter plugged like this before. "That filter is fairly new. How could it have become that dirty is such a short time?"

"I'm going to change your oil, Don. I think someone sabotaged your engine. I'm betting the oil pan is full of some kind of foreign material. It looks like sawdust to me."

"Put the old filter in that bucket and I'll take it outside. I want to keep it for testing."

"I have oil in the truck and I'll fill the pan after I clean it. You don't have to stay if you don't want to. I can finish up here."

"It's OK, I'll stay and buy you a beer when you finish. I need one, too. It's been a long day." Don decided to wait until morning to call Andy Biggs with news of the sabotage of the engine.

Chapter 12

It was midnight when Don crawled into his bed. It was one of those nights when he tossed and turned on his pillow for nearly thirty seconds before falling into a sound sleep. He was awakened in the morning by the ringing telephone. The clock next to the phone gave the time as 8:00 o'clock.

"Hello," he answered in a sleepy voice. It was Lucy.

"Get out of bed, sleepy head. I want you to buy me breakfast."

"I can do that, but I have to shower and get dressed. I'll pick you up at the office in about a half hour. Where do you want to eat?"

"I don't really care. Duncan House is good for breakfast."

"Duncan House it is."

Half an hour later he stopped in front of Lucy's office. She was waiting, looking out the front window. She stepped outside and locked the office door before climbing into his truck.

"You look like you could use more sleep," she said.

"We had a problem with the boat yesterday and I had to get the mechanic down to the dock to fix it. We never finished until midnight."

"Oh, I'm sorry, Don. I didn't know. Would you rather go home and rest a little more?"

"No, I have to meet with Andy Biggs this morning. Let's go have a nice breakfast together without talking business, yours or mine."

"My, my, but aren't we an old grump this morning?" she teased.

Breakfast was pleasant as was the drive back to Lucy's office. "Dinner at my place tonight, Don," she commanded.

"I'm on my way to meet with Trooper Biggs. Call me with a time for dinner." He waved out the window of his truck as he drove away.

It was a short drive to the trooper office in the Homer police station. Andy's patrol car was parked in front of the office. He made his way to

Andy's office carrying the bucket that contained the contaminated oil filter. Andy was at his desk working on a report when Don entered.

"Got a minute for me, Andy?" asked Don Webber.

Andy looked up and smiled, "Sure; have a seat. What's in the bucket?"

"Another complaint, I'm afraid. I had engine trouble while fishing yesterday and called the mechanic when I got in. This is the oil filter out of my boat engine. The mechanic says it's plugged up with, what looks to him like, sawdust. He cleaned my oil pan and changed my engine oil, but he thinks this was a deliberate act of sabotage."

Andy reached for a form from a pigeon hole atop his desk. "Let me see the filter," he asked. The trooper poked at the filter with a yellow lead pencil and studied the object for a long moment. "It does look like sawdust," he said. "Do you have any idea how it got into your oil pan?"

"Not for sure, but I can make a guess. A couple of nights ago I was working on the boat to get ready for yesterday's fishing period. I was about to leave when Willie Hickson came walking down the dock. He made sort of a threat about me fishing on the west side and said he didn't like it. He warned me not to fish there yesterday. I hadn't planned to fish the west side and let it go. I watched him walk back up the ramp and go into the Salty Dawg Saloon. I left and went home to go to bed. I didn't see him come back, but he was in the area and had the opportunity to dump something into my oil pan."

Andy had been writing in his notebook, finally leaning back in his desk chair, "So, you didn't see him come back? Did anyone else see him?"

"I don't know, I didn't ask around. It was late when the mechanic finished last night and I came in this morning to report it to you."

"He will be my number one suspect, but I doubt we will get enough evidence to charge him. I'll go ask around and see if I can turn up anything. Are there any permanent damages to your engine?"

"The mechanic didn't seem to think so. We have one more scheduled opening this week which will be the last one of the season. I plan to fish it and then pull the boat out for the winter. I always have the mechanic inspect the engine and the boat before I put it in storage, just in case something looks like it will break." Don looked out the office window, thinking. "You know, Andy, this has been a really poor season for me and the crew. Then Freddie got hurt and there were the damages to the boat to be repaired and we lost out on that fishing period. This season has been a bust. I'm going to have to find something to do this winter to make ends meet."

"I understand, Don," said Andy Biggs. "I'll pass this on to the DA, but without evidence he probably can't do anything. Hickson is scheduled for trial in a couple of weeks and I suspect you'll get a subpoena to testify. I would almost bet his lawyer will make a deal and have him plead out at the start of the trial. I can't say what the judge will do, but I doubt he will get much jail time, though he may be ordered to pay for your repairs and some kind of restitution to Freddie for his medical expenses."

"I understand, Andy. I've seen these things go to court in the past and no one got what they deserved. If Willie has to pay for my repairs and Freddie's medical expenses I guess I'll be satisfied."

"My advice is, don't expect too much," said Andy. "I'll go down to the docks and ask around and get back to you if I learn anything."

Don stood to leave. "Thanks, Andy," he said as he walked from the little office.

Lou and Eddie were on the boat cleaning the interior of the cabin when he arrived on the dock. The windows had all been cleaned and the deck, fish hold and nets had all been hosed down and cleaned. Don was impressed with the job.

"Dang, you boys saved me a whole day's work. Thanks," he said to the men when they greeted him.

"We thought your week had been bad enough and decided to lend a hand." Lou did the talking while Eddie nodded in agreement. "Did you find the oil pressure problem?"

"Yes, we did. Someone put sawdust or something in the oil. It plugged the filter and stopped the oil from circulating. I saw Willie Hickson on the dock here at the boat that night after you men left. I can't prove it, but I'd bet he was the one who sabotaged the engine. The mechanic cleaned it out and changed the oil. He said we should be good to fish at the end of the week."

"Do you think one of us should sleep on the boat to guard against another attempt?" asked Lou.

"I hadn't thought of that, Lou, but it sounds like a good idea. I can stay here, though. I'm going to pull the boat after the next period, so it will only be a couple of days," said Don.

"Naw, Cap, Eddie and I owe you. We'll both stay on the boat a couple of days and keep watch. Besides, you have a girlfriend to worry about; we don't." Both Lou and Eddie laughed.

Don thanked them and went into the cabin to make a list of supplies needed for the final fishing day. "Thanks again, guys," he said as he left the boat to go shopping. He returned later with the supplies including a pair of huge steaks for the men to cook for their dinner this evening. He stowed the items in the cupboard and small refrigerator and was just placing the last of the food in the refrigerator when his telephone rang. It was Lucy.

"I have a cake in the oven, and I'm making a special shrimp dish for dinner. I think we should have a bottle of wine with the shrimp. Could you stop and get one on your way?"

"You bet, lady. What time do you want me?"

"Give me an hour to ice the cake. I'll wait until you arrive to sauté the shrimp. Bye."

An hour later Don tapped on her front door, carrying a bag with two bottles of sparkling white wine. The front door opened and he was met by his lady friend, wearing a new outfit, wiping her hands on a small towel.

"Just in time," she said, stepping close for a kiss.

"Can I help in the kitchen?" asked Webber.

"Yes, you can open the wine and pour us each a glass while I start cooking the shrimp. Everything else is done. The glasses are there on the counter top."

He uncorked the wine and poured two glasses while watching her drop the shrimp into the hot skillet with melted butter and garlic already bubbling. A fresh cake was on the cupboard, a colorful green salad was in a bowl in the center of the table, and vegetables were steaming in a pan on another burner on the range. Once the shrimp were cooked everything came together almost instantly. They sat, raised their glasses in a short toast and began to eat without speaking. Half an hour later they finished and Don poured another glass of wine for each of them.

"You are a great cook, Lady," he said to her while raising his glass to salute her cooking.

"Thank you, sir," she replied and returned the salute.

After finishing their wine he helped her clear the table and wash the dishes. He enjoyed the domestic activity mostly because he was able to spend time close to her.

"Do you want more wine?" she asked.

"No, thanks, Lucy. I've had enough. Let's just go into the living room and sit a while."

They sat together on the couch, her head on his chest and his arm around her. "This is life at its best," he thought. There was music playing on an FM radio channel. The quiet moment was interrupted by the ringing of his cell phone. It was Lou.

"Your best friend, Willie, is down here, Cap. He's drunk and screaming at everyone on the dock. I think he's working his way toward the boat. You had better come down."

"I'll be right there, Lou." He turned to Lucy, "I have to go down to the boat. There's a problem."

Once in his truck he called Andy Biggs. "Hickson is down at the dock. My crewmen are on the boat, but they say Willie is yelling at everyone on the docks and coming toward the boat. I'm headed there now, but I think we may need you if he's drunk."

"I'm on my way. I'll meet you there." This is fishing season in Homer, Alaska. Never a dull moment if you're an Alaska State trooper.

Don was waiting for him when he stopped at the top of the ramp leading to the docks. "Have you seen him?" asked Andy.

"No, and I don't hear any loud voices either. Glad you're here. Let's go down to the boat and check on Lou and Eddie."

The two men walked quickly down the ramp and across the dock to the boat slip where the *Chilkoot* was moored. Lou was kneeling on the deck beside Eddie who appeared unconscious when they arrived.

"What happened, Lou?" asked Don.

"It was Willie. He was drunk. He started shouting at us and started to climb aboard. Eddie jumped in front of him to stop him and Willie hit him with something, it looked like an axe handle. When Eddie went down Willie ran off. I heard an outboard motor start somewhere in the direction he ran. I didn't leave Eddie and didn't see where Willie went."

Andy reached for his portable radio. "Dispatch, I need an ambulance at the *Chilkoot* on the dock behind the Salty Dawg Saloon. I have a man down and unconscious."

"10-4, Andy," said the dispatcher.

"The ambulance should be here in a couple of minutes. Watch for the medics. I'm going down the dock in the direction Lou said Willie ran."

"Do you want me to follow and back you up?" asked Webber.

"No. Stay with your crewman. If I need help I'll have Homer PD come down here. I'll get back to you as soon as I can." Andy quickly walked up the dock toward the cannery, checking each wing of the dock as he went.

On the last float, across from the cannery dock, a man was standing, waiting for the trooper. "Hi there. I'm Ned Sturtz. Somebody just jumped into my skiff and took off out of the harbor."

"What did he look like?" asked the trooper.

The description matched the one given of Willie Hickson by Lou. "I know who it is, sir. I think we will get your boat back. It may take a couple of days, but he's just running away. I'll send a boat after him. Come to my office and file a formal complaint for me, will you, sir?"

Andy wrote the information as well as the witness' name and ID number in his notebook. "There is an injured man down at the dock. I have to get back there to help the medics. Thank you for your help. Come to my office in the morning."

The medics were on the boat when he returned. Eddie was regaining consciousness when he arrived back at the *Chilkoot*. The medics loaded Eddie on a stretcher to carry him to the ambulance for the ride to the hospital.

"I'm sorry about Eddie, Lou. But I'm really glad you two were here when Willie showed up. There's no telling what he would have done if you hadn't stopped him."

It was after nine p.m., but the sun was still high over the western mountain range. The streets of the Homer Spit were full of tourists and fishermen. The violence on the docks was hardly noticed by the crowd. Don reached for his cell phone to let Lucy know he was on his way to the hospital to check on Eddie. This was not the way he had expected this evening to end.

Chapter 13

Lou was in the waiting room when Don arrived. "The doctors are still working on him, Cap. The doctor initially said he thought Eddie had a concussion, but should be OK in a couple of days. I know we have a fishing period on Thursday, but with the way fishing has been this season I think I can keep up with the catch without finding someone else for one day of fishing."

Don thought for a moment. "I agree, Lou, and I can come out of the pilot house to give you a hand. I hope we get more fish than we two can handle, but I doubt that will happen. Thanks for mentioning it."

Lou just nodded. "The doc said he would come out and get me when he finished treating Eddie."

"You know, Lou, I've known Willie Hickson for a lot of years and never had any trouble with him. My dad had a couple of run-ins with him over the years, but I never did. I wonder what set him off this season?"

"Do you suppose he is just feeling pressured with the lack of fish?" asked Lou.

"I think that's a good possibility. Everyone in the Inlet is feeling the pressure this year. It's not just us commercial fishermen, either. I've heard the sport fishing guides on the Kenai River are having problems too. Senator Price has asked me to be on a panel to travel around the state for hearings about changing the regulations with the intent of protecting salmon stocks. You know as well as I that Alaska Fish and Game hasn't met their own minimum escapement goals for several years and instead of controlling the catch they have lowered the minimums. That doesn't seem like an effective way to manage the resource." Don was speaking thoughtfully and quietly.

"I hope you take the offer, Cap. I don't know anyone fairer than you and you certainly understand the commercial fisherman's side of the argument." Lou was about to say something else when the doctor came to the waiting room.

"Hello, I'm Doctor Pierce. Are you Captain Webber?"

"Yes sir. Eddie and Lou both work for me. How's Eddie doing?"

"He's conscious and has a bad bump on his head. He isn't bleeding, but he's going to have a headache for a couple of days. I plan to keep him overnight just to be sure he doesn't have a severe brain injury. I think you can take him home tomorrow afternoon, but he needs to stay close to home for a couple of days. He probably had some bruising inside his brain and possibly some blood there also. This was a serious attack on his body. You can go back and see him if you have no further questions for me."

"Thanks, Doc, I'll stop and give the girls at the front desk my insurance information. We have a fishing period on Thursday. I'm assuming Eddie won't be able to work it?"

"I would advise against it. His injury is severe enough the effort and exertion could injure him further. He needs to stay home and rest a few days."

"Thanks for the advice, Doctor. I'll see to it he stays home."

The doctor returned to his cubical while Don and Lou walked to the small exam room where Eddie was lying on the bed with an ice pack on his head.

"What did you say to Old Willie to make him so mad?" asked Lou as he entered the room.

"Get out of here and send me a pretty nurse," Eddie replied.

Don stood close to the bed. "The doctor said he was keeping you for the night for safety reasons. He also said you shouldn't fish with us on Thursday. I want you to stay home and be quiet on Thursday, Eddie. I don't want your injury to get worse. I'll see that you get paid. It's my way of saying thanks for stepping up and stopping Willie from doing further damage to the boat."

"Where did he go? Did they get him?" quizzed Eddie.

"No, he ran to the other end of the dock near the cannery and stole a skiff. The owner said he saw him leaving the harbor. I'm guessing he's headed home to Chinitna Bay. The troopers will send someone over there to arrest him."

The following morning a Wildlife trooper, flying patrol on the east side of the Inlet spotted the stolen skiff on the beach in Chinitna Bay where Willie had come ashore the night before. This he reported to dispatch and Trooper Andy Biggs via his aircraft radio on a trooper frequency. He continued his patrol down the shoreline of the Alaska Peninsula, nearly to Kodiak Island before turning around to follow the same shoreline north again.

He was passing Ursus Cove when the call came for him to meet another state aircraft, carrying two troopers including Andy Biggs, on the beach near the spot where he had seen the stolen skiff. By the time he flew the thirty miles to the meeting place the other airplane was landing on the sandy beach in Chinitna Bay. The Wildlife trooper landed his Super Cub on the beach behind the Cessna 185. It was a short walk to where Willie Hickson lived, but they had walked cautiously in case Willie was still feeling belligerent. When they approached the main house they stopped near an outbuilding to keep out of view until contact was made with Hickson. Trooper Biggs used his cell phone to contact the house.

A sleepy sounding Willie answered the telephone. "Yeah, whadya want?" he grumbled into the phone.

"Willie, this is Trooper Biggs. We've met a couple of times. There are other troopers with me. We need to talk. Will you come out and meet with me?"

There was a short pause, then a mumbled answer, "Yeah, give me a minute to get my pants on." Fifteen minutes later out came Willie carrying a cup of coffee and sipping it as he stepped onto the porch.

"Come out onto the yard, Willie, where we can meet face to face," called Biggs.

Without hesitation Willie began to walk down the steps. There was an old, broken down ATV in the front yard where Willie finally sat as he continued sipping his coffee.

Biggs and the Wildlife trooper stepped into view, but the Cessna pilot stayed out of sight behind the small shed. Willie motioned for the men to approach when he saw them. They walked slowly to where he was seated.

"Hi, Andy. What brings you over to my place this early in the morning?" he asked.

"Were you in Homer yesterday, Willie?" asked Biggs.

"No. I stayed here all day 'cause I didn't feel too good. Hangover."

Biggs had his notebook in his hand. "I saw the skiff on the beach over there. It was stolen last night from the Homer docks. How did it get here?"

"Danged if I know. I didn't hear it come in. I was pretty drunk last night, though."

"We followed the tracks in the sand and they lead up to your place," said Andy. "Do you think you could have been drunk and gone to Homer without remembering?"

"I don't think so, Andy. But maybe. What happened in Homer, anyway?"

"There was an assault on the docks last night and that skiff out there was stolen by the guy who did the assault. Three witnesses say it was you." Biggs was now becoming alert.

Willie sipped on his coffee again, "Couldn't have been me. I was here all day and all night."

"Just the same, Willie, I'm going to have to take you back to Homer to let the witnesses get a look at you, just to make sure."

"I don't have time to go to Homer. I have to get ready for the opener tomorrow. Gotta fuel my boat and stuff." Willie made no move to comply.

Andy stepped closer to Willie, "Sorry Willie, you're going to have to come with me to Homer. Once the witnesses see you and tell me it wasn't you we'll bring you home again."

"Naw. I ain't got time today; maybe next week sometime, after fishing season. I have to come to Homer then anyways."

The Wildlife trooper moved up alongside Andy. "I'm afraid I must insist, Willie. Stand up and put your hands behind your back."

As Andy moved closer Willie stood, facing him. When Andy approached Willie raised his coffee cup intending to strike the trooper in the brown shirt. The Wildlife trooper stepped in quickly to grab Willie's hand that held the cup. Without effort he spun Willie to the ground, holding his right arm and snapping a handcuff on his wrist. Andy helped him secure the other hand to the second handcuff and lift Willie to his feet. The Wildlife trooper picked up the coffee cup from the sand and placed it on the porch rail.

"OK, Andy, I'll go with you," Willie said, "but I need to have my deckhand take care of the chores and fuel the boat."

At this point the third trooper, the pilot, stepped out from behind the shed. "Where is your deckhand? I'll go get him."

"It's my son. He's just over there in the cabin. He's still sleeping." Two minutes later the pilot returned with the deckhand and Willie related a list of instructions to him. "OK we can go now," said Willie, calmly.

The Wildlife trooper continued his patrol while Andy and his pilot flew back to Homer Airport with Willie. Once close to Homer he used his cell phone to call Don Webber to have him bring Lou to the trooper office to identify Willie. His second call was to the owner of the skiff, Mr. Sturtz, to ask that he also meet him at the trooper office to identify Willie. In the office Andy took the handcuffs off the prisoner and offered him a chair. He was working on his report when the three witnesses arrived.

"Lou," Andy asked, "can you identify this man?"

"Yes, sir, he's the one who hit Eddie down at the boat in the harbor last night."

"Are you sure?" asked Andy.

"Yes, I'm sure," replied Lou.

Willie instantly jumped to his feet, "That's a lie," he shouted.

"Sit down, Willie and shut up," ordered the trooper. "OK, Don, you and Lou wait outside and send in the owner of the skiff.

Don and Lou stepped out of the office and motioned for the other witness to enter.

When he was inside the office Andy asked, "Sir, is this the man you saw leaving the Homer Harbor in your skiff?"

"Yup, that's him, no doubt about it. Where's my boat?" asked the owner.

"It's still over in Chinitna Bay, but as soon as I finish my reports I can have my pilot take you over there to retrieve it."

When the witness statements had been recorded and signed Andy took Willie into the jail area of the small building where the jailer, a Homer Police Department officer, took control of him and booked him into the jail.

"Hey, Andy, you said I could go home as soon as the witnesses were done," Willie complained.

"Not exactly, Willie. I said you could go back when the witnesses said you didn't do it. That's not what they said. I can't let you go this time. I know you have a fishing period tomorrow, but you won't make it. This is your second assault charge in a few weeks. You haven't even been to court on the first one and now you have a second charge. I am holding you until tomorrow when you go to arraignment. The judge will say whether you can go home or not. You can't go around beating up on people any longer. Most people take offense at it. I'll be back to take you to court tomorrow. The officer will give you a phone call if you want to call your lawyer."

"Yeah, I'm going to call him, Andy."

"You do that, Willie," Andy answered as he left the jail to return to his office. Once there, he called the District Attorney to give him a verbal report.

"I guess we need to be serious about this one, Andy." The DA was chuckling.

"Perhaps we should have been more serious the first time. Now we have two injured fishermen. One may never fish again and the other will miss the final fishing opener of the year for this season. I would guess these fishermen want to see justice done."

"Don't get angry, Andy," said the DA.

"It's time someone got angry," said the trooper. "You people at the courthouse keep claiming you can't afford to prosecute every criminal we arrest. I'll keep arresting them. It's your job to prosecute them. I really don't care if your boss complains about the cost. If he doesn't like it, tell him to take the law off the books and then come to the hospital and explain it to the victims." With that angry statement he hung up the telephone, totally frustrated.

Chapter 14

Don Webber had moved the *Chilkoot* to the cannery dock to load ice by the time Lou arrived. Don called him on the cell phone to inform him of the move and to meet him at the cannery dock. Once the ice was on board Don started the engine while Lou untied the boat and coiled the mooring ropes. It was dusk, but light enough to see as they motored out of the narrow harbor entrance.

Done with his chores for now Lou came into the cabin to sit. There were two plastic foam containers on the small table.

"Breakfast," said Don.

Lou lifted the lid of one of the containers to find hot pancakes and sausage with packages of butter, now melted, and syrup. "Thanks, Cap. I'll finish mine and take the wheel so you can eat."

"It's going to be a long day, Lou. You should relax as much as possible. I plan to work this side below the Kasilof River. It's a shorter trip, and this late in the season the fish should be in that area. After I eat I'll take the wheel and you can get almost an hour nap."

Don was back in the pilot's chair within ten minutes and Lou took advantage of the nap time. He had noted there were few boats out this morning. Most of the fishermen had considered this entire season a bust and many had given up. He found the fish just south of the Kasilof River entrance. He took the boat out of gear and idled the engine to step out onto the deck and check the hydraulic oil in the net reel power pumps. The oil was clean and full. The only thing to do now was to wait for the time to drop the nets. Two other boat skippers had seen him stop and called on the radio. "Did you find the fish?" they each had asked.

"A few, but there will be room for both of you if you want to come over here near me. I'm short one deckhand today, so I'll need some room to operate."

"We're out near the rip and there are no fish showing on the sonar. I'll be coming your direction and Red is nodding he'll be following me. If you get into trouble we'll give you a hand. What happened to the other deckhand, anyway?"

"He and Lou were guarding the boat the other night and Hickson came down, picking a fight. He hit Eddie with an axe handle or something and put him in the hospital." Don didn't want to put too much information on the open marine radio channel.

"Dang, it's getting crazy out here. See you in a few minutes," said the other captain.

At the appointed time Lou was ready and began to deploy the long drift net. Don angled the boat to intercept the fish. In a short time the white corks on the top of the net began to submerge with the weight of the sockeye salmon hitting the mesh. When he thought the net was full he pointed the nose of the *Chilkoot* into the tide and again set the engine to idle, but leaving it in gear to keep the net straight. Once satisfied the boat would be safe he went to the rear deck to help Lou take the fish from the net as it was reeled aboard.

It is back breaking work to pick the commercial nets and the two men worked without speaking. With a small metal hook they pulled the heads of the salmon from the mesh of the gill net, tossing them in the direction of the fish hold. Once the entire net had been reeled in and picked free of fish and the usual debris caught in the net, Don returned to the cabin to, once again, find the fish and make another set. This process went on the entire day. The other two boats stayed in the vicinity and were doing well. Several times each skipper had asked if Don and his deckhand needed help. He did not.

When it came time to reel in the final set of the day both Don and Lou were totally exhausted. "I'm going to motor in to Homer as fast as the water will allow, so be careful out here."

"Will do, Cap. I have my float collar on, just in case, but I'll play it safe."

The other two boats that had fished with them today were following Don back to Homer. The lead boat called to talk to Don, who asked him to use the cell phone and get off the open radio frequency.

Moments later his phone rang. It was Red, the skipper of the second boat to follow.

"Hey, Don, sorry to hear about Eddie. How did you do today?" asked Red.

"Pretty good, Red, not enough to save the season, but one of our better days."

"Same with us, I don't know what's going to happen out here. We can't make a living like this," commented Red. "By the way, I heard you might be on some kind of a committee investigating ways to change the fishing regs and management rules. Is that true?"

"Yes, Senator Price asked me to join the committee. Trooper Andy Biggs is on it, too. The senator is working on an agenda and a schedule. Now that fishing is done he gave me time to take the boat out of the water and a couple of days off and then we go to work full time. I'll try to let you know when the hearings will be held. I'm sure they'll be advertised on the radio and in the newspaper."

"I'm glad you're on the committee, Don. I can't think of a better man for the job. Keep me posted."

"Will do, Red. I'm coming up on the channel buoy right now. I had better pay attention to my business. See you later."

The *Chilkoot* was number six to unload at the cannery dock which meant only a short wait for his turn. He and Lou, as well as the cannery worker, sucked the fish from the hold into a large net and weighed for their tally. The dock foreman came to the boat to give Don his fish ticket and asked him to move his boat for the next fisherman.

Don slowly steered the *Chilkoot* to his slip in the harbor. He shut down the engine and all the equipment for the night. It had been a very long and tiring day. Lou checked the mooring lines and boat fenders a second time before reporting to the captain.

"I think she's all secure, Cap. And I think I'm ready to quit for the day. I'll see you in the morning," he said.

"Take the morning off, Lou. I'll see you here about noon and we can unload the boat and get it ready to take it out of the water. I'll leave it with the mechanic to inspect before taking it to the marine storage yard. It's going to take me a couple of days to total the season and write you a check. It's been a tough one, but I thank you for all you did this season. I couldn't have done it without you. Go ahead and I'll see you tomorrow. Thanks again, Lou."

He was turning out the last of the cabin lights when his cell phone rang. It was Lucy. "Hi there, Big Boy. Are you almost finished for the day?"

"I'm just turning off the lights on the boat. It's been a very long day."

"I was hoping to catch you before you left the harbor. I've made a wonderful stew and thought you might stop by and have some on your way home."

"It's pretty late, but if you can stand a fishy-smelling visitor I'll stop." Don was grateful for the invitation.

Ten minutes later he was at her door. When she answered his knock she stepped out onto the front porch to wrap her arms around him and plant a warm kiss on his lips. Welcome home, sailor." She giggled a little and went into the house with Don following closely.

In the kitchen she told him to sit at the table while she dished up a plate of beef stew for him.

"How was your day?" she asked as she returned to the table.

"Long," said Don, "but we caught some fish. This is the first season I'm glad for it to be over. The fishing has been poor for the most part and with the trouble we had from Willie Hickson it was a bad season. My boat was broken, two crewmen injured, not many fish, and the price is down. It makes me think I should find honest work."

"You're just worn out, Don. In a few days you'll be planning next season. It's in your blood just as it was with your father."

Don took a bite of the stew and a bite of the homemade bread she served with it. "This is what a fisherman should come home to every night," he said after swallowing the mouthful of food.

"Would you prefer wine or coffee?" she asked.

"Coffee. A glass of wine tonight and I'll be sleeping on your couch." He shoveled more stew into his mouth. "How was your day?"

"Busy. Most of it had to do with you and your claims. The company has authorized payment for Freddie's medical expenses and asked for information about Eddie. It appears they're going to OK that one too."

"That's good news, Lucy. I hope they also pay the disability wages. That would take a giant load off my neck." He took a drink of the fresh coffee. "Do you suppose I could get one more helping of that stew?" he asked.

She brought another plateful of stew, placing it in front of him and running her fingers across the back of his neck.

"I suppose you want a tip too," he said between bites. After finishing the second helping of stew he slid his chair back from the table and pointed at his knee. "Come sit here a minute," he asked.

She gladly put one arm around his neck and sat on his lap. "I like this part," she said.

"I've been thinking about our relationship and I have mixed feelings about it. I just had a bad season and can't afford to keep you in a decent lifestyle, but if I get another job for the winter I think we would make out fine. I want you to marry me and raise a houseful of young fishermen. What do you think of that idea?"

"I think it's a wonderful idea. But, you don't have to take care of me. I make a good living at my business and can contribute, too, if you'll let me."

"I'm too tired to fight. Kiss me again and send me home. I need to get cleaned up and go to bed."
Just at that moment his telephone rang. It was Andy Biggs.

"Are you home yet?" he asked.

"No, I'm at Lucy's having dinner, but I'm about to leave. What's up?"

"We have Willie Hickson in jail here in Homer. I talked with the DA and he's going to push for a stiff sentence for this charge. I think old Willie is losing touch with reality. He tried to take a swing at me when we confronted him at his place in Chinitna Bay. He's mad as the devil at me for putting him in jail and not letting him fish today. I don't think his deckhand and neighbor fished the boat today either. I'm hoping the judge will put him away for the winter where he won't have to chop wood or pack water." Andy was expressing concern for the man he had put in jail. "I would like you to come to the office tomorrow to give me a witness statement. Can you do that?" asked Andy.

"Yes, but it will have to be in the morning. Lou and I are going to take everything off the boat in the afternoon and get it to the mechanic for a look-see on the way to winter storage. How about meeting me at Duncan House for breakfast at, say, nine?" Don knew he wanted to sleep late in the morning.

"Good idea. See you there in the morning. Say hi to Lucy for me. Good night, Don." Andy was an understanding man.

Don closed his phone and turned to Lucy. "I have to go. Andy wants me to file a report in the morning. I'm taking him to breakfast. I'll plan to see you when I get the boat out of the water and delivered to the mechanic. I'll think about your offer and give you an answer then.
Thanks for dinner."

"OK, run away without doing the dishes. I understand," she laughed. "You might ask Andy about when they plan to begin those hearings and how much travel you will be doing this winter."

"I'll do that," he said as they walked to the front door where he kissed her passionately.

⇛• Chapter 15 •⇚

Normally an early riser, Don had slept until nearly seven o'clock. Last night he had come home from Lucy's and taken off his fishy smelling clothes and thrown then in a corner. He had showered and fallen into bed. Now he needed to tidy up his small home and put his fishing clothes in the washer. He had finished the domestic chores and had two cups of coffee before leaving for his breakfast appointment with Andy Biggs.

Andy was waiting in his patrol car when Don arrived in the large parking area beside the restaurant. He was talking to someone on his cell phone as Don walked to the driver side of the patrol car. He waited until Andy finished his call to get the trooper's attention.

"Mornin,' Andy," he greeted.

"Good morning to you too, Don. Sorry about the wait, but the DA was on the phone. He said they're going to try for three years in prison for this assault charge. He doesn't know if the judge will go along with it, but he's going to try."

"I really hate to see Old Willie go to jail, but something has to be done with him. I have two injured crewmen because of him and his actions. This last one, when he hit Eddie and gave him a concussion, was deliberate and with rage. It seems to me he is escalating his attacks in both frequency and intensity. You said you thought he was losing it and I agree with you. Next time he might kill someone."

"Well," replied Andy, "it's up to the DA and the judge now. Let's eat."

During breakfast they discussed the committee hearings to be scheduled. "Have you talked to Senator Price?" asked Webber.

"A couple of times. He says Linda has been working on the plan and has a tentative agenda as well as a proposed schedule. I think we should go by his office and talk with him when we finish here."

"Good idea, but I have to be back at the boat by noon. Lou and I are going to take everything off the *Chilkoot* to get ready for winter storage.

I'm taking the boat to the mechanic this afternoon to leave it for a thorough check before we put it away for the winter."

Both men had ordered steak and eggs for breakfast and finished the meal in silence. They were drinking a final cup of coffee when the café owner came by the table to pass the time of day. He spent his day taking orders from customers and taking the cash at check-out. He was always friendly and everyone seemed to like the man. Don paid the tab while Andy left a tip on the table.

Don followed the trooper car from the parking lot and across town to the senator's office. Linda was at her desk when they arrived. "Good morning, fellas," she greeted as they entered. "The senator wants you to come on back to his office. Go ahead and I'll get the files and join you in the conference room."

The senator met them in the hallway leading to the conference room. "Good morning, Don, Andy. Good to see you. I need to go over a few things with the two of you this morning. Linda has been working hard at putting this thing together and we need to see if we have missed anything. Would either of you like coffee or something in the conference room?"

Both men turned down the offer stating they had just finished breakfast. The little group walked the short distance to the conference room. Linda caught up with them as they entered, carrying a thick volume of papers under her arm.

The meeting lasted more than two hours with Linda doing most of the explaining. There were lists of rented halls, dates for meetings, travel schedules and dozens of other details to be reviewed. The schedule was complicated and tight.

"I have checked with your colonel in Anchorage, Andy. He will give you time off from duty to attend the tour. He agreed this was an important undertaking and was pleased you were going to be in attendance. You will be paid full duty pay while working on this project." He then turned to Don, "I have arranged for you to be listed as one of my aides, and you will receive a salary as well as travel and other expenses."

"Thank you, sir," said Don.

It was approaching noon when Webber told the senator he had to leave. When he arrived at the dock Lou was on the boat carrying items from the cabin to the rear work deck. Don saw his progress as he walked down the dock. Still standing on the dock he called to Lou. "Hey, Lou, how is it going?"

"I have most of the stuff out of the cabin except for the electronics. I figured we could unload them and this stuff when we get the *Chilkoot* on the trailer."

"Good," replied Don. "I'll get the truck and back the trailer down the ramp. You can drive the boat to the other end of the harbor and wait for me."

"OK, Cap. Take your time; I have a couple more things to bring out here."

Don didn't answer, but returned to the parking area where the trailer was parked behind his truck. He climbed inside the truck and drove to the other side of the harbor and backed down the ramp, submerging the trailer in the salt water of the harbor. When he stepped out of the truck he could see the *Chilkoot* making its way past the boat slips to the loading ramp. It took only a few minutes to load the big metal boat, secure it and pull it to the top of the ramp where the two men loaded the items stacked on the rear deck into the pickup bed. Don climbed aboard and began to take the many electronic devices from the instrument panel. Lou carried each one to the truck and stowed them in the rear seat of the four-door vehicle. When finished both men climbed into the front seat.

"After we drop the boat at the shop, I'll buy you lunch," said Don.

"Good, I'm hungry. I slept late this morning and missed breakfast. I guess I should find some nice young girl to cook for me. But on the other hand, if I did that I would have to work year around. I probably wouldn't like that part." Lou was in a good mood today and talking more than usual.

"I've been thinking of doing just that, Lou. I think a lot of Lucy and she likes me, too, I think. I'll see how she feels at the end of winter. If she's still speaking to me I'm going to ask her to marry me in the spring." It was out of character for Don to be this open with Lou.

"Well, congratulations, Cap. I plan to spend the winter in Hawaii working for a friend of mine who owns a marlin fishing charter boat. Let me know if and when you get married. I want to come back for that event," replied Lou.

Don stopped the truck in the yard of the repair shop. "Go inside and ask where they want me to park the boat."

Lou stepped out of the truck and entered the office side of the boat garage returning a minute later. "Over there," said Lou, pointing to a vacant spot on the front side of the lot. "I'll guide you in," he said as he walked ahead of the truck.

Once parked Don left a list of instructions for the mechanic, "Have him call me if he finds anything and let me know when he's done and I'll pick up the boat and take it to storage.

"Let's eat," said Lou as Don climbed behind the wheel of the truck. "After lunch I'll help you store the electronic equipment."

After lunch Don drove the truck to his house where Lou helped him carry all the expensive equipment into an unused bedroom for safe keeping. "I plan to work on the books this afternoon, Lou. Your check could be ready by morning. I'll call you later."

"Thanks, Cap, I thought it would be a few more days before I got paid. I'll be home making arrangements for a flight to Hawaii."

Back at the harbor parking area Lou opened the door to step out when Don called to him.

"Hey Lou,"

"Yeah, Cap?"

"I just want you to know how much I appreciated you after all the bad luck hit us. You're a good man, Lou, and I hope you will fish for me next year."

"You can count on it, Cap. I get treated pretty well on your boat. See you later."

Don watched as Lou walked to his own truck and drove away. Lou's season had ended and he was carefree. Don on the other hand had to pay his men, pay his bills, buy net for next season, pay his taxes and hope there would be enough left over to keep him through the winter. The scheduled list of hearings with Senator Price should take up some of the shortfall, luckily.

From the Spit he drove to Lucy's office. Addie, Lucy's receptionist greeted him when he entered. "Hello, Mr. Webber, good to see you again."

"You, too, Addie. Is it possible for me to see Lucy for a minute?"

"She is always in for you, sir." She picked up the phone to announce Don's arrival. "Go right on back, Mr. Webber, she's waiting for you."

Don walked into Lucy's nicely appointed office, closing the door behind him.

"This must be serious," she said as he neared the desk. "You closed the door."

"It could be," he teased as he walked around the desk to kiss her.

"Perhaps I should lock the door as well," she returned the teasing. The two of them laughed a little.

"I just pulled the boat out of the water and took it to the shop for an annual checkup. I'll pick it up next week and take it to storage. In the meantime, I thought it might be nice for the two of us to get away for the weekend. How would you like to go to Anchorage? We could stay in a good hotel, have dinner at a good restaurant and maybe take in a good movie or something. It's been a long season and I would really like to spend a weekend with you."

"The most pressing claims I have right now are yours. If you can afford to delay your settlement two more days I can go with you. It sounds romantic, exciting and adventurous. Let me tell Addie I'll be out of town this weekend." She called to tell her receptionist to clear her calendar for the next two days.

"I'm glad you consented. I thought I would have to kidnap you. I'm going to the hospital to see Freddie. I think he is being released to go home today. They are furnishing him a day nurse to care for him, but he'll be alone at night. After that I have to go to my little office and work on the totals for the year and make a final payment to Lou, Freddie and Eddie. If you get me a big enough settlement from the insurance I will be able to eat this winter. By the way, the Senator is hiring me as an aide for the hearings around the state. That should stop me from having to ask you for a job this winter." Don was only half joking. "I'll talk with you later."

He felt elated as he left her office to drive up the long hillside road to the hospital where he walked directly to Freddie's room. He was sitting on the edge of his bed, a wheelchair beside him.

"Are they letting you go?" asked Don.

"Yes, my day nurse is out at the desk getting my release papers. She ordered a van to take me home." Freddie offered. "By the way, how was fishing yesterday?"

"It was good, not great, but good. We pulled the boat this afternoon and took it to the shop for inspection before we take it to storage next week."

"Wish I could be there to help, Cap."

"Everything is done, Freddie. Your job is to get well. Do you need anything?" asked Webber.

"No, the nurse said she would do some shopping for me. Lucky for me your insurance is paying for all this luxury. I can't thank you enough for what you have done through all this, Cap."

"You're a good hand, Freddie. I'm just sorry you got hurt. Old Willie goes to court next week on your injury case. The DA said they were going light on this one, but when Willie attacked Eddie at the boat the DA said he was going to attempt to get the judge to give him a long jail sentence on the new charge."

"He's just a crazy old loner living over in the Bay. I think like the DA, he is getting nuttier by the day." Freddie looked up to see his day nurse coming through the door.

"Are you ready to leave? she asked.

"Load me up and haul me out of here," exclaimed Freddie.

"I'll be seeing you Freddie. Call me if you need anything." The nurse was seating Freddie in the wheelchair when Don left.

Chapter 16

That same Friday evening, in Seattle, a meeting had been called in the back room of a high dollar restaurant across the West Seattle Bridge on the Alki Beach Road. The Phoenecia Restaurant was chosen for the privacy afforded these patrons. There were three attendees at this meeting: Sam Nelson, Eric Goodloe and Ioshi Morita. Each was the owner and CEO of large fish processing companies. Each owned a fleet of commercial fishing vessels as well as processing plants up and down the west coast and in Alaska. Sam Nelson owned the largest fleet and the most canneries. Sam owned five canneries and more than a hundred boats in Alaska as well as several fish tenders, large fish processing ships in Cook Inlet and the Bering Sea.

The men met regularly at this restaurant and always in the small banquet room in the rear. The owner assigned himself as waiter and server for the meeting. Without asking he brought a tray of drinks for the group. Sam thanked him and asked for privacy before they ordered dinner. The owner agreed and said he would be near the door when they finished the business portion of the meeting.

Once the owner exited the room Sam sat at the head of the large table sipping his tall glass of Johnny Walker Blue. "OK, fellas let's get down to why I called this meeting."

The other two men stopped their private conversation and sat, each taking up their own glasses.

"What's this all about, Sam?" asked Eric Goodloe.

"I just received some disturbing news from Alaska. There is a move afoot to change fish allocations and a lot of other regulations up there. This move is being headed up by Senator Dalton Price of Homer. He carries a lot of weight in the State Senate. He is in the process of setting up hearings to change the way fish are allocated as well as season openings based on fish return numbers. He wants to eliminate many of the commercial fishing permits. There are some other items on his agenda, but those will affect us the most." Sam took another drink of his liquor.

Ioshi Morita was of Japanese descent, but was one hundred percent American. He was the first to ask the question: "Where did this information come from, Sam? If they are only now proposing hearings it can't be an emergency."

"I have a close friend at Alaska Fish and Game. He is the head of the Commercial Fish Division for Cook Inlet. He has had inquiries from Senator Price's office. From his discussions with the folks in Price's office we could be in big trouble. You both own canneries in Alaska, you know how it is to do business up there. We have been able to persuade Fish and Game to open periods of fishing in order to keep the labor crews busy. I don't have to tell you how we do it, but we have all made a lot of money and kept a lot of our boats working by applying pressure to the fish managers at Fish and Game. My informant is saying that Price is attempting to change that authority. We put a lot of cash into the Alaska economy and will still have a great deal of say in who gets the fish, but if they change the laws we will be in jeopardy of losing our influence. We can't have that. We need to devise some means of controlling these hearings."

"Can we buy Senator Price?" asked Goodloe.

"I don't know, Eric. We can try." Sam made a note on his pad.

"This has been tried before and failed," said Ioshi.

"That's what has my informant worried. We may not be able to stop it this time. I called this meeting to get ideas on what to do about the situation. Assuming the threat is real, I want your ideas on what to do about it." Sam Nelson took down the last of his glass of scotch.

"We need to find out who is on the panel holding these hearings and see if we can buy any of them," remarked Goodloe.

"If we can get a list of these hearings we could seed the crowd and disrupt them, you know, get the crowd on our side. Cash would do that." Ioshi believed in the influence of the dollar.

"Both good ideas and my informant will keep us abreast of the panel's progress. I won't lie; this thing has me worried. My man at Fish and Game is worried. He says this is the most serious threat he has ever seen. He can usually beat these things down, but he says everyone in Alaska is angry and afraid of the dwindling fish stocks. I'll keep the two of you informed of what's going on. I just wanted you to be aware we are facing the greatest threat we have ever had. If we lose Alaska I can move most of my fleet to Peru and Chile, but I can't possibly make that kind of money down there." Nelson hung his head. "I'll do my best to keep you apprised of this situation and I want both of you to keep your ears open for any indication this is going to happen. Your skippers should be hearing about this soon and start reporting back to you."

"I don't like threats," said Goodloe, "and I think I have someone who can eliminate Senator Price if it comes down to it."

"Let's not get that extreme just yet," stated Ioshi Morita.

"I called this meeting to inform you of the situation and you now know most of what I know. All we can do now is wait to hear of further developments and pray nothing happens, but we have to be ready for any eventuality. Now, let's have dinner and another drink." Sam needed another drink.

An hour later the three men drove back into Seattle, each going to their respective homes. Sam Nelson had done all he could do for tonight. Tomorrow he would call his contact in Alaska and ask him to stay on top of the developments.

Early Sunday morning Nelson direct dialed the home of Winston Dugan, director of the Commercial Fish Division of Alaska State Fish and Game Commission. It was an hour earlier in Alaska and a sleepy voice answered the telephone.

"H'lo," answered the voice.

"Winston, it's Sam in Seattle. We need to talk."

"Yeah, Sam. What's up?"

"This is important, Winston. Wake up," demanded Nelson.

"OK, OK, give me a minute to go to the bathroom."

Sam waited patiently while the phone was dead. Finally he heard footsteps and a voice came on the line.

"OK, Sam, what is it?" Winston Dugan was now awake.

"The boys and I had a meeting last night and we're worried about these hearings you said were in the works. We will need more detailed information before we can plan an attack. I don't care how you do it, but you have to get that information for us. Like always, I'll pay, but it will be up to you to furnish us with the intelligence we need. You know as well as I that what's happening could put us out of business in Alaska. If the proposals you have mentioned become law we'll be forced to close all our canneries and sell or move our fleets. We can't allow this to happen."

"What do you want me to do, Sam?" asked Dugan.

"We need a detailed schedule for the hearings, times, sites and dates. We need to know the agenda and who will be directing the meetings. If you come up with a method of ending these hearings, let us know right away. We're still in the dark and can't make any decisions without more information." There was a great deal of frustration in Sam Nelson's voice.

"These are set to be fact-finding hearings. The panel, at least to this point, is going to be the Senator, a commercial fisherman from Homer, Don Webber, an Alaska State trooper, Andy Biggs, someone from the river guide outfit, someone from the sport fishing community, I think it will be the president of Trout Unlimited, and one of my Fish and Game resource managers. I don't know which one I will send along, but it will be my job to pick him." Dugan had just given a mountain of information.

"Who is invited to testify at these hearings, Winston?"

"I'm not sure, but I understand it is open to all interested members of the public. I'll try to confirm that for you."

"Good, I know it's the weekend, Winston, but this is very important to all of us. If this comes to fruition it will be devastating to our profits and likely cause us to move all our operations out of Alaska. I am depending on you to get me as much information as possible and keep me up-dated on the status of the panel. I don't want any surprises. Once I get a schedule, I can plan to have agents at the meetings. I will expect daily reports." Sam Nelson had always been a careful man, a man who knew how to make money, a ruthless and dedicated man. "I want all this as quickly as possible. You know my private number."

"Sure thing, Mr. Nelson. I'll call you as soon as I learn anything." Both men hung up the telephone wondering where this would lead.

That Sunday morning in Anchorage Don and Lucy awoke in the Sheraton Hotel to a sunny and bright day. They were in love, officially. After a shower and dressing and with an occasional kiss, they discussed where to have breakfast. They decided on a small café a few blocks from the hotel. After breakfast it was a day of shopping, downtown for clothing for Lucy and Costco for necessities for Don. They left Anchorage just after two in the afternoon and planned to eat an early dinner at the Sunrise Inn in Cooper Landing on the trip back to Homer.

Though it was getting late in the summer the traffic was terrible. Motorhomes were slow moving and hindering the movement of faster traffic. Though the state had provided slow traffic turnouts to allow passing, few drivers chose to use them. It was nearly four thirty when the couple pulled into the full parking lot of the Gift Shop, Motel and Restaurant. The lady who had purchased the complex only a short three years ago had turned it into a very nice stop with good food and wonderful views of the mountain and Kenai Lake. Arden, the owner, met and greeted them as they entered.

"Hi, folks, sit wherever you like. My waitress will be right with you. How was the traffic today?" she asked.

"Not too bad, considering. We're headed to home in Homer and still have nearly two hours of travel today," answered Don.

"I love Homer," said Arden as she placed glasses of water on the table. "Can I get you something to drink?"

They each ordered a huge blackened bleu bacon burger, one with regular fries and one with sweet potato fries. They settled for drinking the water on the table. The place was full of tourists enjoying the wonderful Alaska summer. Because of the number of customers it took some time to get their order. They chatted like good couples do while waiting.

"I've had a wonderful two days with you, Don. I can't remember when I've been so relaxed. Thank you for inviting me to come along." Lucy stared dreamy eyed at him across the table.

"It's been nice for me, too, Lucy. I'm glad we had this weekend. The senator will be asking me to go to work on the hearings for him at the middle of this week and I don't know when I'll have another weekend off to be with you. Once I have a schedule of these meetings and know when they will end, I think we should plan a wedding. What do you think?"

Surprised by the statement, Lucy sat open-mouthed. "I think that will be wonderful, Don. Do you want any say in the matter or are you leaving it all up to me?"

"I'm leaving it mostly up to you. I prefer a small, family style wedding, but I put you in charge and I'll go along with whatever you want." Don reached across the table to hold her hand.

Their sandwiches came and they ate in silence, though they smiled and passed secret glances to each other. At one point Arden came by to ask how they were doing and they replied, "Great." Upon leaving the café they stopped by the gift shop to look around but didn't buy anything.

The trip from Cooper Landing to Homer was nearly three hours and both were exhausted by the time the purchases were unloaded at Lucy's home. They said good night and Don drove to his place to unload the things he had bought. He hardly noticed the chore as he thought about the weekend and his love for Lucy.

⋙• **Chapter 17** •⋘

Linda was in the office early on Monday. She had been working for more than an hour when the telephone rang. It was Winston Dugan.

"Good Morning, this is the office of Senator Price. How may I help you?"

"Good morning, Linda. This is Winston over here at Fish and Game. How are you this morning?"

"I'm fine, Winston. The Senator hasn't come into the office yet, but he will be here shortly. Is there something I can do for you?"

"Perhaps. I have heard rumors the Senator is setting up a statewide series of meetings to discuss changes in the fisheries management plan. Is that true?" asked Dugan.

"Yes, the agenda and schedule haven't been finalized yet. I'm sure he will want you to participate." She wondered where he had learned of the meetings.

"Since the topic is about how I run my office I think I or my representative should be involved in the discussions. I would like to ask the Senator why I wasn't included in setting the agenda." There was coldness in his words.

"I'm sorry Mr. Dugan. That would have been my fault. There have been so many facets to this that I just hadn't gotten around to calling you. I'm sure, given the scope of these hearings, the Senator will want you on the panel." Linda knew the Senator had deliberately not called him knowing he would do his best to resist any changes needing his cooperation. She also knew his participation would be required.

"Thanks, Linda. Please have Dalton call me when he gets into the office." It was meant as a directive from a department head.

As she hung up the telephone she looked at the clock and decided she should make fresh coffee for the Senator. He was going to have a very long morning. She had just returned to her desk when he parked his car in front of the office.

"Good morning, Linda," he greeted her as he entered. "I see you're hard at it this morning."

"I've been here for nearly two hours making a list of things to confirm for our tour around the state. I had a call from Winston Dugan this morning. I think he's angry he hasn't been invited yet. He asked to have you return his call when you came in."

"We knew this was going to happen. I wonder what took him so long. Maybe our secrecy has been better than we thought." Senator Price chuckled as he walked to his office. "Get him on the phone for me, will you Linda?" he said as he walked away.

Dalton Price was at his desk with a fresh cup of morning coffee when his phone rang. "Good morning, Winston. I understand you called this morning. I just came into the office. How are you, my friend?"

"I'm good, Dalton. I called because I learned you were planning statewide meetings to discuss changing fishing regulations and commercial fish allocations. Since this is my area of responsibility, I wondered why I haven't been told and asked to participate in these hearings?"

"Consider yourself asked, Winston. So far we are only in the planning stage of this. I have been asked by several user groups about why something hasn't been done to preserve the fish stocks and why commercial fishing seems to take priority over all other groups. We are attempting to put an agenda together that will give all these groups an opportunity to be heard. Once the agenda has been established we would have called you. I realize how important your office is in this discussion. I apologize if you felt slighted. It was purely unintentional. We just haven't finalized the agenda as yet. When we have a schedule we will contact you and furnish you with a list of locations and dates. I hope you will attend personally. You would be a great addition to the scope of the panel."

"Dalton, I know BS when I hear it and this is BS. I think you are trying to set this up without input from me or my office. Commercial fishing has the largest stake in this process and deserves to be part of the planning." It was clear Winston Dugan was angry.

"Calm down, Winston. You will be given a chance to add or change things in the program, but the overall scope is with the intent to preserve the fish. I am hoping that is the same goal you have for your department. In the end we are on the same page. I'll have Linda send you a copy of the confirmed portions of the agenda and schedule, but remember all this is tentative pending final work-up. Let's work together, Winston. We're on the same page and have the same objectives."

"I'm glad to hear it, Dalton. I'll be waiting to see those plans. Get back to me as soon as possible." Dugan hung up without further comment.

The Senator called Linda to his office. He was laughing when she arrived.

"Was it that much fun, Senator?" she asked.

"Yes, it was," he replied, still chuckling. "Old Winston is really put out we had gone this far without his knowledge. I guess we should send him a copy of the schedule of meetings and the proposed agenda. Invite him to be a part of the official panel. That should make him feel important enough." He was still laughing quietly.

Now Linda was chuckling. "I'll get on it right away, sir. Is there anything else?"

"No, just keep at the programming. I'll call Andy and Don to let them know we've heard from Winston. Once they have reviewed the schedule we can begin to advertise the meetings."

Don Webber was up to his ears in bookkeeping when the phone rang.

"Hello, Don, Dalton Price. I wanted to let you know I just had a call from Winston Dugan. He's pretty upset at us because he hasn't been invited to our meetings."

Don chuckled. "I thank you for that, Senator. I don't mean to be rude, but I think he's a big part of our problem. I guess, since he's in charge of all commercial fishing in this part of Alaska, he should be invited. How is everything else?"

"It's going well. Linda has an agenda planned and is busy setting up venues and meeting dates. She is the best coordinator I've ever seen. It will be done right. You will get a copy of the schedule as soon as it's completed. Once done you and I will have to have some meetings to discuss strategy. Andy has been cleared to go to all the meetings with us. I plan to add a Wildlife trooper to the mix within the next couple of days. That, with Winston should fill the panel."

"I have to admit, you have done a great job of organizing this thing. I was apprehensive at first, but now I'm excited and looking forward to getting something done."

"Say, Don, isn't today the date for Willie Hickson to go to trial?"

"Yes, in fact I have to leave here in a few minutes to testify. This is for the first offense. The second one will be next month. I hope they only have to deliver him to court from the jail." Don had been so engrossed in his accounting work he had lost track of the time. "I have to deliver checks to my three deck hands today before I go to the court."

"It sounds like you are a busy man. I'll let you get to it. I'll be talking to you in the next couple of days and Linda should have your schedule and copy of the agenda by then. See ya." Senator Price held some guilt for stopping Webber from his accounting tasks.

Don finished making his entries in the ledgers and writing a check to each of his three deckhands. He planned to personally deliver each of the checks before going to the court, though Lou would be there in court with him.

It took only a minute to deliver the check to Eddie, who was grateful for the bonus money included. The stop at Freddie's home was another story. His personal caregiver answered the door and invited Don into the small house. Freddie was happy to see his boss.

"Give us some time alone, Geneva," he told the girl. "We have some business to discuss."

"I'll be around if you need me, sir," said the caregiver.

He turned toward Don saying, "Man it's good to see you, Cap. She's a nice girl, but she fusses too much. How is everything going?"

Don gave a short summary of the past few days including the court date this afternoon. "Sorry you can't be there. The word from the DA is that he will go easy on Willie for this charge, because your injury was unintentional, but he intends to throw the book at him for beating Eddie with an axe handle. I hope the judge sees it differently and sends him away for a long time for your pain and suffering. I guess it's up to the jury today."

"Wish I could be there, Cap, but the doc won't allow me out of the house for that long at a time. I'm getting up and walking every day, though, and I'm feeling stronger."

The two men reminisced for more than an hour when Don excused himself by saying he had to be at the court soon.

"Thanks for the generous check, Cap, and come back soon. I like the company." Freddie was studying the figures on the check when Don left the room.

Court was scheduled for three in the afternoon and Don was seated on a bench in the hall talking with the DA at 2:30. The DA was prepping him with the kind of questions he would ask and guessing at the questions the Defense Attorney would ask. "Wait out here until I have the bailiff come out to get you," said the DA. Don waited patiently.

The court proceedings, including the jury deliberation took just under two hours. The jury finding was guilty on all charges with no recommendations for sentencing. The judge had studied all aspects of the case prior to trial and in accordance with the wishes of the DA he levied a very large fine on reckless endangerment for ramming the *Chilkoot*. He demanded restitution for all damages inflicted on Don Webber's boat, his machinery and fishing gear.

The judge wasn't so nice about the personal injury to Freddie. The judge ordered Willie to pay the equivalent of Freddie's lost wages including wages during his recovery period as well as restitution for all medical expenses incurred by Freddie and Don. The total would amount to several hundred thousand dollars. The final nail in this coffin was 45 days to serve in jail at the state institution, Wildwood Jail Facility in Kenai, Alaska. He was to be remanded this day. Andy was tasked with delivering the prisoner to jail in Kenai. He seemed pleased with the job.

"Court adjourned," said the judge as he gathered his papers and left the bench.

Before leaving the court with his prisoner, Andy Biggs spoke to Don. "About what you expected?" he asked Don.

"More than I expected," he replied. "I sort of feel sorry for Old Willie, but he screwed up and it cost him dearly. I hope it changes his attitudes toward me fishing on his side of the Inlet."

"I have to drive the prisoner to Kenai. I'll call you tomorrow and we can discuss the other matter we have in common." Andy stepped to the defense table to place handcuffs on Willie Hickson.

"Have a nice drive to Kenai," said Don to the trooper.

It was nearly half past five when he drove past Lucy's office. Her car was parked in front of the small building. He stopped and went inside to ask her to have dinner with him. The receptionist had gone for the day and they were alone in the office.

"Did you have your day in court today?" she asked.

"Yes, I did, and the judge threw the book at poor old Willie. I spent all the rest of the day doing my fishing reports and writing checks to my helpers. I was a busy man today, Lady."

"Oh, you poor thing, you. What are we having for dinner?" she said smiling widely.

"Whatever you want at the steak house; I missed lunch and I'm hungry. We can talk about other things later, later," said Don, teasing his girlfriend.

"Why you dirty old man. You should be ashamed. Let me turn out the lights and I'll be ready."

⇒• Chapter 18 •⇐

The rest of the week had been filled with stops at Senator Price's office to collect stacks of papers related to the up-coming series of hearings. First was the agenda which took Don two days to digest. It was long and complicated, forcing him to think in broader terms than his commercial fishing experience. Two days of study and data collection were needed to understand the long list of items on the agenda. He readily understood the needs and wants of commercial fishermen, but it was difficult for him to comprehend the broad effects on the state's economy of guided and sport fishing. It was a revelation to realize sport fishing was done in both fresh and salt water, in federal waters and state waters, by residential and non- resident fishermen, by guides and week-end anglers. There was also a huge class of fishermen who, by federal mandate, took precedence over all other groups. This latter group of personal use and subsistence fishermen was also the most difficult to manage and the most abused segment. He spent hour upon hour studying the agenda and the consequences of each item. He finished the statement two days later.

The mechanic had finished his annual inspection of the F/V *Chilkoot* and Don welcomed the chance to get away from his desk to deal with the mechanic and move the boat to winter storage. He paid the mechanic and was grateful the bill was not as large as usual, due mostly to the work already done while repairing the fish reel damaged by Willie Hickson. Satisfied with the outcome of the inspection he towed the vessel to the marine storage yard to be covered with plastic wrap for the winter. This was new for him, but he had decided to try it this year.

He was returning to his office at home when his cell phone jingled. It was Lucy. "Where have you been?" she asked. "I haven't heard from you in a couple of days. Don't you love me anymore?"

"Hi, Lucy, yes I still love you. I've been up to my ears with the stuff from the senator's office and I'm just now coming back home from the boat yard.

And you thought I did nothing in the off season but drink beer and tell lies like a good fisherman should."

"How did you know what I was thinking?" She giggled a little. "I was thinking it would be a good night for me to stop for a pizza on the way home and for you to come to my place and help me eat it."

"You really are a sweet talker. What time do you want me there?"

"I should be home and ready by 6:30 if you can be there by then."

"What can I bring?" he asked.

"Just your gorgeous self. I'll see you then, bye." She was giggling again when she hung up the phone.

He was at home and just stepped out of the shower when his telephone rang once more. It was Andy Biggs. "Have you seen the proposed agenda, Don?"

"I just spent more than two days attempting to digest all of it. I was surprised at the depth of the list. I wonder how long the wish list will be after the hearings end." Don was wiping water from his hair as he spoke.

"I'm glad I'll be exempt from most of the questioning and debate. Have you heard who the Wildlife trooper will be?" asked Andy.

"No, I haven't. Have you?"

"Just got a call from my captain. It will be Sergeant Galen Carpetti. I've known him a long time. He has a good head on his shoulders and speaks his mind. That last fact sometimes gets him into hot water. I respect him and I think you will, too." It was a good evaluation by Biggs.

"I think I've met him somewhere, but I really don't know him. I'll be anxious to meet him. The senator said he was the last addition to be named to the panel. I wonder how soon we'll have a meeting with our entire panel?" Don speculated.

"I don't know, but I think it will be soon."

"Say, Andy, how did Willie like the ride to jail?" asked Webber.

"He was mostly quiet, but resigned to his fate. He admits he was wrong and he's dreading the next trial. He told me he thought the judge was mad at him and would probably give him life without parole for attacking your deckhand." Andy snickered at the statement given by Willie.

"I gotta go, Andy, but I'm supposed to get more stuff from Linda tomorrow. Why don't you meet me at the senator's office and we can pick up our packets at the same time and perhaps talk with the senator."

"Good idea, see you around ten at his office."

Don finished drying his body and put on clean clothing for his date with Lucy.

Dinner was wonderful and the conversation even better. Lucy was in a good mood to match that of Don, but he seemed preoccupied in his thoughts all evening. As he drove Lucy to her home she asked, "Are you coming inside for a while?"

"Sorry, Lucy, I can't tonight. I still have some things to review before I go to the senator's office in the morning."

"So, you love the senator more than you love me?" she teased.

"Of course not, Lover, but this bunch of public hearings is turning out to be a full-time job. It's so much more complicated than I ever thought it was going to be. I'm beginning to regret taking the job. I'll learn the schedule for the hearings tomorrow. I've been studying the scope of the testimony to be taken and the proposed questions to be asked and they are mind blowing. By the end of the hearings I think every fisherman from every side of the argument will hate my guts." He looked at her and smiled. "At least Old Willie Hickson will have a lot of allies."

"I know you took this position because you wanted to help, but if you think it is going to be too much work I suggest you quit now, before you're in too deep to pull out."

"You know I can't do that, Lucy. I can't be a quitter."

"I know, Don. That's one of the things I love about you."

In the driveway of her house he kissed her good night and watched her walk to the door before pulling out and driving home.

The following morning Andy had called to confirm a time to meet, giving Don enough time to stop at the Duncan House for breakfast. He slept well last night and was rested and ready for the day. Andy was waiting in the parking lot when he arrived at the state office complex.

Inside, they each greeted Linda. She asked them to have a seat while the senator finished a phone call he was taking. "Want some coffee?" she asked.

Both men turned down the offer and waited in the visitor chairs across the office from the reception desk. They waited ten minutes before she called them to follow her down the hall to the senator's office. She placed two large packets of papers, each bound in heavy covers, on the senator's desk and went back to her desk.

Senator Dalton Price was writing notes on a yellow legal pad and didn't look up until he had finished. "Good morning, Gents," he said. "That was my counterpart in Fairbanks on the phone. He's heard about our little tour and asked to be kept abreast of the progress, or lack thereof, as we proceed from meeting to meeting. Are you fellas ready to start in two weeks?"

"If the captain says I can be there I will be. I'm kinda excited about this," said Andy Biggs.

"That's at least two weeks earlier than I had anticipated, but I'm ready. I've been studying the agenda and realized how wide a scope we will be dealing with. Andy may have his hands full when they all start shooting at us." Don was only half joking.

"That is the way these things always work. They start with a simple idea and morph into a hornet's nest. This one is going to be more volatile than most because of the emotion attached to each user group. Each group claims to own the resource and none wants to give up anything, but take it all from the other groups. You're right, Don, there could be some fireworks at these meetings." Price was voicing his candid opinion. "Are you still in it for the long haul?"

"I'm in Senator, I've complained enough. I can't back out now."

"Good. Then take these packets and study them. They contain the schedule of dates, times, and places for the meetings. They will each be advertised on the radio and television as well as in the local newspapers for each meeting. The names of the panel members will not be in the published ads, but I suspect it will be one of the first questions the TV reporters will be asking. You should be prepared for some unflattering phone calls. If you receive any threatening calls, I want to know about them immediately, whether you think them serious or not; understand?"

Both Don Webber and Andy Biggs nodded in compliance, but Andy had a question.

"Excuse me, Senator, but I have to ask as part of my responsibilities; have you or your office had any threatening calls?"

The Senator smiled, grateful Andy was taking the suggestion to heart. "None that I'm aware of, but I'll ask Linda and get back to you. Do either of you have any questions for me?" No reply came from either man.

"Good, then go home and adjust your personal schedules for the next couple of months. Don, I want you to stop at Linda's desk and sign employment papers in order for you to get paid."

Andy and Don had only been gone from the senator's office a few minutes when Linda notified Dalton Price he had a phone call from Winston Dugan. He moaned and picked up the telephone.

"Winston, how are you this morning?" he began.

"I have two large packets on my desk. It looks like I will be joining you at the hearings. I haven't had a chance to review the agenda, but I did look at the schedule and have been told by the director I was to attend all the meetings. I assume you must have talked to my director."

"Yes, I did, Winston. I told him you would be an important part of the panel. I expect you to be the one to field all questions from the public regarding the role of Fish and Game both in past actions and in future planning. Is that satisfactory with you?"

"Thank you, Senator. It's far more than I expected. I thought you just wanted a whipping boy and so I wasn't looking forward to being on the panel. I appreciate your giving me dedicated responsibility. I'll do the best I can to help meet the objectives of your panel, even though it seems its purpose is to change the scope of responsibility of my department." There was a great deal of sarcasm in his tone.

"Don't be offended, Winston. I'm looking for true experts in each area I except to cover with these hearings. It is my intention to revise the way the entire fish stock is managed. I want you to be a major part of that planning. The one thing stopping this in the past is each stakeholder only wanted to protect their own kingdom at the expense of all the other kingdoms. When this is over, I expect every stakeholder to be both angry at their losses and happy with their gains. There will be no winners and no losers from the changes we make, however it is our objective to protect the remaining spawning fish stocks.

"I am tasking this panel to find the best and least painful way to accomplish that goal. The other members of this panel are experts of sorts in their area of responsibility, just as you are for commercial fish management. When the hearings are finished it will be up to this panel to draft new policies and it will be up to me to draft new legislation with those goals in mind. I hope you will agree with these objectives and support the end result of these hearings. I expect individual groups to pressure each of the members of this panel and attempt to sway the end result. None of the other members has shown an interest in any preconceived results and I hope you will not be the first. I want you to engage in this panel with an open mind. Is that clear, Winston?" Dalton hoped he had sufficiently explained to the fishery manager how he expected him to conduct himself while on the panel.

"Those are pretty lofty goals, Dalton. Our biologists have always done their best to protect the salmon stocks. I will not sit still for this panel or any other agency to degrade the work of my department." Winston was now becoming angry, feeling his ability to control the hearings the way he had been able to do in the past by claiming scientific knowledge would be at risk.

"I'm telling you how this panel is to function, Winston. If you can't agree with this policy I suggest you tell your boss to find someone else to replace you." Senator Price felt good to exercise his own authority.

"I'll serve on the panel, gladly, if only to protect my agency. You said you wanted no preconceived conclusions. I expect the same from you and this panel. I can be objective as long as the process is honest and not intended to place blame or eliminate any group of users. I appreciate your honesty, Dalton. We understand each other. I'll be on the panel and withhold open warfare as long as no one takes a shot at me. Thanks for your time, Senator."

After ending the call Dalton Price faced his computer and began to note the time and content of the call. He personally hoped this hostility would not seep into the panel or the hearings. "Linda," called the senator, "close up the office and let's go to lunch. I need to cool off after that call."

Chapter 19

The first meeting was scheduled in Valdez on the first Saturday in September. It was to last the entire day from 9:00 in the morning until 8:00 in the evening. The local newspaper had advertised the meeting and PSAs were noted daily for a week on the local radio station. Valdez is a small community, but the crowd of interested participants came from shoreline communities around the region. The largest group was from the little fishing town of Cordova where a large fleet of commercial vessels was based in addition to a large cannery facility. Cordova is the base for a large portion of the Prince William Sound area fishing fleet.

One of the features of Valdez Sound, second only to the Alyeska Pipeline Terminal, is a cannery established by, some say, 'THE' smartest man in the world. Across the road leading to the Pipeline Terminal is a small pond where warm outfall water from the gasoline refinery drains. It is fresh water from the cooling towers of the refinery and without any sort of contaminates. Fresh cold water is added to the pond from spring water dripping from the rocky cliffs behind the pond. The "smartest man in the world" obtained a permit to plant pink salmon in the pond. He then built a cannery with a fish ladder below the culvert under the pipeline terminal highway. Once the fish stock was established the fish returned to the same pond to spawn each year, swimming up the fish ladder into the cannery, thus eliminating the need for a commercial fishing fleet. It is an awesome sight to see nearly a million fish swimming around in front of the cannery waiting to swim up the fish ladder into the facility. A spawning stock is allowed to enter the pond and naturally produce eggs for the next generation of salmon.

It seems every predator in the Valdez area awaits this huge school of fish. There are sea birds of all description, seals, sea otters, sea lions, sharks, and other predators getting fat on the returning salmon. Tourists gather each day to watch the fish swimming around the enclosure meant to deter the predators from entering the proximity of the cannery.

In a large conference room in the hotel near the harbor in downtown Valdez, the panel was ensconced in a lush setting with coffee, water, pastries and other amenities furnished by the hotel. Each panel member had a room reserved in the hotel eliminating the need for travel outside the hotel for business reasons. It was a very convenient arrangement.

The first evening the panel had dinner together at a large banquet table furnished by the hotel. Linda had made the arrangements for them with the hotel furnishing many extras for the panel members. Don and Andy had made a tour of the meeting room before dinner and admired the detail given to the meeting by the hotel.

The first order of business at the opening public meeting was introductions conducted by Senator Dalton Price. The audience filled the hall with standing room only in the back of the room and many attendees standing in the hallway.

"I would like to introduce you all to our select panel at this meeting. First of all, I am Senator Dalton Price of Homer. I will chair this meeting. I expect all participants to be cordial and precise with their statements. I will direct all responses to the member of the panel best suited to answer your inquiries and statements." Senator Price paused a moment to be sure everyone understood. "Next I would like to introduce Alaska State Trooper Andy Biggs. He is in charge of security and will not tolerate any wild behavior."

Andy stood, waved his hand and reseated his large frame.

"Next I would like to introduce the head of the Commercial Fishing Division of the Alaska Department of Fish and Game, Mr. Winston Dugan."

The introductions went on through the entire list of the panel: Commercial fisherman Don Webber; Sport fish representative from Trout Unlimited Bill Ordman; Sport fishing Guides Association Herb Bissett; Subsistence and personal use representative Raymond Seals; and finally the senator's aide and record keeper for the meeting Linda Barton.

"This is going to be a very long day and I hope you will keep your statements as short and succinct as possible. My assistant has compiled a list of registered requests to speak and she will call on you in the order you registered. Please try to be positive in your statements." There didn't seem to be any objections to his introductions. "In the interest of saving time you have been furnished a statement of intent for this meeting, therefore I will forgo that explanation." He turned to Linda saying, "Please call the first name on your list."

And so it began. The first speaker was a commercial fisherman from Cordova. "I'm Augie Stevenson and I been fishing out of Cordova for more than fifty years. I ain't goin' to sit around and listen to you if all you want to do is put me out of business. Them foreign boats are killin' us and you ain't never done nothin' to stop them people. My catch was down by thirty five percent this year and the price was more than thirty percent low. We can't make a livin' with income like that. I got a boat to keep and gear to replace and my family to feed. What are you goin' to do about that? You don't do nothing about them big Korean factory boats neither. I betcha you don't even know how many fish they take. I'm a Alaskan fisherman. Who is looking out for me?"

"I think this is a question for Winston Dugan, but the high seas fishing you refer to is under the direction of the federal government about which we in the state of Alaska have little say." With this statement he handed the question over to Dugan.

"Mr. Stevenson," Winston began. "You make a valid point. We are all concerned for the well-being of our Alaska commercial fishermen. The state has no control over the prices paid for fish and I cannot address the fish prices, but if you have fished for as many years as you profess you know the returns vary widely from year to year. We do our best to manage the forecasted returns, but we are always behind the curve by the nature of the business. Limited entry guarantees you will be able to fish, but, as you know, you will have good years and you will have bad years. Some fishermen are better at the trade than others. We at Fish and Game do our best to predict fish returns in the various districts and set openings to intercept them. Global warming has played a big factor in the fish returns and for that we can only make suggestions to the federal managers. This panel is charged with attempting to correct some of that shortfall by changing the number of fishing boats in a district as well as the number of hours you will be allowed to fish. We can get a more accurate count of returning spawners after they return to the rivers, and a great many of those returning fish are harvested by other user groups such as personal use fishermen and sport fishermen. These play a tremendous negative factor on returning fish that have already passed the commercial fishermen. Every commercial user is affected by them. We as managers must allocate fish stocks to all groups, but the federal government says subsistence users have priority over everyone else. We on this panel are as frustrated as you about matters that are out of our hands."

Augie Stevenson was shaking his head. "You ain't tellin me nothin'. I want to know what you're doin' about it?"

"That is why we're here, sir. We have come to gather ideas from you and other users to correct the inequities you are facing. I would be happy to hear any ideas on how to go about this task. Do you have any suggestions, Mr. Stevenson?"

"Yeah, go home and stop wastin' my time." With that statement he turned and walked to the door to exit.

The next eight speakers were much like the first, with similar and broader concerns. The speaker on the floor was making his appeal when there was a disturbance in the hallway outside the room. Andy Biggs stood to go see what the problem was when a very stout man in a three piece suit entered the room, pushing others out of the way to enter.

"Who are you and what do you want, sir? This is an open and official meeting. You must wait your turn to speak." The senator held his hand out to stop Andy from leaving the podium.

"I'm Irving Boswell and I own three canneries in this neck of the woods. It is beginning to sound to me like you are only here to justify ways to put me and other cannery owners out of business and to allow the foreign fishermen to take over the entire industry. I have a large investment in the state of Alaska and I am a major employer. If you plan to cut the number of fish I can purchase from the commercial fishermen you will be cutting millions of dollars in revenue currently being paid to the state as taxes on wages and income from fish sales. You are only hurting yourself. I don't want to close any of my facilities, but I won't operate at a loss. I need these fishermen and you people need our money. It will be your choice if you cut us or our fishermen." Irving Boswell was now sweating and red in the face, angry and frustrated with having to wait in the hall and not being able to make a solid point that he and his fishermen were the most important people in the room.

Don Webber listened to the remarks becoming more heated and when a small break appeared, he asked the senator for permission to enter the fray. The senator approved hoping he could calm the agitated parties.

"Mr. Boswell, I am Don Webber. I am a second-generation drift fisherman in Cook Inlet. I have suffered the same declines as you and my income is showing the effects of the low fish numbers. I agreed to take a position on this panel in an effort to find ways to change the trends we are seeing. If something isn't done there will be no fish for us to catch. We have all contributed our share to the decline of fish. I am not here to determine who is to blame, only to find a solution. I appreciate your attempt to define the problem, but we must also look for solutions. If it means fewer fishermen or fewer canneries, then that is what we will have to do, but the loss will not be to one user group. Every user group will be forced to change. If we fail to find our own solutions the loss of fish will put us all out of business. Let's attempt to find reasonable alternatives without threats or mayhem. We, as reasonable people, should be able to adjust our own system so that most of it will survive. If we don't, I fear we all will fail. I suggest we work together to this end."

"Wise words from a second-generation drift fisherman," said Senator Price. "I think this would be an excellent time for us to take a lunch break and give us all a little time to cool off. We will resume the discussion at 1:30." He slammed the gavel and stood.

The entire panel had their lunch at the hotel restaurant. Don sat with Dugan, Linda, Price and Biggs during lunch. While waiting for their food the senator asked Don what he thought of the proceedings thus far.

"I thought that cannery guy was going to start a riot. I guess I didn't realize, though I should have, just how much hostility would be voiced at these hearings. I'm beginning to learn how much those kingdoms you told me about are in play. Everyone wants to fix the blame and not the problem."

"Don't take all this guff personally. You didn't create the problem and we're searching for ways to resolve the issues. A judge once told me when you go fishing you put the bait in the water: sometimes you get a bite and sometimes you don't, but at least you were fishing." Senator seemed very philosophical about it all.

Similar conversations were taking place at other tables. Linda excused herself to go to the ladies' room to freshen up for the afternoon session. When she had left the table Don turned to Andy. "I thought you were going to have to shoot that cannery guy, Boswell."

Andy chuckled, "This is a public meeting. We only pepper spray them in public meetings."

"Nonetheless, Andy, I admire your quick response to the prospect of a threat. Thank you." It was the senator once again, thinking he had made a good choice of members of this task force.

⇛ Chapter 20 ⇚

After lunch the meeting continued much as it had in the morning session—mostly local commercial fishermen voicing their opinions and feelings about the low fish returns and low prices, blaming sport fishermen for killing the spawning salmon and foreign fishing fleets for over-harvesting on the high seas. Few offered suggestions for improving the returns or limiting their own participation. It was the fourth participant in the afternoon who stirred things the most.

He introduced himself as Dwayne Pooter, a commercial fisherman from Yakutat. "I'm a commercial fisherman; have been all my adult life. Things used to be good for us, but now we can't even make a living. I operate a cannery boat out of Yakutat and this year I didn't even make minimum wage. All I want to do is fish, but it looks like all you want to do is stop us from fishing. The canneries pay my wages based on my catch. If the catch is down so is my paycheck. I'm glad I don't own a boat these days. I couldn't even pay for the fuel. If it doesn't improve soon the canneries will have to close and I'll be out of business. You guys have to listen to the cannery owners. They have the most to lose and pay the most fishermen. You can't just come in here and shut down fisheries and close canneries without it costing the local people their livelihood." The senator directed the response to Don Webber.

"I'm a commercial fisherman myself, Mr. Pooter. I own my own boat, as did my father before me. I agree with most of your argument, sir, but in my experience the cannery owners are a big part of the problem. You know as well as I that the cannery owners have been forcing Alaska Fish and Game to continue opening fishing periods when the runs have dwindled to nothing and minimum escapement has not been met. They think with their pocketbook and don't care about the fish. They don't want to lose their labor force and have to rehire when the next run appears. It costs them too much money. They look out for the dollar and not for the fish. No one is protecting the fish. That's what these hearings are about: changing the way escapements are managed. You won't have future runs worth putting a boat in the water if you keep reducing minimum escapement to keep the boats, yours and mine, in the water. We need to find a way to take some loss now to protect the future. I don't mean to argue with you; I'm on your side, but somewhere we will all have to give a little for the betterment of the future. If we don't there won't be a future for either of us."

The next speaker was a local guide, with a twist. His business owned fish wheels for taking subsistence fish on the Copper River.

"Jud Perkins," he said into the microphone. "I operate several fish wheels where city people can come and get their allotment of fish for subsistence purposes. I try to be a sort of game warden and only let them take the number of fish allowed by permit. Subsistence fishing is traditional on the Copper River. The federal government even put subsistence above other fishing. I operate several wheels and take the customer to and from the site and regulate the number of fish they take. This reduces the amount of river traffic and improves safety on the river for the fishermen as well as other operators out there. What you say is mostly true, but I worry that my business will be shut down by new regulations.

"Everyone seems to think that just because we operate in the river we are raping the spawning beds. We're taking free swimming fish on their way to the spawning beds, but is that any different than a drifter or set netter or even a high seas fisherman taking free swimming fish in the ocean or a sport fisherman taking a free-swimming fish with hook and line in the river? It boils down to when and where you count the fish returning to the spawning beds. The federal government says my fishermen take priority over all others. I'm here to make sure they remain at the top of the list."

"You make an excellent point, Mr. Perkins. I will be sure your comments are noted in our findings."

"Thank you for allowing me to speak and not treating me like some nut. Thanks for giving me the time."

As he was leaving the table to exit the room, Perkins was pushed aside by a group of five men. Andy, once again stood to move on the intruders.

The intruder in the lead saw Andy stand to confront them and held up his hand, pointing a finger at him. "Sit down, Trooper. We're commercial fishermen and we came to stop this goat rope. You guys in Juneau think you have all the answers, but you don't ever get anything right. We're going to have our say and it will take more than one fat trooper to stop us."

Andy Biggs said something into the lapel mike on his shirt and stepped out from behind the table. "I'm here to keep the peace and you have disrupted our process. You will have an opportunity to speak, but in the order you register. You will not be allowed to come into the hearing at your own pleasure for the purpose of disrupting the proceedings. I am ordering all of you to leave the hall at once or you will be arrested. Turn around now and leave. There's a sign-up sheet on the table in the hall and you are free to sign it."

"I and my friends are staying and I, for one, am not taking orders from you, so go back to your seat and shut up."

"What's your name," asked Andy as he stepped off the podium platform to confront the man.

"I'm Einer Jacobs and I told you to stay seated at the desk." The fisherman now took a step forward with two other men following.

"That's it, Jacobs. You and your gang are under arrest for disorderly conduct. If you don't want further charges you will turn around and go out to meet the four officers entering the front of the building as we speak."

"He's bluffing, guys, let's get him," ordered Jacobs.

He was taking long strides over the short distance between them when Andy took the canister of pepper spray from his belt and at a distance of less than two feet sprayed the charging fisherman. The men behind him stopped and took a step backward as Einer Jacobs screamed and tried to wipe the solution from his eyes and face. Andy quickly spun him to the floor face down and applied handcuffs just as the four local officers arrived on the scene. He instructed the city officer to take all five of the unruly fishermen to jail and to have Jacobs treated for his encounter with the pepper spray.

The rest of the attendees had retreated back into the hall away from the confrontation and now formed a pathway for the officers to lead the detainees out of the hall. Jacobs was screaming and crying during the entire event and could be heard sobbing after he was outside and on the street.

Once the five fishermen were out of the building Andy made an announcement. "OK, folks, I think this is over. Let's take a fifteen-minute coffee break to cool down. We will reconvene in fifteen minutes."

He made his way back to his seat at the table where Senator Price shook his hand. "You handled that situation splendidly, Andy. I was sure someone was going to be hurt. Let me get you a soda or coffee and thank you again." The senator sent Linda for refreshments to be brought to the table.

Don Webber was seated next to Andy and poked him in the ribs when he was seated, "You move pretty good for an old fat guy," he teased.

"It's easy when you're as scared as me," he replied only half joking.

"Honestly, Andy, I was impressed with how you handled the situation. Good job."

Sitting on the other side of Don was Galen Carpetti, the Wildlife trooper who now leaned forward to speak with Andy. "Good job, Andy. I got out of my chair to back you up when you went into action. You're pretty smooth, old man. I think I would have just shot him."

"I thought about it, but I think the senator would have been upset so I just squirted him with the pepper spray. Fortunately, everyone had moved out of the way and I had a clean shot without filling the hall with the stuff. This new stuff isn't as bad as the old mace we used to have. An old trooper I know once sprayed a small puff of mace inside the air ducts at the Kenai police station and it migrated across the hall where seven police chiefs were meeting. It was funny at the time seeing all seven of them running out of the building and into the parking lot. My friend got a letter in his file for that one. But it was still funny."

Linda returned with a large tray on wheels containing coffee, donuts, a bucket filled with ice, and cokes. Minutes later, the meeting resumed in an orderly manner. The next person on the list stepped to the microphone to give his testimony. The speakers continued all afternoon and into the evening. By eight p.m. the last of the speakers was finished, and Senator Price declared adjournment.

Linda and the senator were scheduled out of Valdez on the first flight to Anchorage the next morning. The rest had driven private vehicles with Andy riding with Don Webber. Don dropped Andy at his home and drove directly to Lucy's office, not realizing the time of day. The office was closed. He cursed and drove to her house. He knocked on the door and she answered it almost immediately.

"Honey, I'm home," he said when she opened the door. Without answering she wrapped her arms around his neck and kissed him. "I like the way you say hello," said Don.

"I don't greet everyone that way," was her reply. "Have you had dinner?"

"No, I haven't even been home yet. Would you like to go out?"

"No, I have things here to fix. Come in and tell me about your trip." She stepped back from the doorway to allow him to enter.

"It was certainly more than I expected. It was confrontational and informative, for the most part. I was glad Andy was there to keep the peace. I can tell you the members of the panel have as big a difference of opinion as how to solve the problem as the folks who came to testify. The senator did a wonderful job of keeping order, though. The meetings are going to be stressful if they continue like the first one, and I expect them to."

"Well, then let me give you some good news. I have a check at my office for you. The insurance company gave you everything I asked for in the insurance settlement and said they would negotiate with the hospital directly about the medical expenses for Freddie. Congratulations, you're rich again." She giggled a little. "I've been looking for a rich boyfriend."

"I'm too tired to argue with you; just keep the check and feed me," he said in a sarcastic tone.

She fussed over the stove for several minutes making a nice omelet of ham, cheese, mushrooms and onion. Whole wheat toast and honey were set on the table. She kissed him on the forehead and sat across the table from him. "Will that make you feel better?" she asked.

"Just being here with you makes me feel better," he said as he dished his portion of the omelet.

"Are you going to stay a while tonight?" she asked.

"Sorry, Lucy, not tonight. I have a full day of report writing tomorrow as well as a meeting with the senator at nine a.m., but I'll buy you dinner tomorrow night, if you like."

"Come by the office and I'll have you sign for the checks you will be getting." She dabbed her mouth with a napkin and stared across the table. You look really tired, Don. You should get a good night's sleep tonight and call me in the morning."

"That sounds like a good idea. I have to shower and do some laundry though before going to bed. It's a long drive from Valdez."

"Where is the next meeting?" she inquired.

"King Salmon on the Alaska Peninsula," acknowledged Don. "That one will be air travel."

She stared at her hands folded on her lap. When she looked up and into his eyes she looked sad. "I'm worried about you, Don. I've been thinking about how much emotion is involved in what you're doing and some of these people are not very nice. I have a great fear that you could be in danger. I couldn't stand it if you were hurt. Please don't take any chances and be extra careful, for my sake?"

He smiled and reached across the table to take her hand to comfort her. "You're right about there being an element of danger involved in this process. I saw it in Valdez. Please don't worry. Andy is always ready for trouble. He stopped a potential bad situation this week and I know he can handle it. Please don't worry about me." Don had not thought about how distressing this was to Lucy. "Kiss me and send me home," he said.

⇒● Chapter 21 ●⇐

The next scheduled hearing for the senator's panel was two weeks away, but there was a great deal of work to be done in the meantime. Linda had been working on the notes for the Valdez meeting until very late each night. Don Webber and Andy Biggs were assisting her as best they could. Galen Carpetti had submitted several suggestions for the next meeting in King Salmon. The senator was helpful in the planning and made some procedural changes for the meeting. Everyone knew the fishermen in Bristol Bay would be a vocal and an active group at the hearing. The senator was attempting to prevent any mass attacks similar to the one by the five fishermen in Valdez.

The senator, Don and Andy were in Senator Price's office as was Linda, holding an electronic file in front of her. "Have you two thought of any way to improve the tone of the next meeting?" asked the senator.

"I haven't," spoke Andy, "but now we have some idea about how the objections will be voiced. I don't expect any violence, but as you know, Senator, those Bristol Bay and Bering Sea fishermen are a fiercely defensive bunch. Troopers in Dillingham, Naknek, and King Salmon are overworked during fishing season with fights, shootings and all manner of violent behavior both out in the Bay and in town. I've asked to have the local troopers and VPSOs available in case of trouble. This time of year the colonel doesn't have any men to spare and can't send extra officers to King Salmon during the hearings. I think your suggestion about having those who wish to testify wait outside the meeting hall until their turn is going to help with control more than anything else."

"It should keep the gallery from some of the heckling we saw at the last meeting," said the senator. "A majority of the nonresident fishermen have gone back home, not waiting for the meetings to take place. I didn't plan it that way, but that's what's happening."

"May I make a suggestion?" asked Linda.

"You sure can, Linda. You're a big part of this panel. What is it?" asked Price.

"I was thinking: We have the speakers sign a registry sheet in order to be allotted a time slot. Do you think it would be helpful for them to note what category they wish to address such as sport fishing, commercial fishing, subsistence or personal use fishing? It might minimize the number of conflicting groups sitting outside the hall." Linda had been frightened by the confrontations in Valdez.

"What do you think, Andy? You're our security expert," said the Senator.

"I think she may be right. It could reduce the number of confrontations while they wait to get inside to speak. We can try it. It certainly won't increase the hostility."

"Good. Make a note to add that to the sign-up sheet, Linda."

This planning meeting went on most of the day as it usually did. The senator was doing his best to cover each detail before it became a problem. The purpose of the hearings was to gather information and opinions from all factions of the fishing community; evaluate the statements at the end of all the hearings; and make recommendations for changes in the laws and regulations that would protect the fishermen as well as the fish.

Later, during the afternoon of the same day, Linda entered the office of the senator carrying a stack of mail. "I have to ask what to do with all these letters, sir."

The senator looked puzzled, "What kind of letters, Linda?"

"They all have to do with the hearings. Some are suggestions, some are complaints and some are threats. The threats are the ones that concern me the most."

"We get threatening letters from kooks all the time, Linda. What makes these different?" he asked.

"These are more graphic and to the point. Some have very definite and specific threats, not like the ones we usually get from angry citizens or just plain nuts. My personal opinion is that we should give them to Andy Biggs and have him check out the senders of some of them."

"Can you give me an example?" asked the senator.

She sorted through the stack, "Here's a short one, but a good example." She handed the letter to him to read.

As he read he began to frown. When he finished he handed the letter back to her. "I can see why you're concerned and I agree with your suggestion. I'll call Andy and ask him to come back to the office. When he gets here we'll both talk with him. I think you made a good judgement call on this one, Linda. Thanks."

A half hour later Andy came back into the office. Linda instructed him to go on to the senator's office. She gathered the stack of letters and followed. In the office she and the senator voiced their concerns and gave the pile of letters to the trooper.

"I'll let you deal with these as you see fit. I would like a report on the total, but not individual letters. I will leave it up to you as to what to do about each one. We get crank letters in my office all the time, but these deal directly with our hearings and refer to specific threats. I'm sure most are from nut cases, but we had better be certain."

"I'll see what I can do and get back to you, Senator." Without further conversation Andy left the office. He was a trained investigator and would follow up on each letter mailed locally and forward others to the areas of origination for other investigators to look into.

In his own office Andy read all the letters. He determined the senator had made a good call—the letters were real threats. He sorted the letters, kept three to investigate personally and forwarded the rest to other trooper posts for investigation. Two went to Valdez, one to Glennallen and two to Anchorage.

Of the three he kept the one with clues about the sender but unsigned and the other one that was signed. The first unsigned letter would be difficult to determine exactly who the writer was without searching for DNA or other scientific means of investigation. Also, the letter did not contain specific threats. After reading it twice Andy set it aside without action.

The other two letters were different. One had no signature, but gave hints as to the writer and his location. Andy called his trooper post and asked them to find the address of the sender and get back to him. The last letter had been signed, and Andy recognized the man's name as that of a commercial fisherman from Yakutat. It was one of the men in the confrontation at the meeting in Valdez. Andy thought for several minutes before calling the trooper stationed in Yakutat. The trooper, Casey Spurgeon, listened to Andy and replied that he knew the man.

"Do you think he's a real threat?" asked Andy.

Spurgeon thought a moment before answering, "He could be, Andy. He's a troublemaker down here. You know, bar fights, confrontations with other fishermen, pulled a knife on another fisherman once and some mischief we could never prove he committed. You know the type, a tough guy."

"I hate to fly to Yakutat to interview him, but it sounds as if he could be a real threat. He was one of the men trying to force themselves into our meeting in Valdez. Can I impose on you to interview him and get back to me?" asked Andy.

"Sure, Andy. It's been quiet around here for a few days. It'll give me something to do. I'll get back to you as soon as I finish the interview."

Andy knew that, in most cases, a visit from a uniformed trooper was all it took to dissuade blowhards from making more threats, but if he was really serious about his rhetoric it could put the trooper in danger. He didn't feel easy about putting Spurgeon in that position, especially since he had no backup in Yakutat.

He was writing notes in the file about his conversation with the Yakutat trooper when his telephone rang. It was his dispatch at headquarters in Soldotna. "Hello, Andy. This is Gina in the Soldotna office with the information you requested. I'll send it to you by FAX in a few minutes, but I'll give you the contact information if you have a pencil handy."

Andy reached for a notepad and his pen, "Go ahead, Gina." Andy wrote the information on his pad. The address for the writer of the last letter was Anchor Point, Alaska, only sixteen miles from Homer. He thanked her for the information and turned to find the letter and read it again. It contained very specific threats to all members of the panel, but singled out Don Webber and Senator Price. In the letter he made life threatening statements toward these two men. He looked at the clock above his desk. It was now after five and he should be quitting for the day but was concerned enough about this letter, so he decided to drive to Anchor Point to talk with the man, Gustav Bjornson. Bjornson was a commercial fisherman and fancied himself a leader in an anti-enforcement group.

After the FAX with complete information came in, he took a copy and walked out of the office to his patrol car to drive the sixteen miles north. When he arrived in the small fishing town he immediately recognized Bjornson's pickup truck in front of the local bar where some of the fishermen he hung out with were regular customers.

Andy used the radio in his patrol car to notify dispatch of his location and his intent to interview Bjornson. The fisherman and two of his cohorts were seated at the bar when he entered. Andy approached Bjornson and quietly asked him to step outside for a talk.

"What the hell for? I didn't do nothing wrong," answered the fisherman.

"I don't think we should have this conversation in here, Gustav. Let's do it outside, just between you and me. It shouldn't take long if you've done nothing wrong."

"OK, let's go outside," said Bjornson. "I'll be right back fellas," he called to his drinking friends.

The two men walked to the door and stepped out into the evening sunshine. Outside the fisherman stopped to take a deep breath of the evening salt air. Andy took a few steps in the direction of his patrol car and stopped with the fisherman following a moment later.

"OK, Trooper Biggs, what is it you want?"

"I came to ask you if you wrote a letter to Senator Dalton Price in the last few days?" asked Andy.

"Yeah, I wrote him a letter. He's having hearings about us fishermen. Any time the gov'ment does that they want to put us fishermen out of business. I just wrote him to say so," explained Gustav.

"I saw the letter and it sounded like you were going to attempt to stop him if he continued the hearings."

"You betcha I did. He needs to leave us alone. We got too many regulations now. We don't need no more."

"It's alright to tell the senator you don't like his hearings, but you can't threaten to shoot him. That is against the law, Gustav."

"I ain't shot at him yet, Trooper, so you can't arrest me."

"I don't want to arrest you, but I don't want to have you shoot the senator either. Were you serious about that?"

"You betcha, Biggs. If he keeps holding these meetings I'm going to find him and fix his wagon."

"Do you have a gun with you now?" asked Biggs.

"In my truck, not on me," said Bjornson.

"Is your truck locked up now?" inquired Biggs.

"Yeah, I always lock it when my gun is in there. Too many crooks out her want to steal stuff."

"Well, Gustav, I am going to have to take you into Homer and have you spend the night in jail and see the judge in the morning."

"You're gonna arrest me?" commented Bjornson, "What for?"

"I guess you hadn't heard it's against the law to threaten an Alaska State Senator. Turn around so I can put the handcuffs on you. You can call your lawyer when we get to Homer." Biggs pulled the handcuffs from his belt.

A stunned Bjornson turned around to allow the trooper to place the handcuffs on his wrists. "I ain't never heard of nothin' like this," he said.

Andy placed the fisherman in the back seat of his patrol car and stepped over to his truck to check the doors. They were both locked. In the driver seat of his patrol car, Andy reported to dispatch that he was returning to Homer with a prisoner.

From the back seat of the patrol car Bjornson asked again, "Are you really going to arrest me for writin' a letter to the senator? I can't believe it, I just can't believe it."

⇛ Chapter 22 ⇚

The morning after Andy arrested Gustav Bjornson the word reached Sam Nelson in Seattle. He waited until a reasonable hour and called his two cannery owner friends to a meeting in his office near Lake Union in the city. The meeting was held in Nelson's own private office.

"If you want coffee get it now. We have urgent business to deal with," said Sam when the two men arrived.

Eric Goodloe and Ioshi Morita both refused the offer, wanting to get to the reason for this early morning meeting which held such urgency. The office was plush with large overstuffed leather covered chairs for seating. They each took a seat with Nelson taking the third of four chairs in the office overlooking the locks leading to Puget Sound where many fishing and private vessels passed each day.

"OK, Sam, get to it. What is so important that we couldn't take care of it on the telephone?" asked Eric Goodloe.

"I had an urgent call from one of my men in Alaska. He was arrested last night and taken to jail in Homer." Sam looked directly at Eric, "If these meetings are too much for you and you don't want to be involved, I can take care of it without you, but you will be sharing the costs. I don't have a problem making a decision without you."

"Don't get testy, Sam. We just need to know why we get a call to an urgent meeting in the wee hours of the morning. Ioshi and I are both in this with you. Now, why was your man arrested?" asked a defensive Goodloe.

"My man is a fisherman out of Homer, but lives a few miles north. He was out drinking with some other fishermen when a trooper asked him about a letter he wrote to Senator Price about those hearings. Apparently, there were threats in the letter against the Senator. He doesn't know how they figured out it was him writing the letter, but Gus isn't the sharpest knife in the drawer and probably gave them his identity. At any rate, he was one of the men I sent to Valdez to break up the meeting. He wasn't successful at that job either. We have other hearings coming soon in King Salmon and I need him out there. I also want him out of jail before he gets cold feet and cuts a deal with the DA and implicates me." This was the brief explanation Sam furnished the other two cannery owners.

"I can now understand your need for urgency, Sam," commented Ioshi. "What kind of solution do you propose?"

"The first thing I should do is get a lawyer down to Homer to deal with the DA's office. I have one working for me out of Anchorage. I can send him to Homer, but it will be expensive. He has one advantage. He owns his own airplane and can be there within hours. He is also already up to speed on the root of this problem and will be representing my canneries in the hearings in King Salmon. I have two canneries in Bristol Bay and I can't have them messing with the way we do business out there." Nelson was silent for a few moments, then, continued, "It does give us one more option, though. If something were to happen to Senator Price, the investigators would immediately look at Gus as a suspect. We could be sure he was in the area when the incident took place."

Eric Goodloe sat upright in his chair, "Hold on there, Sam. Now you're suggesting murder and that's not what I signed on for. I don't know about Ioshi, but I'm not willing to go that far."

Ioshi was nodding his head, and added his comments when Eric finished speaking. "I agree with Eric. I will go along with many things, but I refuse to be involved in any murder plan. You are right about expecting us to be at a disadvantage if changes are made to the fishing regulations, but we could survive, making less money of course, but we would survive. If we are caught committing murder we cannot survive. Even if we are not arrested there could be a cloud cast over our connection to the situation that would cause our customers to stop buying from us. We cannot do this. We are not the Mafia."

"Very well, what is it you want me to do now?" asked Sam Nelson.

Goodloe looked toward Morita before answering. "I think you should get your lawyer down to Homer and shut that fisherman up. Get him out of Alaska if need be, but quiet him today."

Ioshi added his comment also: "We pay those legislators in Juneau a great deal of money to watch out for our interests. It's time for them to earn what we pay them. Let this Senator Price hold his hearings. He will still have to draft bills and get them passed and signed by the governor. There are many steps we can take without murder."

"You do have a point, Ioshi," said Nelson. "I made a suggestion and was outvoted. We will find another way to deal with this problem. I'll call the attorney in Anchorage as soon as he gets to his office. I'll let you know what takes place. Any more questions?" he asked. Neither Goodloe nor Morita had any more to say.

"Good, then let me get to work. I'll call you when I hear from the lawyer."

Without saying a word, both the visitors stood to leave. Once they were out of the office Nelson returned to his desk to make the call to Anchorage.

Lester Goode had represented Sam Nelson in hundreds of cases during his career. Nelson paid well and never asked how he won the cases. Nelson had become somewhat notorious for his dealings in the fishing and fish product industry, due in part and by way of this, his attorney, Lester Goode.

"Good morning, Les," greeted Sam when the lawyer came on the line.

"Good morning, Sam. What gets you out of bed at this hour?" replied the lawyer.

"I have a somewhat urgent problem, Les, and I need your help."

"How urgent?" he asked.

"Now," replied Nelson. "A fisherman who does odd jobs for me has been arrested in Homer and I need to get him out before he starts making deals with the DA."

"I can arrange bail by telephone Sam, now tell me the rest of the problem."

"That's why I like you, Les." Nelson went on to explain in detail what had happened and why he didn't want the man talking with the District Attorney.

When he finished Goode replied, "I'll fly my 206 to Homer. I'll be there in about an hour and a half. Have someone meet me with a car at the transient area of the Homer Airport." Without further conversation Lester gathered the paperwork he would need and filled a briefcase with them and a bundle of cash for bail. He made a phone call to the Homer court to learn the time for Bjornson's arraignment. He had just enough time to make to the court building if his driver met him at the airport as he had instructed.

It had been a pleasant trip from Merrill Field in Anchorage to Homer. He had chosen to fly inland over the Kenai Peninsula, skirting the mountains on the eastern side of the peninsula and arriving over Kachemak Bay roughly fifteen miles north east of the city. The aroma of salt water and fish filled the cabin of his Cessna making him feel at home.

He landed and taxied to the transient parking area and tied down the aircraft for safety. His driver was waiting when he arrived.

"Are you Mr. Goode?" asked the driver.

"Yes, I am. I need to be at the courthouse in a few minutes, and I should talk with my client before court time. We had better get going." The driver had not volunteered his name, but said he would wait and drive him back to the airport when Goode finished.

Homer is a very small city and the courthouse meets its needs perfectly. Inside the court building a trooper was waiting with his prisoner. Lester approached the lawman and asked if this was Gustav Bjornson. The trooper confirmed he was and allowed the lawyer to consult with his client. A couple of minutes of conversation was all it took with Gus and he returned to talk with the trooper, Andy Biggs.

"I will need a copy of the charges against my client," said Goode.

Andy searched through several folders he held, pulled a sheet of charges out of one and handed it to the lawyer. Goode read it thoroughly and handed it back to the trooper.

"I'll need a copy of this," he said.

"I'll have the clerk make you a copy, sir. I can allow you to confer with your client in an interview room here in the lobby if you like."

"Thank you, that would be very nice," replied Lawyer Goode. Gus had said nothing.

Andy locked the two men inside a small room with a table and two chairs while he went across the hall to have the clerk make a copy of the charging documents for the lawyer. While alone with Gus the lawyer instructed his new client as to what and what not to say in court.

"I don't need to hear your side of the case right now, but I don't want you to explain it in this court today, either. You plead 'not guilty' when the judge asks and don't say anything else. I'll do the talking. I'll have the judge set bail and get you out of here. We'll discuss particulars later. Understand?" he asked.

"Yeah, I guess. Who sent you here for me?" he asked.

"The man you work for," was the answer. "They will read the charges and ask if you understand and you will say 'yes.' The judge will set bail and I will agree to it. Then the judge will set a court date for your trial. During all this you will keep your mouth shut. Got it?"

"Yeah, I got it."

At that point Andy came to take the prisoner to the courtroom. The entire hearing took only ten minutes with bail set at $5,000, cash only. Cash only because of who had been threatened. Lawyer Goode paid the cash to the clerk and the two men walked out of the courthouse, but had to return to the jail to be released. Once that was done Goode offered to take Gus to lunch at Fat Olive's Restaurant. The lawyer didn't discuss the case while at lunch, but waited until they were outside, sitting in the small car the driver had brought and the driver was away from them.

"The judge said you couldn't leave Alaska, but I think I had better get you out of Homer. I have a small cabin up near Sutton and I want you to stay there until your court date. You can fish on the lake and walk all you want, but I can't have you drinking. Do you understand what I'm saying?" asked Lester.

"Yeah, I can't drink any beer. I don't think I'm going to like this very much."

"If you get convicted you won't be able to drink anything for a lot of years. You threatened a government official. They take that very personally. I think we can get you off with a short jail sentence, but only because you don't have a police record. I don't think you really understand where you stand here. You could be doing twenty years if you get convicted. I'm going to try to get you off with only a couple of months. You had better think about that and, at least, try to stay out of sight until your court date. Do you have a cell phone?"

"Yeah, I got one." Gus reached into his pants pocket to display the phone.

"Put the number on this card in your speed dial list. You will be able to get me any time. Don't call anyone else. There are a few neighbors around the cabin and you can visit with them, but don't say anything about why you are staying there. Got it?" Goode asked again.

"Yeah, I got it," agreed Gustav Bjornson.

"OK. I'll have the driver take us to the airport and I'll fly us to Anchorage and then drive you to the cabin. If you need anything you call me. Got it?"

"Yeah, I got it."

➣• Chapter 23 •◄

Lester Goode flew his Cessna back to Merrill Field with Gus in the right seat. After tying down the aircraft he climbed onto the driver seat of his Buick to drive Gus to his cabin site near Long Lake ten miles east of King Mountain on the Glenn Highway. The cabin is small, but modern with a generator for electrical power. It is heated with a wood stove, but no heat would be needed at this time of the year. Lester stopped at a Safeway store in Palmer to buy groceries and supplies to make Gus' stay pleasant, but did not include alcohol in the list of provisions he provided.

At the cabin the two men carried the supplies in, including a change of clothing for Gus. "There's a small aluminum boat tied to the dock and fishing gear in the shed at the side of the cabin. There are grayling and trout in the lake if you want some fresh fish to eat. The radio works, but there is no TV reception here. You should find it quite relaxing. I love coming up here to get away from all the turmoil of the city." Lester looked around the cabin to see that everything was in order and walked to the door. "Do you want anything else?" asked the lawyer.

"No, I'm good. How long will I have to be here?" inquired Gus.

"I'm not sure, but my boss wants me to keep you out of sight and out of trouble until your court date. He told me he had work for you soon and didn't want you in jail when the time came. I have no idea why, but he likes you." Lester reached for the door handle, "Use the cell phone if you need me for anything." Without saying any more he climbed into his car and drove back to his office in Anchorage where he used his desk phone to call Sam Nelson.

"He's out, Sam. I have him at my cabin up on the Glenn Highway. His bail was five grand and I had to do some shopping for him, but he seems satisfied to hide out for a while. What's next?"

"I'm not certain, Les. The next hearing is Friday and Saturday of this week in King Salmon. I want him there with his friends to make some noise and interrupt the proceedings. I don't want any violence at this hearing, but a lot of noise. Those Bristol Bay fishermen might just take the hint and provide a commotion of their own. I have two canneries on the Alaska Peninsula and I'll get word to some of those boys to do what they can at the hearing." Nelson knew some of the fishermen working for his cannery didn't have much respect for the law or for Alaska Fish and Game. He felt he could count on them to disrupt the meetings.

"I've told you before, don't let them connect you with any illegal acts. The state could shut you down for getting involved. The courts will go after your assets as well as sentence you to prison. You have to use men like Gus to do that for you, to insulate yourself from the acts of violence of any kind." Lester was giving his client sound semi-legal advice.

"I'm on my own with this one. The other two owners are backtracking and won't go along with what needs to be done in order for us to stay in business," said Nelson.

"I've told you in the past that the secret is not to stop the hearings, but to keep their recommendations from becoming law. The disruptions will help to that end by making our objections public. Our friends in the legislature will be able to use that to bolster their arguments if we feel a bill that's introduced is detrimental to our ends." Lester, again cautioned Nelson.

"Nonetheless, it will take a combination of all these efforts to get the job done. I want you to send Gus to King Salmon on Wednesday. The hearings are scheduled for Friday and Saturday. That will give him two days to prepare and to enlist his helpers." Nelson was adamant about his course of action in spite of the warning from Lester.

"OK, Sam, if that's the way you want it." Lawyer Lester Goode was not at all sure this would turn out well.

In Homer Senator Price, his aide, Linda, Trooper Andy Biggs and commercial fisherman Don Webber had spent the day assessing the information they had gathered and preparing for the meetings to be held at the end of the week. An old friend of the senator in King Salmon had heard about the meetings and offered to send one of his airplanes to pick up the members of the panel and take them to the Alaska Peninsula on Thursday.

The plan was for Ray Seals, representing subsistence fishermen and Bill Ordman, sportfish representative, to be picked up in Anchorage. Winston Dugan, Commercial Fishing and Fish and Game representative along with river guide Herb Bissett would board in Kenai. The aircraft would then proceed to Homer where the rest of the panel would board the twin engine turboprop passenger plane. The passengers would be taken to King Salmon Airport only a short distance from the hotel where they were to stay. The meetings would be held in the banquet room of the same hotel, minimizing the need for travel while there. The return trip would be the reverse of the first trip on Sunday morning.

"My friend offered to furnish the travel for free, but I'm not allowed to take such gifts; therefore all expenses for food, lodging and travel will be billed to the State of Alaska. I hope we don't suffer the type of disturbance we had in Valdez, but those fishermen out there on the Peninsula are a close family and we should be prepared for any eventuality. I'll get back to each of you regarding the time to meet the plane on Thursday. I appreciate all the work you have done to prepare for this meeting. I don't expect any of the rest of the meetings to be as volatile as the first two, although the one in Kenai will certainly be entertaining. I think the reaction by commercial fishermen will be the same, but we will be dealing with an organized group of fishing guides with many years of experience in fighting with commercial fishermen. I don't think the panel will be the target of any rage, but these two groups may butt heads. Any questions for me?" asked the Senator.

"Not about the meetings, but I want to know if you have had any contact with Gustav Bjornson since he was bailed out of jail?" It was Andy Biggs doing the asking.

"Not a word, Andy. These things usually just fade away. I don't expect him to make any more trouble."

"Perhaps, Senator, but I want you to notify me right away it you hear from him or have any other threats."

"I will, I promise, Andy."

After the meeting Andy returned to his own office while Don drove to the office of his insurance agent, Lucy Hardy. "Hi, Addie, is she in her office?" asked Webber.

"Yes sir. She said to send you back if you came in." The receptionist giggled a little saying, "She has sure been in a good mood lately. You have been good for her."

"Thank you, Addie. I'll tell her to give you a raise." Don snickered as he walked to the little office at the rear of the small cement block building. He tapped on the door as he entered. She looked up and smiled at him. "All finished with your meeting?" she asked.

"Yes, until Thursday when I go to King Salmon for the weekend." He parked his bulk in the chair in front of her desk. "Who's cooking dinner tonight? You or me?" he asked.

"I don't know. What are you cooking if it's you?" she asked with a smile.

"I have a new recipe for salmon in wine sauce we can try, and after dinner I can take you to MacDonald's for an ice cream sundae." How does that sound to you?"

"You talked me right into it," she said, motioning for him to come around the desk for a short kiss.

It was late when Don brought their ice cream to the table. "I'm sure glad fishing season is over. I never thought I would ever feel that way, but this year was a disaster for me. I'm just happy to be sitting here with you. I have nearly two months of hearings left to attend, but when they end I think we should take a trip somewhere for a few days. I need to be alone with you."

He was scooping chocolate out of the bottom of his dish when she answered. "A small wedding in a Las Vegas chapel would be nice around Thanksgiving time and would make a good get-away." She was giving him a coy look across the top of her plastic dish of ice cream.

He moved his empty dish away and reached across the table to take her hand. "Really? You would go to Las Vegas with me to get married?" asked the astonished fisherman.

"I've thought about it a lot, Don. I don't want a huge wedding with a lot of people there. My business will be slowing down by then and it will be close to winter. We could take a little time for ourselves and enjoy the city. And, when we get back I want to spend the rest of my life with you."

"This is wonderful, Lucy. When we finish with the hearings I'll buy the tickets and make arrangements for rooms and such." He squeezed her hand. "You have made me very happy, Lucy. I promise to make you happy for the rest of your life."

"You're a fisherman. I'll bet you say that to all your girlfriends." She was teasing him again.

"There is something I should discuss with you."

"Four," she said.

"What do you mean, four?" asked a confused Don.

"Children, the number of kids we can have." She was giggling again.

Now Don was chuckling too. "That wasn't the question I had in mind, but I agree if that's what you want."

"I was only kidding you Don. We can take that as it comes. What was it you wanted to discuss?"

Still smiling about it all he said, "It was about the Senator. He has been hinting at me to come to work for him this winter as his aide. Normally I wouldn't even consider it; I'm a fisherman, but with the fishing business being so uncertain, I am thinking about doing it. The legislature finishes in time for me to get the boat ready and I could still fish. I would have less time to get the boat ready, but I have two good deckhands to pick up the slack. Do you think I'm crazy?"

"No, in fact I think it shows a great deal of forethought. You know what has to be done to make the fishing industry sustainable and if you took the second job you could work on the problem from both ends. I admire your thinking, Don. I guess that's why I love you so much." Now she was squeezing his hand.

They stared into each other's eyes for a long moment. "Let's take a drive out to the end of the spit and watch the tide come in," said Don, softly.

It was getting late and they had enjoyed a nice walk on the sandy beach. The sun was getting low in the northwest sky and the temperature was cooling by the time they returned to Don's truck. "Let's go to your place for a while," said Don. This had become an evening he would remember the rest of his life, as would his bride-to-be, Lucy Hardy.

≫• Chapter 24 •≪

Gus Bjornson was happy to be boarding the Penair flight bound for King Salmon on this sunny Wednesday morning. He had contacted an old friend and fishing partner who was to pick him up at the airport when he arrived. George Gibson was the operations manager for the cannery owned by Sam Nelson. It was located in Naknek, ten miles by dirt road from King Salmon. George was waiting inside the airport terminal building when Gus arrived.

George greeted his old friend with a huge bear hug. "How the heck are you, Gus?" he asked.

"I'm good," replied Gus.

"Did you just come to visit or is there something else?"

"I'll tell you when we get to the truck," Gus answered while looking around the lobby of the terminal.

"OK, I'm living in one of the cabins at the cannery. I opened the one next door for you to use while you're here. How long do you plan to stay?"

"Just a few days, I'm here for the fish hearings starting on Friday. I'm being paid to disrupt the proceedings. Can you find four or five good men to back me up?" Gus didn't mention who was paying him.

"We can stop for a beer on the way home and probably find all you need at the saloon." George was grinning, "Boy, it's good to see you, Gus. What's it been, three years?"

"I think it's four. This is my first trip back since I sunk the *Daisy Mae* down at the mouth of the Kvichak River. It makes me sick every time I think about it. She was a great boat."

"I run the operations for the cannery and we have a couple of boats for next year, if you want one. You can take your pick if you want to come back to Bristol Bay."

"I appreciate it, George, but I'm running a cannery boat out of Cordova. I like it down there and there aren't as many Californians running boats there. I hate those guys. They have no soul. They only fish for money."

"You say you came out here to attend the fish hearings. I heard about them, but nobody seems to know what to expect from them. How come someone wants them stopped?" George was curious and was suspicious it could cause a change in the cannery schedule and lead to his losing his job.

"I can't tell you much about that, but Senator Price wants to cut the number of fishing days for the entire commercial fleet. That's the drifters and the set netters. If that happens it will mean the end for more than half the canneries still working. It's a really bad thing for fishermen and for canneries, George." Gus spoke with a sad tone.

"So, do you want to stop for a beer and see if we can find you some help?" George asked once again.

"Sure, why not?" said Gus, not having had a beer for several days.

The saloon, as George called it, was a dimly lit smelly beer hall that also served a short menu of food.

"Order us a beer while I try to find a couple of guys I know," said George as he walked away from the table toward a back corner where a group of men were playing pool. Two minutes later he returned with two rough looking men with him.

"Gus, meet Ole Larson and that's his brother Olaf behind him. They're both fishermen with their own boat."

Gus stood and stuck out a hand. "Pleased to meet the both of you," he said over the sounds of the crowd.

"They will follow us to the cannery where we can talk in private," George informed his partner. "I'll give them a signal when we finish eating."

An hour later the four men met in Gus' cabin to discuss what was to be done. The group discussed the situation and came up with a plan they hoped would not get them arrested in the meeting. They told Gus they could provide two more trustworthy men to back the play. They all agreed to meet at the banquet room at one in the afternoon on Friday. It would be after lunch and the players on the panel would be sleepy and sluggish—he hoped.

At noon on Thursday Andy, Don, the senator and Linda waited at the airport terminal building for the Penair Metroliner to arrive. Don sat on a bench with the senator discussing strategy while Andy and Linda discussed security measures. A half hour later the plane stopped in front of the only loading gate in the terminal. The little group walked over and boarded the small passenger plane. All the other panel members were already on board. There was also a young lady flight attendant offering sodas and coffee once they reached a safe altitude. Slightly over two hours later they touched down at King Salmon Airport. A small white tour bus came out to the airplane to give them a ride to the hotel where they would be staying. Most of the members preferred to take a nap before dinner. Don was one of them.

Prior to dinner the Senator called a meeting of the panel in the banquet hall to discuss the agenda for tomorrow's meeting. More than eighty names had been entered on the participant list. Linda had been busy all afternoon arranging the names and allotted time segments for the speakers. It looked as if the King Salmon area hearings would be lively and well attended.

Andy spoke to tell the delegates there would be decent security at the meeting, but none would be inside the meeting hall. Wildlife troopers had two officers in the office at the State of Alaska compound only a few blocks from the hotel where the meeting was to be held. In the same compound were Fish and Game enforcement officers as well as federal Fish and Wildlife officers. There were two Alaska State troopers in town, but one had been called out to a village to investigate an incident there. Andy was confident that if there was another incident like the one in Valdez he would have backup almost immediately.

The meeting was short, only about half an hour, and they adjourned for dinner. Since the senator was paying for the dinner there was no alcohol served. Don thought a glass of wine would have been nice with dinner, but drank coffee instead.

After dinner Don and Andy went outside the hotel for a walk to settle the great prime rib dinner. They strolled along the roadway past the airport and continued on down to the river bank. It was after nine, but the sun was warm, though the mosquitoes were beginning to swarm along with the small bot flies known locally as white sox. They had planned to walk for more than an hour, but because of the insects they turned around at the river bank to return to the hotel.

In his room, Don called Lucy to report on the trip so far. She was elated to hear from him. He finished his call to turn on the television. Once there was only recorded programing in this fishing town, but now the hotel was connected to the satellite programming and he was able to find Fox News on his screen. Only a few minutes of this and he was ready to go to bed.

Television was not Don's favorite evening activity. He showered and fell into bed not waking until five a.m.

The staff was just opening the hotel restaurant when he came downstairs. He was the first customer of the morning shift. Don was sipping his coffee and awaiting his order of ham and eggs when Andy came into the dining room, asking permission to sit with him. He agreed.

"How many white sox bites do you have this morning?" Andy asked.

"I didn't find any, but I had put on some bug dope before we went for a walk. Did you get bitten very bad?"

"I should have known better, but, you remember, I had on a short sleeve shirt. I have four bites on my left arm and two on the right. I always get infected from them." Andy pulled up his shirt sleeve to show Don his bright red welts.

The two men finished a leisurely breakfast and returned to their respective rooms where Don brushed his teeth and then called Lucy to say good morning.

Don and Andy walked to the meeting hall shortly after eight and found Linda and the senator already in their seats reading the list of speakers scheduled for this morning. There was coffee available on a table at the side of the seating area where both Don and Andy helped themselves before sitting at the head table with the senator and his aide. The rest of the panel filed into the hall within minutes. A crowd began to form outside the banquet room making it necessary for Linda to go into the hall and begin organizing the speakers list. One of the hotel staff was tasked with keeping the crowd peaceful and directing them to their seats.

The vast majority of the names on the list of today's speakers were commercial fishermen from Bristol Bay, though they gave addresses of towns from Bethel, Dillingham, Naknek, Pilot Point, and other towns on the Alaska Peninsula. It was to be a large crowd. At precisely nine o'clock Senator Dalton Price banged the gavel to open the meeting. He gave a short statement outlining the nature of these hearings and explained this was a fact-finding group and nothing in the way of legislation had yet been decided. He asked only that the speakers remain polite and observe the time limits allotted to each speaker. He asked for questions, but there were none. He turned to Linda and asked her to call the first speaker.

The concerns voiced by these fishermen were along the same general lines as those expressed at the meeting in Valdez. Most of those speaking were articulate and referred to notes on points they were intending to make. The morning passed quickly and Linda seemed pleased with the number of speakers they had heard from. At noon the senator recessed the hearings for a lunch break. The panel had a table waiting in the main dining room where lunch was preordered. Most of the members sat to drink iced tea after lunch, but two of the members went outside the hotel to smoke.

They had not had time for a cigarette when they returned to the dining room to report a van with five or six men had arrived outside and they had overheard the leader giving orders about how to interrupt the meeting after lunch.

"This is your department, Andy. I think you should call in your troops, just in case." The senator had feared there would be a demonstration and was dreading this confrontation.

Andy dialed his cell phone to alert the officers a few blocks away at the state office compound. The local trooper on duty said they would be right outside if he needed them, giving him a radio channel to call him into the building.

At exactly 1:00 p.m. Senator Price reconvened the meeting with a thump of his gavel. The first speaker gave his testimony without a problem, but the second speaker had only just taken the floor to speak when a commotion occurred in the hallway outside the banquet room. Immediately Andy pressed the button on his radio to call for help from law enforcement officers waiting outside.

Andy made his way through the crowd which was now standing to see what the disturbance was about. A group of men was shouting and pushing bystanders out of the way. Andy immediately recognized Gustav Bjornson among the group. He elbowed his way through the crowd. Most of them were attempting to leave the area. By the time he made his way to where Gus was muscling a member of those awaiting a chance to enter the hall, Andy shouted at Bjornson, ordering him to stop pushing folks around.

Gus turned to swing at Andy when the trooper and his posse entered the hotel. Andy was bringing up his arm to defend himself when another of the invading men slugged him from behind rendering him unconscious and slumping onto the hallway floor among many pairs of feet.

Hearing the intensity of the confrontation in the hallway, Don jumped to his feet to follow Andy into the hall. He saw Andy being punched as he came out of the banquet room and into the hall. Andy's attacker was about to give the trooper a savage kick when Don reached around his neck and tripped him with one leg, riding the attacker to the floor. Another local fisherman, seeing what had happened, came to the aid of Don who was rolling on the floor with the man and attempting to subdue him. The late-comer noticed the handcuffs on the fallen Andy's belt and reached for them. He was able to retrieve them and help Don apply more weight to him and get the handcuffs on the offender.

The trooper and other law enforcement men entering the building were able to corral the attackers, six in total, with Gus putting up the greatest fight with the officers.

Once the attacker was cuffed up, Don stepped over to see if Andy was alright. He was beginning to regain consciousness, but groggy. He had a small cut on the back of his head from the blow, but Don could see the man's eyes were beginning to focus again.

"Are you OK, Andy?" asked Don in a very concerned tone.

"I don't know, but I think so," said a dazed Andy.

Don saw one of the other officers nearby. "Hey, officer," he said to get the attention of the new lawman, "I think we need to get Andy an ambulance and have him checked out at the hospital."

This officer was one of the Alaska Wildlife troopers. He knelt to look at Andy and reached for his microphone to call medical assistance for the fallen trooper. "Stay with him, I have to help the rest. EMTs will be here in a minute.

The melee lasted only a couple of minutes after the local officers arrived, and minutes later they were leading the offenders out of the hotel.

The senator had everyone take a seat while he went into the hall to assess the damages. The first thing he saw was Andy lying on the floor with Don hovering over him. As he approached from the banquet room the medics were entering from the other end of the hall. Price watched as the medics checked Andy and decided to take him to the hospital for a thorough examination. By now most of the people who had been gathered in the hallway to get inside to speak had left the hotel.

"Come on, Don. Let's see if we can salvage any part of this meeting." Senator Price was wishing he could close the meeting and go home, but that was not an option.

Once back in the meeting room the senator called the meeting to order and ordered a fifteen-minute break to re-organize. Don went to the table at the side of the room for a cup of coffee while Dalton Price conferred with Linda.

Most of the crowd had left the hall leaving the list of speakers for the rest of the day very short. The meeting ended at three in the afternoon, but, the senator announced, they would continue as scheduled at nine a.m. on Saturday morning. "I apologize for the ruckus today, but some people don't understand what we are attempting to accomplish. I look forward to a more peaceful meeting tomorrow." He slammed the gavel to adjourn and leaned back in his chair. "I need a drink," he said to Linda.

⤛ **Chapter 25** ⤜

The following day, Saturday, was filled with speakers having both opinions and questions. The session was scheduled to end at three p.m., but no one was there to speak during the last hour. The panel members sat in the banquet room eating pie and drinking coffee while recapping the discussions of the two-day hearing.

"I don't expect there to be any more wild sessions like we had here and in Valdez. The one exception could be the hearing in Kenai where we will have more commercial fishermen as well as personal use fishermen and, loudest of all, river guides and sport fishermen. Bristol Bay is the largest group of commercial fishermen, but the Kenai River hosts the greatest number of sport fishermen. The numbers of river guides has dwindled in recent years because of decreasing numbers as well as the size of Chinook salmon. One advantage there is we also have more law enforcement available to us. I just hope we don't need them." Senator Price looked around the room at the tired faces. "Does anyone have questions for me?" There were none.

"OK, I'll call Penair and have them warm up the airplane. I want to thank every one of you for your participation." He looked at Don Webber. "Don, would you check to see if we can take Andy with us?"

Don nodded and left the room to call the hospital to check on the injured trooper. He was put through to the attending doctor who told him Andy could go home, but should not return to duty if he suffered a headache or blurred vision. Don informed the doctor he and the others would be there to pick up the ailing member within thirty minutes.

At about this same time, in his office in Seattle, Sam Nelson had waited all day for word from his paid henchman in King Salmon. It was near four thirty in the late afternoon when his phone rang.

"Hello, Sam, it's Lester Goode."

"That's not good, Lester. Where is Gus?"

"That's what I called to tell you, Sam. I just had a call from him and he's in jail in King Salmon. The story he told me was that he hired five other men and went to the afternoon hearings yesterday to break them up. Those were his words, not mine. They went into the hotel and started pushing people around and were headed into the meeting room when that trooper from Homer came out of the hall to confront them in the hallway. Gus got physical with him and they scuffled. One of the other men Gus had brought slugged the trooper and knocked him out. Gus said he didn't know where the law came from but several cops showed up and took the six of them into custody. They are all in jail in King Salmon now. They were arraigned in court and, of course, all pleaded not guilty. The magistrate set bail at ten thousand each, because of the injury to the trooper.

Gus just now came from court and was back in jail, but used his phone call to call me. I guess my question is what do you want me to do about him and the others now?"

"This just keeps getting worse and worse," replied Sam. "What do you suggest, Lester?"

"There are no good options, Sam. He's out on bail for harassment of the senator and this same bunch of people. The officer who was injured was one of the members of the senator's panel and the same one who arrested him in Anchor Point. I don't know the others, but I think the judge will paint them all with the same brush. They were a bunch of toughs trying to stop the hearings. I can't see a good outcome for any of this. I don't know if it's even wise to try to separate Gus from the others in this one." Lester was truly at a loss as to what he should do.

"At this point I don't care what happens to those men, but I don't want to be connected to them in any way. I have a cannery there and the publicity alone would ruin my business. Personally, I don't think the charges there are going to amount to much on their own, but with Gus being out on bail for threatening the senator, I think the court in Homer will want to throw the book at him. Talk with the DA there and try to make the best deal you can. Get Gus out of there and back to your cabin until he goes back to court in Homer. Gus is becoming far too expensive to keep around. Call me when you have some answers. Thanks for the up-date, Les."

Penair flew directly to Homer where Linda, Senator Price, Andy, and Don stepped off the plane, and it continued on to Kenai and then to Anchorage. Don was concerned for the wellbeing of his friend, Andy. He didn't think it was a good idea for him to be alone for a few days, considering his possible concussion.

Linda was the one to speak up. "I have a few days owed to me by the senator, Don. He and I agree with you, he needs some personal care for a few days. I told the senator I would volunteer my time if he would allow me to work on the King Salmon report at the same time. Andy can rest and I can have some quiet time to finish the final draft for the senator."

The senator had been standing to one side away from the conversation, waiting for Linda to finish when his cell phone vibrated in his jacket pocket. He checked the caller number which was a Juneau prefix.

"Senator Price," he answered.

"Hello Dalton, it's Waylon Goff, the lieutenant governor. Do you have a minute to talk?"

"I'm still on the tarmac at the Homer Airport, Waylon, but I can talk a minute. What's the problem?"

"I wouldn't have called you on this phone except we got word of the disturbance at your meeting in King Salmon. And I have been getting calls from the corporate offices of several cannery corporations. These folks want to know what's going on at these meetings, and frankly, so do I. You've stirred up a hornets nest, Dalton. Commercial fishermen are screaming their heads off, cannery owners are having fits, the river guides are asking questions I can't answer, and I don't like getting questions I don't have an answer for. You and I need to talk face to face. Can you come to Juneau right away?"

"It's too bad that I embarrassed you, Waylon, but one of my personnel was injured in that disturbance and one of the men responsible was arrested earlier for sending me a threatening letter. He happens to be a fisherman from Cordova who works for the cannery there. The same man who owns the cannery in Cordova also owns a cannery near King Salmon. Don't you think that is a huge coincidence?" Dalton Price was becoming angry. He took a couple of deep breaths and resumed his conversation. "I'll wager that you had a call from that cannery owner and other owners as well. Every commercial lobbyist in the state has called me to ask these same questions.

I'm not going to stop the hearings. If you and the governor don't like it, too bad; cut off my funding. I don't believe you'll do that because of all the negative publicity it would generate. I'm not trying to solve a political problem. I'm trying to solve a resource problem that has been ignored far too long for political reasons. My answer to your question is no, I'm not travelling to Juneau to be bullied by you, the governor, the fish lobby, or by cannery owners. Sorry Waylon."

"I admire your dedication, Dalton, but it will not sit well with the governor. I think we will be having another talk very soon. Good day, Dalton." The line went dead on the Juneau end.

"Linda," Price called to his assistant. "We have to go to the office for a while. Can you have Don take Andy home and stay with him for an hour?"

Linda looked at Don Webber who nodded agreement. "Go ahead, Linda," he said. "I'll have Lucy come to Andy's place and bring me back to the airport to get my truck."

Don walked to where Andy had been standing on the parking apron and picked up his small bag. "Looks like I'm driving you home, Andy. Do you need to stop anywhere on the way?"

"Thanks, Don, but no. I'm just really tired and I need to go home and lie down. Here are the keys to my patrol car. Don't scratch it on the way home."

Andy was in worse shape than Don had suspected. At Andy's home Don helped the ailing trooper to his bed and covered him with a quilt. Andy fell asleep almost immediately. It didn't seem right for him to leave the sleeping man alone and called Lucy to tell her he would be a little late getting to her place. Nearly two hours later Linda tapped on the front door of the home. Don opened the door to an apologetic Linda.

"It's OK, Linda. I called Lucy and told her I'd be late. Andy went to bed as soon as we got here and has been sleeping since. I'm worried about him."

"We could call his captain in Soldotna and have him contact his local doctor to come over and check him out," Linda suggested.

"That's a good idea. Do you know the number?"

"Yes, I have it here in my directory. I'll call him if you want to leave and meet Lucy."

"I think I'll stay a while, at least until the doc takes a look at him." Don had a worried look on his face.

"I'll make the call. You go to the kitchen and make some coffee."

By the time the coffee had run through the Bunn coffee maker Linda came to the kitchen to report the doctor was on his way. The two friends checked on the patient every couple of minutes, not really knowing what they should do for him. Within a half hour there was a knock on the door. The doctor had arrived.

Don and Linda waited in the living room while the doctor examined the injured Andy. Finally, the doctor came out of the bedroom to confer with the two caretakers.

"I'm going to call the EMTs and have him transported to the hospital. He needs constant watching and he has a severe concussion, possibly a skull fracture. I'll have to review the X-rays from King Salmon to be sure. He's a tough old bird to stay on his feet until he got home."

"Is there anything we can do for him, Doc?" asked Don.

"You can stand by here until the medics arrive, if you will. Thanks." With that comment he pulled his cell phone from his pocket and called the Homer EMTs. After the call he asked, "Do you have any more of that coffee?"

Don nodded and went to the kitchen to bring the doctor a cup of black coffee. Minutes later the ambulance arrived without sirens or lights. The medics carried a large wheeled stretcher into the house, conferred with the doctor, who showed them the way to the patient, and loaded the sleeping Andy on the cart. They lifted him carefully into the waiting ambulance and drove away.

"I had better follow them to the hospital and check him in. Thanks for the coffee. I'll call the both of you if there is any change in his condition." The doctor shook Don's hand, picked up his small satchel, and walked to his car.

Don turned to Linda: "I guess we can lock Andy's house and go home. I would appreciate it if you would give me a ride back to the airport to get my truck. I'll let Lucy know the plan is changed."

"You're right, Don, I'll be happy to give you a ride." They locked the house and climbed into Linda's little car.

"You know we have never worked closely together in the past, but in recent days I have learned to appreciate your ability to take charge of any situation. I think the senator picked the right man for this job," she remarked as she drove.

Don smiled, "Thanks for the vote of confidence," he said.

"I mean it, Don. If you would take the job, I would recommend the senator hire you as his aide and chief of staff."

"I thought that was your job," said Don.

"One of them, but in fact, I'm his assistant. I have far more responsibility and duties than I can handle. I would like to see you take over the chief of staff position. You would be good at it." She had given him her honest assessment.

As they approached the airport parking area Don replied, "Fishing is suffering a horrible downturn and I should look for some kind of work to do in the off season. I'll give the offer some serious consideration."

"Good, I'll ask the senator about it." She stopped her car alongside his big truck. "I'll call you if the doctor has anything new to say. See you later and thanks, Don."

Don stood beside his truck, thinking this would be a wonderful opportunity. The smell of the salt air from Kachemak Bay was comforting, making him truly feel at home.

≋• Chapter 26 •≊

On the east side of the road traversing the Homer Spit is a beautiful bicycle path used by everyone from tourists walking their dogs to bicycle enthusiasts and joggers. Hundreds of people use this pathway each day in the summer months. As Don drove toward town he recognized one of the pedestrians walking slowly along the trail. It was Freddie, his deckhand. Don was only a few feet from a place he could turn off and park for a few minutes. He stepped out of his truck and called over the guardrail to his employee and friend.

"Hey, Freddie!" yelled Don. "Hold up a minute."

Freddie looked up to see who was calling him. When he saw Don he smiled and stopped walking, waiting for Don to come to him.

"What the heck are you doing out here on the spit, Freddie?" asked Don, sticking out his hand to shake with him.

"The doctors said I should start walking to strengthen my back. I have been walking short distances and this is my first day attempting to walk the distance to the end of the spit."

"Are you going to make it? Do you want a ride back?"

"No, but thanks Cap. I feel pretty good and I think I can make it out and back. If I get too tired I can flag someone down for a ride home. I heard you were on some kind of committee with Senator Price. It seems like you are getting to be awfully important these days."

"Don't believe everything you hear, Freddie. I'm still just a fisherman."

"It's good to see you, Cap. I think I should keep walking right now, though. I don't want my back to stiffen up. Maybe we can get out and have lunch or something."

"You bet, Freddie. I'll call you one day this week. Good to see you out and walking." He waved at Freddie and walked back to his truck to continue the drive toward town. He drove directly to the hospital where he wanted to learn the condition of Andy.

The nurse at the admitting desk had no information for him except to tell him he had been assigned a room number. Don thanked her and walked down the hall to the room she said he should be in. The doctor was in the room when Don arrived.

"How's he doing, Doc?" he asked.

The doctor was adjusting an oxygen hose and finished the job before stopping to answer the question. "He's doing well. He does have a severe concussion, but no fracture in his skull. The blow would have killed most men, but old Andy is in pretty good shape and survived. It's going to take him a while to recover, though. I'm glad you called me when you did. We're treating him for possible blood clots in his brain. This was a very bad injury. He will have twenty-four hour nursing care here and I'm on call if they need me. It will be two or three days before he shows any improvement. I'm going to keep him sedated to minimize the chance of aggravating the brain bruising. I'll call you if there's any change."

"Thanks, Doc. Andy is a good friend. I don't want anything to happen to him. Call me when I can talk to him."

Don left the hospital to drive to Lucy's office. It was late, but her car was parked in front of the building. Addie was gone for the day leaving it up to him to let Lucy know he had come into the office.

"Honey, I'm home!" he called out.

Lucy was smiling when she stepped out of her office. "You're a smarty pants," she commented as she came to him and planted a kiss on his cheek.

"One of my more endearing qualities," he replied.

"How was the trip?" she asked.

Mostly pretty good, but there was a sort of riot in the hallway at the hotel and Andy got punched. He has a concussion and some related injuries and is in the hospital here in Homer now."

"Is he going to be alright?" Her face showed her concern.

"The doctor says he will, but it will take a few days. They are keeping him sedated so he won't move around," explained Don. "How would you like to go out to dinner tonight?"

"I'd love it. Give me a few minutes to finish a report and I'll close the office. You can wait in my office or you can come back in about a half hour; your choice, big boy."

"Now who's being a smarty pants?" Don said he would come back for her. He was going home to unload his bags out of the truck. They had a nice dinner and went back to Lucy's place to spend a quiet evening.

In the Seattle office of Sam Nelson on Monday morning there was another strategy meeting with the other two cannery owners present.

"Well, Sam, how did the meetings in King Salmon turn out?" asked Eric Goodloe.

"Hmpff!" grunted Nelson."That clod I hired gathered five other men and started a fight in the hotel. The local police contingent came in and arrested them all. My lawyer is going to try to get them out on bail, but it doesn't look good. That Trooper Biggs, the one who sits on the panel, got hit on the head and was taken to the hospital. I don't know how he is, but they frown on that sort of thing in Alaska."

"Can they connect those men to us in any way?" asked Ioshi Morita.

"Not unless my man talks and I don't expect him to do that. My attorney is working on what to do with the whole bunch."

"This situation is going from bad to worse, Sam. I didn't like this idea in the first place and now you see why. We need to find another way to deal with this." Goodloe was now speaking his mind.

"I am doing that very thing now. I am attempting to convince some political friends of mine to stop the hearings. I'm hoping it will work out. I have word that the lieutenant governor called Senator Price and told him he didn't like how this was going and would attempt to stop his hearings. We pay those boys a lot of money and it's time we had a return on our investment."

"I like this tactic better than the last one," said Goodloe.

"As do I," commented Ioshi Morita.

"I asked one of our Juneau friends to come to my office, here, for a meeting. I want the two of you here for that meeting. It will be on Wednesday afternoon. It could be expensive."

"I'm beginning to think it would be more profitable to sell my Alaska holdings than to get into a fight over it. We may not win in either case." Eric was expressing his frustrations.

"Be here on Wednesday, Eric. You can't pull out now. We have the fishermen on our side and they are going to do all the public protesting. All we have to do is keep the legislators in line and we will win the day. It will cost us, but we will win." Sam now sounded like one of the politicians he was paying to shipwreck the process. "Be patient, both of you. We are going to come out of this as winners and make a lot of money."

"I hope you're right, Sam," said Ioshi. "If this blows up we could all go to prison for a very long time. There would be no profit in that. I'll be here on Wednesday." The meeting adjourned and Sam Nelson decided to go the several blocks down the street to his club, located on Lake Union, for a drink and try to relax a while.

Tuesday morning the doctor called to tell Don he could come in to see Andy. "He's awake and asking for you," reported the doc.

Don called the office of Senator Price to tell Linda he would be late to the morning meeting as he was stopping at the hospital to see Andy. She was pleased the trooper was awake and able to take visitors.

A nurse was tending to Andy when Don arrived. "I'll be finished in a minute and you can visit. Don't let him get excited," she ordered. "The doctor doesn't want him out of bed just yet, so don't let him get up to go to the bathroom. He thinks he's tough and smarter than the doctor." She finished getting his vitals and noted them in the portable computer she pushed around in front of her as she went out of the room, humming some old tune.

"Good to see you awake, Andy," said Don when she had gone.

"Man, I've got a headache," commented Andy. "I've been told that guy hit me with his fist, but he must have used a baseball bat. I've never been hit that hard. I don't remember much of the trip from King Salmon. I must have been in worse shape than I thought."

"We have all been in the office working on the final report on the meeting. Those six men are all being charged with felony assault. It seems the judge took it personally when they tried to break up a meeting chaired by an Alaska senator and injured an Alaska State trooper. The judge doesn't know you well or he might have thanked them instead."

"Thanks for the sympathy, Don. I'll be back in the office with you in a couple of days. The doctor said I should get out of here on Thursday. He said they scrambled my brain pretty bad and doesn't want it to start bleeding inside again. I really want to thank you and Linda for looking out for me." Andy reached out a hand to shake hands with Don.

"The least we could do, Andy. Can I bring you any magazines or something else to read?"

"No, I don't want to read. My head hurts too much yet. I don't even want to watch the television."

"You have my number if you change your mind. I have to get back to the office and do some work. Get well quick, partner," said Don as he stood to leave the room. "See you later." He returned to the legislative affairs office to give a report on Andy to Linda and the senator. Both were pleased to hear of his progress.

Linda explained, "Don, I've got all the information I need right now and I have to compile the statistical data from both our Valdez and King Salmon meetings. It will take a few days to finish the reports. I've talked with the senator and now would be a good time for you to take a few days off, if you want to."

"Actually, I do need to tend to a couple of personal things, thanks," replied Don.

"Good, that shows good judgement on your part, Don. I would like to have a short conversation with you this morning, though, if you have time?" said the senator.

"Sure, sir, I have time."

"Linda, would you mind leaving Don and me alone a few minutes?" asked Senator Price.

"Of course, sir," she said and began gathering her files to leave the office.

When she had gone and closed the door behind her the senator turned to Don. "I know you see yourself as a commercial fisherman. You have made a career of fishing. That is why I chose you for the position on the panel. I have no wish to take that vocation away from you, but I would like to offer you a position on my staff. It would pay pretty well and because of my legislative schedule we could arrange for you to continue your career as a fisherman during the season. Do you think you could be interested in working with me?"

Don blew out a long breath and stared at the ceiling a moment. "To be honest with you, Senator, I was considering finding work to make up for the poor fishing season. I would like to have until tomorrow to weigh the options, but right now this sounds like a wonderful offer. I enjoy working with you and Linda. What position did you have in mind for me, if I might ask?"

"I was thinking that you would make an excellent chief of staff."

"Holy smokes, Senator! Do you think I'm qualified for that position?" asked a surprised Webber.

"We have been working together for several weeks now and you have proven to me that you have a good head on your shoulders. You have proven to me you can handle just about any situation. I like your decision-making qualities and your ability to calm a volatile situation with some ease. I admire your ability to do those things and those are the qualities I need as a chief of staff. I hope you will join me."

"Like I said, Senator, I do have to think about it, but at this point I can't think of a reason to say no. I'll have an answer for you tomorrow." Don stood to leave.

"Sit down a minute, will you Don?" The senator had a worried look on his face. "There is one thing I must tell you and it's something you should consider in your decision. I had a call from the lieutenant governor who made some veiled threats. These hearings are generating a great deal of resistance from some very influential people. I suspect some of the members of my own party are being influenced by bribe or threat from that faction. I would rather not say who I think the threats are linked to, but I have very good reasons to suspect them. If I'm right you could become a target the same as me. I don't expect physical danger, but I do expect character smears coming my way and very soon. You should be aware this could affect you as well if you take the job. This threat is one of the reasons I chose you for the position. I believe I can trust you."

"Thanks for the vote of confidence, Senator. I'll add this to the list of things to consider. I do appreciate your honesty and your trust." Again Don rose to leave. "I'll have an answer by morning."

This was a decision he must discuss with Lucy, since she would soon be his wife and directly involved.

⇒● Chapter 27 ●⇐

Sam Nelson had arranged for his secretary to hire a caterer to bring fresh Danish rolls and latte-style coffee to his office for the Wednesday morning meeting with the three expected guests. Sam was behind his desk when the first of the men arrived. His secretary announced him and escorted the well-dressed, fifty-something man into the office.

"Mr. Waylon Goff, sir," the secretary announced. Once the man was seated she left the room, closing the door behind her.

"Good morning, Sam," Goff greeted, reaching out to shake Nelson's hand.

Taking the hand for a shake he replied, "Good morning to you, Waylon. How about some coffee and rolls? I purposely asked the others to come a little later in order to have a quiet talk with you."

"Coffee and rolls sound good. I haven't eaten breakfast this morning. I came in on the red-eye and only had time to change clothes before coming here. I assume the private talk is about Senator Dalton Price?"

"As a matter of fact it is." The two men went to the coffee bar and each filled a plate and cup. "I know you have been made aware of the disturbance at both the Valdez and King Salmon meetings he is holding."

The two men carried their plates and cups to the large conference table where Sam sat at the head and Waylon sat to his right. Sam took a sip of his latte before continuing. "My business associates and I sort of encouraged the fishermen who instigated both those incidents. Our intent was to discourage the senator from going on with the meetings. Obviously that tactic didn't work as well as we had hoped. Frankly, without resorting to direct violence, I'm not sure how to go about ending the hearings. I'm very worried he is going to introduce legislation that will gravely impact the cannery and fish processing business. I cannot allow this to happen. I was hoping you would have some suggestions on how to go about ending the hearings."

Waylon Goff gave a short chuckle. "Sam, you old dog, you and I have been in business together for years. I have spread a great deal of your cash around the capitol, both as a lobbyist and now as the lieutenant governor. Since there is just the two of us here let's cut the hogwash and get to the point. It will cost a lot of cash to get the votes to stop Dalton. He's popular in Juneau and has a lot of followers. Our only ally in this fight is the fisherman's lobby. The guide association hates the hearings, too, but they don't have the legislative backing to do any good for themselves. We, you and I, have managed to do some very beneficial things for ourselves in the years we have been associated. I would like to see that arrangement continue."

Sam Nelson was smiling, "I think we understand each other, Waylon." He walked to his desk to take a large envelope from the center drawer. Coming back to the conference table he dropped the packet in front of his guest. "That should buy a couple of votes with a little left over for the ringmaster."

Goff hefted the envelope, "Yes it should," he said, stuffing the fat envelope into an inside pocket.

Sam looked at his watch. "The others will be here momentarily. We will have some of this conversation again with them, but they aren't as direct as I."

They were filling their latte's again when the others arrived. The meeting was short, but productive and the two late-comers each brought the state official another thick envelope. Goodloe and Morita stayed only until official business was complete and made a hasty exit. Nelson furnished Goff with a large padded envelope to place the three smaller packets inside.

"Would you like to go to my club for lunch, Waylon?" asked Sam.

"Sorry, Sam. I have another appointment downtown in an hour. I'll take a raincheck on the lunch. I have a, sort of, following in Juneau. I think I can convince them to vote against any adverse legislation Price may introduce. Thank you for the "advice" I can pass on to my followers. I'll keep you apprised of the results." Goff shook hands with his host and walked from the office.

Sam Nelson returned to his desk where he sat thinking this was a very productive meeting. He checked his watch and decided he would go to his club alone for lunch.

In Homer Don Webber was returning to his truck in front of Lucy's office when a new blue color GMC truck stopped beside him. The driver rolled down the window and spoke. It was Willie Hickson.

"Hey there, Webber, hold on a minute, I want to talk with you."

"I don't think we have anything to talk about, Willie," said Don.

"Hold on, Webber, I came to apologize, not to cause trouble. That stretch in jail made me see some things differently. Please, give me a minute."

"I don't have much time, Willie, but make it short."

"Look, I know I done you and your crew wrong. I told my lawyer to pay all the expenses from that deal. I was drinking pretty good before and I'm really sorry your crewmen got hurt. I really am, but I think I can make some of it up to you. I met some guys in jail who are out to get you. In fact, they asked me to join up with 'em. I ain't gonna do that, but they're out to get you. One of them said he started a fight in Valdez at a meeting you was at. He said he was hired by some big money guys and they paid him to do that. He knew who you were and said he would get you and all of you on the commission. I don't want any part of that and I wanted to tell you."

"Thanks, Willie, I guess I misjudged you. Who was the guy who tried to recruit you?"

"His name is Gus Bjornson. He fishes a cannery boat out of Cordova. He said the guy who owns the cannery is the one who hired him to go to the meeting and make trouble."

"Thanks Willie; that's useful information. I'll pass it along to Senator Price."

"Uh, Don?" stammered Willie.

"Yes, Willie, what is it?"

"Those two deckhands of yours, the ones I hurt, are they going to be OK?"

"Thanks for asking, Willie. Freddie, the one with the broken back, is out of the hospital and I saw him walking on the bike path on the spit. He seems to be doing well. Eddie the one you hit with the axe handle is OK. Honestly, Willie, I have no intention of harming you in any way. I hope that, since you have stopped drinking, you will see things differently. We're the same, you and me, just fishermen, that's all, just fishermen." Don was granting Hickson conditional forgiveness.

"You getting me thrown in jail is probably the best thing that ever happened to me. I took some AA classes and I've promised myself to never drink again. I thank you for that. I'm selling my boat to my deckhand and getting out of the fishing business. I think I can sell my property in Chinitna Bay and get enough to retire. I'm too old to fight the fight any more."

"Thanks for the information, Willie. I wish you luck for the future." Don opened the door of his truck and climbed inside. Willie drove away, waving his hand as he went.

Don sat in the driver seat of his pickup for several minutes thinking about what Willie had told him about Gus Bjornson and decided this was information he should relay to the senator. He started his truck and drove back to the legislative affairs office. In the office he found Linda at her desk.

"Hi, Linda, I've just learned something I think both you and the senator should hear."

"OK Don, let's go to his office." She rose from her desk chair and he followed her down the hall to see Senator Price.

"Hello, Don, what brings you back here?" he asked.

"I just bumped into Willie Hickson in front of Lucy's office. He looked me up to apologize for hurting my crewmen. The reason I came back here was because he gave me some very good information."

"What kind of information?" asked Price.

"I know you remember the guy who wrote those threatening letters to you. His name is Gustav Bjornson."

"Yes, of course. The fellow Andy arrested and then he showed up in King Salmon and was arrested again," replied the senator.

"That's him. I just learned from Willie that Bjornson fishes a cannery boat out of Cordova and works for the owner of the cannery there. It got me to thinking: Do you suppose the cannery owner is the one paying these men to disrupt the hearings?" Don was nodding his head indicating he believed it was possible.

"It is certainly an interesting possibility," stated Linda.

Dalton Price was massaging his chin thoughtfully and said, "It not only could be possible, but probable. I've run into him, if it's the same person, in the halls in Juneau. He owns several canneries in Alaska. I think he lives in Seattle, but he spends a lot of cash in Juneau. The rumor is that he has bought several of the legislators and uses them to influence votes concerning the fishing industry. His name is Sam Nelson. I remember his name because I threw him out of my office in the capitol and told him to never come back. He had made some remarks that I took as an offer of a bribe. I reported it to the capitol police."

"It could be the same man, Senator. It sounds like the kind of tactic he would try," commented Don.

"Come to think of it, it fits with the phone call I got from the lieutenant governor the other day. He asked me to stop the hearings and, in essence, quit attempting to promote this legislation. It makes me wonder if the lieutenant governor could be on Sam Nelson's payroll."

"Is there anything we can do about this, Senator?" asked Don. "Come to think of it, do you suppose this goes even higher in the state government?"

"I can tell you it doesn't. If the governor heard what was said here today he wouldn't even ask for verification. He would fire Waylon Goff instantly," said a smiling Dalton Price.

"What do you think we should do, Senator?" asked Linda.

Again Dalton rubbed his chin. "When does Andy get out of the hospital?" he asked.

"He should be released in the next couple of days. Why?" asked Don.

"This is his area of expertise and I think we should let him handle it. That way it's a police matter and not a political one. It might keep us from agitating any old enemies. If these hearings lead to new legislation and regulations we don't want any retaliation by a 'nay' vote."

"I never would have thought of that, Senator. I guess I have a lot to learn if I'm going to be your aide."

"Ah, good. It sounds as if you have decided to take the job," said the pleased senator. "If you have, then contact your lady friend and we shall celebrate over dinner at the steak house. Linda, of course you're invited. We can't have an office party without you."

Don left the office and drove the few blocks to Lucy's office to give her the news and to invite her to dinner with the senator and Linda. Lucy was thrilled to know Don had accepted the position.

"Do I need to dress up?" asked Lucy.

"This is Homer. Dressed up in this town is wearing a clean shirt and shoes. Of course, you have to dress up."

Lucy giggled and picked up her phone to call the receptionist, Addie. "I'm leaving a little early today, Addie. Lock the office when you leave."

＃ Chapter 28 ＃

Lester Goode, lawyer for Gustav Bjornson, was in King Salmon to confer with his client. He felt at a loss as to what to do about him. The man paying the legal bill, Sam Nelson, had given up on Gus. After his interview with the fisherman he had decided to post bail for all six defendants, but only represent Gus in court. The judge took a plea of guilty from Gus, fined him $5,000 and ordered him to pay for damages at the hotel, which amounted to roughly one thousand dollars. Lester was elated. The judge had obviously not read the report of the injured trooper nor the previous charge in Homer pertaining to the threats by mail. Lester paid the requested amount to the clerk of the court and hustled his client out of the court and to the airport where the two of them boarded a flight to Anchorage.

On the flight Lester, as tactfully as possible, explained to Gus he should return to Cordova as quickly as he could get there. He had luckily escaped further jail time and he should avoid any further contact with the law.

In Anchorage Lester paid for a plane ticket to Valdez and left the fisherman in line at security while he returned to his office to report to Nelson. The cost of this affair was beginning to add up to a considerable sum. Lester also suspected he would never need to represent Gus again in matters pertaining to Sam Nelson and company.

"Hello, Sam," he began when the call was answered. "I just put Gus on a plane for Cordova. It was costly, but I was able to get him out of King Salmon without jail time. I'll send you an itemized accounting of the costs. I suggest you don't use him any longer."

"I'll take that advice, but I don't want you to charge me for it. What about the other men?" Sam asked.

"I bailed them out, but didn't represent them. If they go to court as scheduled, I'll get my bail money back. I'm charging you for the bond fee."

"This has turned into a very expensive can of worms, Les. My partners have almost left me out in the cold on this one. I'm going to change tactic, as my partners had suggested in the first place, and forget about the hearing process. I think I can buy enough votes to stop any legislation to come from these talks. Anyway, send me a statement and I'll send you a check. I'll be talking with you soon."

At the Homer hospital Andy called Don. "I'm being released today, Don. Can you pick me up and take me home?" he asked.

"That's wonderful news Andy. How are you feeling?"

"I still have a pretty good headache, but other than that I feel good. The doctor says the ache will hang on for another few days and I shouldn't do anything too physical. I'll be ready to go back to work with you guys by tomorrow."

"I'll be there in an hour. Have the nurse bring you down and I'll be waiting at the door. Do you want me to buy you dinner on the way home?"

"No, I just want to go home and flop in my own chair. See you in an hour."

Don called Linda to let her know Andy was being released and that he was picking him up at the hospital. She was pleased with the news and said she would pass the word on to the senator.

The following morning Don met Andy outside the senator's office. "Good morning, sir," greeted Don.

"Good morning to you, too. It sure is good to be outside and moving around."

"I think Linda and the senator will be glad to see you also. In fact I'm betting the senator is about to give you a special job. Let's go inside and get some coffee."

"Good to see you back on the job, Andy," said Linda as they entered the office. "The senator is waiting for you. Do you men want some coffee?"

"That's why we came early," admitted Don.

The four met in the coffee lounge where the senator invited them to his office for a short meeting.

"How are you feeling, Andy?" asked Senator Price.

"I still have a headache, but other than that I feel fine. Don says you may have some work for me." Andy minimized the huge headache he was suffering.

"What I am about to tell you is only suspicion on my part. I don't want any of it mentioned outside this office. Agreed?" he asked and received three head nods. "I've been around Juneau for many years and I have had suspicions of bribery among some of my colleagues over the years. The events of the past few weeks have amplified my feelings. I'll cover some of the background in a moment, but the thing that triggered these new suspicions is a phone call I had from the lieutenant governor. He was trying to pressure me into dropping the hearings and said some of his friends in Juneau were unhappy with the direction they were taking.

"I know Waylon Goff. In my estimation, he has had too close a relationship with some cannery owners in southeast. The main one is Sam Nelson. Nelson has used Waylon to press his issues since he was a lobbyist for the fisherman's fund. I have never seen a money transaction personally, but I've heard the bragging by several of the legislators in the past. I suspect the cannery owners are the ones paying those hoodlums to interrupt our hearings. I can't report this to the capitol police without proof. They would call it political sour grapes and forget it. I'm asking if there is a way for the troopers to investigate my claim as a possible crime. I would hope they could do this as an anonymous tip for now and not publish the source of what little information I have. Do you think any of this is possible, Andy?"

Andy had listened intently. He sipped his coffee before answering. "Senator, I think you have a legitimate issue here. I'm going to need more specific details before I can take this to my superiors. We have an entire division dedicated to fraud, money laundering and other money crimes. If legislators are being bought these men can find out about it. They can trace money to its source and check bank accounts for deposits and check credit records for inordinate purchases whether they're real items, cars and yachts or Caribbean cruises. They are very good at what they do."

"I'm glad to hear you say that. If you can stay a while I'll give you a list of names of people and corporations I suspect, both bribers and bribees. I must put in one thing I also suspect and that is that I believe the governor is completely innocent of any wrongdoing. I believe him to be an honest man with a bad sidekick. I also believe that if any concrete proof is found the governor will terminate Waylon Goff instantly."

"Sure, Senator, I can stay. After all I'm still on official sick leave."

"Good. I'm really happy to have you back on the job, Andy. Welcome back." The senator picked up his coffee cup and held it high in a salute to the returning Andy Biggs. "Remember gang, we have a hearing in Kenai next week. This one could be a wild one because of the diverse user groups involved. There will be guide groups, sport fish groups, personal use groups commercial fishing interests and who knows what else. We had better have our ducks in a row for this one. We have a lot of work to do. So, let's get to it. I couldn't do this without all of you."

"Do you want me to call Winston Dugan and Galen Carpetti to give them a heads up about this meeting?" asked Don.

"That's a good idea, Don. Get with Linda to make a list of items they will probably encounter in the meeting." The senator was pleased with the way Don Webber took charge to get things done in an orderly way. He was going to make a good chief of staff.

"I'll get right on it, sir," replied Don.

"One other thing, remind all the panel members that this meeting in Kenai will last four days instead of two. It has been extended due to the number of speakers asking for time. Even with the extra days we may have some very long days ahead."

In the front office Don and Linda began the list of phone calls and notes for the meeting. It was noon when Andy and Dalton appeared. Andy carried a yellow legal pad filled with notes.

"Linda and I have a Chamber of Commerce meeting to attend," voiced the Senator. "Otherwise I would take the three of you to lunch. We will have to get a move on, Linda. The meeting starts in ten minutes. I'll see the two of you later."

Outside the office Don asked Andy, "How do you feel, Partner?"

"I'm getting puny," replied Andy. "I think I'll skip lunch to go home and rest for an hour. The senator handed me a bucket of worms and I have to go to Soldotna for a meeting with one of the specialty units. My meeting is at three. That gives me an hour to rest. Take my advice, Don. Don't ever get kicked in the head; it hurts. I'll see you later."

Don watched Andy drive away, thinking this wasn't so bad after all. He would call Lucy and invite her to lunch on the beach. She accepted the invitation, leaving Don to stop at McDonald's for two Big Macs and fries and two chocolate milkshakes.

There is a small vehicle parking area on the right as you drive onto the Homer Spit. The gravel in that area is clean and makes a nice area to sit on a sunny day. Lucy was parked in the lot when he arrived and met him as he stepped out of his truck carrying two large McDonald's bags. With his arms full he couldn't defend himself from the vicious kissing attack she waged upon him.

"You could have at least said hello first," he teased.

"I wanted to get you before your hands were free. Give me one of the bags. I'll help you deliver lunch."

The two lovers sat on a log watching the waves wash against the beach. It was a relaxing interlude with little conversation.

"I have to go back to the office and do some work this afternoon. I don't know how you can work inside all the time without going crazy." Don was only making conversation.

"What makes you think I'm not crazy?" she replied as she leaned over to kiss him.

"I'll have a couple of days off this weekend, would you like to go silver fishing?" he asked.

"Where would you like to go?" she asked. "Salt water or river?"

"I still have my old fiberglass cabin boat in the harbor and the weather looks good. Seas are predicted to be only one foot and a moderate tide. I can pick you up at your place at around five Saturday morning."

"I'll be ready. I'll bring lunch and coffee. Do I need fishing gear?" she asked.

"No, I have enough on the boat. I only have to buy some herring for bait in case we want to jig for sea bass over in the rocks."

"It's a date then. Thanks for lunch. I have to be getting back to the office." He watched her walk back to her car before gathering their trash from the spot on the log where they had eaten lunch. He had just started the engine on his truck when his cell phone rang. It was Andy. "Hey, Partner, do you want to ride to Soldotna with me. You can sit in on this meeting I'm having."

"What meeting is this?" asked Don.
"Come on over. I'll tell you about it when you get here. You're gonna like it." Andy was laughing as he hung up.

When Don arrived at Andy's home and knocked on the door Andy answered, looking terrible. "Is your head bothering you, Andy?"
"Yes, it is. That is one of the reasons I called you. I want you to drive me to Soldotna. I don't think I should be driving yet."

The two men climbed into Don's pickup and headed toward trooper headquarters in Soldotna. While travelling, Andy explained the case for bribery and fraud described by the senator. When he finished relating the details he turned to Don. "We have no idea how far this goes, but it could involve several legislators. I'm going to meet with Jim Steadman at the office. He's the best there is in this kind of investigation. You can sit in on the meeting because I trust you with the information. If something happens to me you can take over to help the senator and Jim."

In the office introductions were made and the business began. Trooper Steadman had stopped several times to make phone calls to investigators in Juneau. His efficiency impressed Don, who had never been around an investigation of any kind. It was after six in the evening when Andy finally said, "I think you had better take me home. I'm getting tired."

An hour and a half later he dropped Andy at his front door. Assured the injured trooper was only tired and not in distress he drove to his own home for a shower and some television news.

⁂ Chapter 29 ⁂

The following Wednesday the full panel convened in the Visitor Center in Kenai. The meeting room was spacious, but it was plain to see there would be standing room only. At 8:00 a.m. sharp Senator Dalton Price dropped the gavel to bring the meeting to order. The hubbub of conversation ceased while the senator outlined the goals and rules of the meeting. Linda had the list of names of speakers who had signed up prior to the meeting. When the senator finished his remarks Linda called the first speaker.

"Curtis Benson," she announced.

Benson was seated in the back of the room and rose to take his place at the microphone. He had some note cards in his hand. Introducing himself, he began. "My name is Curtis Benson. I own Busy Bee Charters, a sport fish guiding business out of Soldotna. I have fished the Kenai River for thirty-five years. When I first started guiding only a few guides were on the river. Everyone knew everyone and helped each other. Spence DeVito showed the guides how to make money at this business and it became a business rather than a sport. Spence was a prince of a man, helping other guides and even hiring some when they didn't have a boat or something went wrong with theirs. But make no mistake, he was there to make money and taught others how to do it. He's gone now, and it's sad to see what the river has become. In the early days the average size fish was 42 pounds. Today it is around 15 pounds. Sixty-pound fish were caught regularly in those days. Few sixty-pounders are caught today. It has been a constant battle to maintain the numbers of king salmon viable. Alaska Fish and Game met escapement goals by reducing the numbers of fish required on the spawning beds. When commercial fishermen ruined their own area on the west side of the Inlet Fish and Game moved them to the east side and extended the nets out from shore in order to do so. When the nets are in the water no fish of any kind can enter the two big rivers on the east side, the Kasilof and Kenai Rivers.

They are choked off by commercial nets. Those nets target sockeye salmon, but they catch any fish swimming by. The commercial nets catch far more king salmon as incidental catch than sport fishermen catch each year. When the king salmon return drops they close the river to sport fishing while at the same time tell the public that sockeye salmon are running late and allow the set net sites to continue fishing with extended days and hours."

Benson stopped speaking long enough to take a drink of water from a bottle on the table. He then continued. "This is common practice with Fish and Game, and I believe it is unfair to the guides, the sport fishermen, and to the personal use fishermen who net their fish for food in the lower river. As a guide I see this as a poor management practice for the sole purpose of protecting the commercial fishing industry at the expense of all other user groups. A regulation was passed to prevent this practice which states if the river is closed due to low escapements the commercial fishermen must pull their nets.

"Fish and Game has circumvented this rule by restricting river catches with catch and release, no bait, fewer hours, and other silly regulations when we advocate closing the river. At the same time they allow extended hours and days to commercial fishermen who catch those same king salmon as incidental catch. It makes no sense. Commercial fishing in Alaska exports six BILLION pounds of fish annually. The sport fish catch, mostly used by residents of Alaska, total only one percent of that amount and yet Fish and Game chooses to reduce sport fishing while at the same time extending commercial fishing in Cook Inlet.

"The federal government wants to take over fish management in Cook Inlet, but their record is even more dismal than the state regulators. It is my opinion that the fishery is managed to protect pocketbooks and have forgotten that without the fish we will all be out of business. I ask for you to propose regulations to increase the numbers of returning fish. I ask that this be done by reducing the numbers of fishing sites allowed from the beach as well as the numbers of drift fishermen allowed. Methods and technology have improved the catch numbers for those fishermen. We have enough fish to support a healthy commercial and sportfish industry, but we do not have enough fish to support an unlimited fishery we allow at this time. Senator Price, I ask you to help the fish. Without them there will be no commercial, sportfish or subsistence fishermen. We must protect the fish. Thank you."

"Thank you, Mr. Benson," said Linda Barton.

Senator Price stood to speak. "I thank you Mr. Benson. What you have stated is the very reason we are having these discussions. It is not the aim of this panel to assign blame, but to solve problems. We are here to define the problems and do our best to correct them. The items you have addressed are the reason we are here today. I assure you I will do my best to attempt to resolve these inequities."

Benson nodded approval and left the speakers table.

"The next speaker is...," called Linda. Another sport fishing guide with another plea, though not nearly as eloquent as the first, for more restrictions on commercial fish and more latitude for sport fishermen and personal use fishermen. The list continued until after seven o'clock that first evening. Sport fishing was the most represented group to be heard, but several commercial fishermen testified during the day. The entire panel was totally exhausted by the end of the first day of hearings.

Andy was completely worn out from the long day and asked to be excused to go to his room to rest. Don worried he would not go out to eat and vowed to bring him a meal when he returned from the restaurant.

The other members of the panel were starved and had reserved a large table at Louie's in downtown Kenai. The food was excellent, the drinks were wonderful, and the waitress was pleasant and efficient. Don had finished his prime rib dinner and was enjoying a cup of coffee when a tall, middle-aged man approached the table. It was Jim Steadman.

"Where is Andy?" he asked Don.

"He went to his room to rest. Can I help you?" asked Webber.

"Not here, but I would like to see you when you finish," replied Steadman.

"I'm going to take some food to Andy. Give me a minute to pick up his dinner and we'll go up to his room."

Don excused himself and asked the waitress for his "to go" order, paid his bill, and walked out to the hotel lobby where Jim Steadman was waiting. The two men climbed the stairs to the second floor where all the rooms were located, found the door of Andy's room and knocked. In a moment a sleepy Andy answered the door.

"Oh, hi, Jim," he said when the door opened. "Come on in guys. I've been napping."

"I brought you some dinner, Andy. A burger and fries. I thought you might be hungry after your nap."

Don handed the bag of food to him.

"Thanks. Did you bring coffee?"

"In the bag," said Don.

"What are you doing here, Jim?" he asked.

"I came by to give you a progress report on the investigation. It looks like your suspicions were well founded. Some of your legislative friends seem to be involved in money transactions leading back to three cannery owners. We're still tracking money, but figures don't lie and they lead directly from the cannery lobbyists to, so far, several of your legislators. They have tried to camouflage the money trail, but we are beginning to match the footprints. In each case the tie-in is legislation affecting the fishing industry. We have uncovered links to at least four legislators, at this point, with direct ties to the industry lobbyists. In two cases Waylon Goff was the lobbyist working for three cannery corporations. The investigation is in its early stages, but I came to tell you we do have concrete evidence, but have yet to trace all the leads to specific suspects."

Andy was munching his burger and dipping a French fry into a puddle of ketchup. "You know," he said finally after swallowing, "that Cordova fisherman involved in the disturbance in Valdez and again in King Salmon, he's one of the cannery's boat captains. He works for that Nelson guy from the cannery. I wonder if he works directly for Nelson doing odd jobs?"

"I'll follow up on that one, Andy. My advice to you is to get some rest. I'll get back to you in a few days."

"I'm glad you stopped by, Jim. I needed some good news for a change." Andy then continued to eat his sandwich.

"I'll let you finish your dinner, too, Andy, said Don. I'll see you at breakfast." With that he and Jim left the room together.

In the hall Steadman commented, "He looks pretty tough. He really shouldn't be doing this hearing."

"I think you're right, Jim, but he won't listen to our advice."

As Steadman walked toward the stairwell Don walked the other direction to his own room to call Lucy.

The following morning the hearings resumed. The opening speaker was a board member of the local Sportfishing Association. "I am not here to represent the Kenai River Sportfishing Association, but as a resident of the area and an avid fisherman myself. I have listened to the statements of the other speakers and I agree with almost everything said. I would just like to add a couple of things. First, we must reduce the number of fishing permits allowed to fish in Cook Inlet. If this is not done the fishery will collapse. There are not enough fish to sustain this size fleet. Limited entry was supposed to control the number of fishermen in the Inlet to a number the returning spawning population could support: it was dubbed maximum sustainable yield, but the number of beach nets as well as the number of drift fishermen grew as did the efficiency and fish detection technology. The fishing industry grew until today the catch is far greater than the resource is able to sustain. The management system is broken. Without change the resource will be destroyed forever.

"In Canada fish farming is allowed, but even there the brood stocks are not keeping up with the decline in returning fish. This is an international disaster. The federal government wants to put management of these stocks in their hands. It has not worked elsewhere and we believe we must fight to keep our fishery managed by local agencies and the science that we know works. We need to defend Alaska management of Alaska fish. There is room for a commercial fishery, but not at the scale we have today. The fish must be shared by all user groups and all groups must be considered equally by management agencies. Thank you for allowing me to voice my opinion. I wish you luck in what you are attempting to achieve."

"I thank you, sir, for your thoughts. I believe you and this panel want to accomplish the same result, to protect the fish in order that future generations of fishermen will be able to enjoy the magnificent, wild salmon we enjoy today.

The statements continued the rest of the day into the early evening. The last scheduled speaker was a small woman of obvious oriental descent. She was small and thin and extremely nervous to be speaking to such an audience. Linda called her name and she slowly stood to walk to the speakers table.

"There is no need to be uneasy, Mrs. Coogan," said Linda, noting her hesitation. "We are all here for the same reason. We are not here to criticize but to gather information and, hopefully, solve your problem. Please speak your piece."

"I live in Anchorage. My name is Viola Coogan. My husband is retired from the army. He lost his leg in Iraq. I don't say this for sympathy, but rather to illustrate my need for the personal use fish I take each year. We no longer have children at home, but we eat many fish. My husband and I are allowed twenty- five fish each year in the dip net fishery on the beach not far from this building. My husband is unable to do the fishing because of his war injury so I do the fishing for us. Sometimes it takes us more than one day to get our fish, but we stay until we have what we are allowed. I know some abuse the dip net fishing, but we do not. Twenty-five fish is about two fish a month for us to eat. We eat a lot of fish. My husband gets a pension from the army, but it isn't very much and the fish helps us to make ends meet. In the recent years fishing has become more difficult. There are many more fishermen and less fish. The cost to come to Kenai for three or four days is great. We eat every fish we catch. We don't waste the fish or even sell our fish. We eat it to survive. Please, I ask of you, don't take this away from us. Thank you." When she finished, she quickly turned to go back to her seat.

"A moment, Mrs. Coogan," said the senator. "I would like to ask a question of you."

She stopped and returned to the speakers table. She didn't speak, only nodded her head.

"You say your husband is an army veteran, wounded in the Iraq war. I cannot help but think there is other help for you within our state and federal governments. We are about to adjourn this meeting, but I would like to ask you to stay a few minutes and speak with my assistant, Linda. I don't know if we can help you, but I will be happy to look into it, if you would like."

"Oh, yes, I would. Thank you."

"Please have a seat there and when the hall clears Linda will come talk to you." The senator returned his attention to the crowd and stated, "I declare this session adjourned, and we will reconvene at nine a.m. tomorrow morning. Thank you all for coming and for participating in these hearings. We will see you tomorrow." With that he banged the gavel ending the meeting. He turned to the rest of the panel, telling them to go on without him. He and Linda would take a few minutes to speak with Mrs. Coogan.

Outside the hall Don asked Andy how he felt.

"Not too bad," he replied. "I think I was just tired out yesterday. Maybe I'm not as well as I thought," he said, grinning widely at Webber. "Let's go eat."

≥• Chapter 30 •≤

Sergeant Gary Wilcox headed up the investigative arm of the troopers for southeast Alaska. In his career he had been in charge of hundreds of investigations, about half of which were white collar crimes. A twenty-four-year veteran of the force he was not intimidated by those of rank or position. His reputation and tenacity were legendary in the state. At fifty-two years of age he was beginning to fear the end of his career. In his early years as a young trooper he was involved in a high speed chase with a fleeing felon when a teenage cyclist rode out of a side road on his bicycle directly in front of the speeding patrol car. Reacting instinctively Wilcox whipped the wheel to the left sending the speeding patrol car over a high, steep embankment. He was hospitalized for several weeks and off duty for several months due to his serious injuries. Upon his return to duty in Fairbanks his supervisors assigned him to investigations while he continued to regain his strength and agility. During this time he acquired the knowledge as well as a reputation for superb investigating skills. On his twentieth anniversary as a trooper he was transferred to Juneau as a sergeant to head the investigations division of the Juneau post.

Jim Steadman had worked with Gary Wilcox on many occasions and had great respect for his ability. Friday morning he called the sergeant. "Good morning Gary. Have you had your coffee yet?"

"Jim, you old dog, how have you been?"

"Busy; that's why I called you. What are you working on these days?" asked Steadman.

"Oh, right now I'm reviewing a cold case I've been working for several years. What do you have?"

"Are you alone in your office? This is sensitive stuff."

"Yes, I'm alone, but I'll close the office door; hold on." A moment later he returned to the telephone. "OK, Jim, go ahead."

"I have been asked to investigate a situation that started simple enough. Senator Dalton Price from Homer has received some threatening letters. I learned who had written them and thought that was the end of it, but it wasn't. That person not only wrote the letters he was also involved in a physical incident at some public hearings in Valdez and was arrested for disorderly conduct. When I asked Andy Biggs to ask the senator about the threatening letters, the writer, a man by the name of Gustav Bjornson, was located in Anchor Point. Biggs interviewed him and arrested him for making threats. Some lawyer bailed him out and he showed up at one of the senator's hearings in King Salmon. He was involved in a disturbance there and was arrested again, and again the judge slapped his wrists and released him. Pretty simple stuff really. I was called again after the senator received a call from Waylon Goff, the lieutenant governor, asking him to stop his hearings. I think this is turning into a big case with big names and I want to ask you to investigate some aspects there in Juneau. Goff appears to be involved with some corporate bigwigs and I think they are paying off Goff and some other legislators. This is one of those cases that could get you fired."

"I don't think we should say any more about this on the phone. Can I meet you in Anchorage?" asked Wilcox.

"I was about to suggest the same thing. Let me know when you will be there."

The Friday segment of Senator Price's hearings took a slight change of course. An environmental group took the floor to praise the Department of Fish and Game for a job well done. The speakers criticized sport fishermen for trampling the salmon spawning beds with their hip boots and destroying all the good and hard works the biologists had done. This triggered an outburst by several sport fish enthusiasts in the audience. The senator did his best to control the meeting, but it became very loud and laced with profanity by both sides. Andy leaned over and whispered in the senator's ear, he nodded and banged his gavel.

"I want order in this hall," demanded Price. "I am declaring a thirty-minute recess to allow tempers to cool. This behavior will not be tolerated in this meeting. Cool off and come back in a half hour." Again he slammed the gavel on the table.

The entire panel went to the dining room to have coffee in a more private setting. "Dang, I thought all these meetings were going to be boring," said Herb Bissett, the representative for the sportfish guides seated on the panel. He had said little during the entire sharing process, but had written pages of notes during the several meetings. "I wish the fish board hearings were this much fun."

The senator snickered and turned to Andy: "Do you think there will be trouble when we reconvene?" he asked.

"Probably not, but you can never be sure. We'll have a different speaker when we return to the meeting. That, in itself, should change the tone of the meeting. When we return to the hall I'll stay in the back of the room for a while, just in case there's another outbreak." Andy hoped there wouldn't be any further disturbance since he was not yet completely well from the last encounter.

Back in the meeting room the senator called the meeting to order. Linda called the next speaker to the table. It was Dennis Rugby, a river guide specializing in trout fishing. He defended the trout fisherman as a breed apart and should not be considered part of the group depleting salmon stocks, but rather as one of the solutions. His claim was that, though trout eat a great many salmon eggs which deplete salmon stocks, trout fishermen catch and release most of the fish they take, thereby teaching the trout to stay out of the spawning beds. This argument left most of the other fishermen in the audience scratching their heads.

The next speaker was an environmentalist who was angry that there were so many guides on the river. The exhaust from the guide boats was contaminating the river with hydrocarbons and stirring river silt from the bottom, thereby suffocating the eggs on the spawning beds as well as making it impossible for young salmon to ingest enough oxygen from the water.

And so it went, speaker after speaker giving the individual rendition of what makes the Kenai River the great fishing river it is. Representatives from both the Kenai and Soldotna Chambers of Commerce spoke to defend the value of tourism and non-resident fishing to the local economy. Few speakers, however, came to defend the fish, but to defend their own use of the salmon and asked to be exempted from any reduction of quotas assigned to the group they represented. It seemed to Don Webber that each speaker was attempting to fix the blame and never the problem. The days were becoming long.

On the last break of the day Don called Lucy to check on her well-being. "Hi Lover, how is your day?" he asked in a cheerful tone.

"I miss you. When are you coming home?" she asked.

"One more day. We finish tomorrow evening. I'm ready to come home."

"I'm ready to have you home. How is it going? Do you think it's productive?" she inquired.

"Actually, I think it is. The senator is planning to use this information to draft new legislation and management rules based on protecting the salmon. I'll wait until I see the bills he submits to the legislature before I judge our success. I have to get back to the meeting now, but I'll call you before I go to bed." Don hadn't realized how much he was missing his new companion.

Saturday, the last day of hearings in Kenai went like the first three. A full schedule of speakers was on the list, and like the previous days, a diverse variety of backgrounds were slated to give testimony. Linda Barton, the senator's aide was showing signs of exhaustion as was most of the rest of the panel. At the end of the day Senator Price excused all the panel members and thanked them for their time. "I will be in my office on Monday to take individual reports and suggestions. Thank you all for participating in this long week of testimony. This meeting in Kenai should be the most difficult of the five we have scheduled. The next one is in Anchorage in two weeks. I'll have Linda notify you of the housing arrangements. Thank you again," he said in closing.

Don turned to Andy. "Do you feel like driving home tonight or shall we stay here and get rested?"

"You're doing the driving I'll leave it up to you. I can sleep all the way back to Homer," he responded.

"That being the case, let's get something to eat and head home." Dinner was the day's special at Louie's Restaurant with both men drinking iced tea with the meal.

The luggage had already been loaded making it a quick exit from the city of Kenai after dinner. Andy made conversation for about twenty miles before going to sleep. Don was anxious to get home to call Lucy. He would have to be in the office with his, now, boss on Monday morning. He planned to spend at least part of Sunday relaxing with Lucy.

Sunday evening Jim Steadman had a call from Gary Wilcox to tell him he was arriving in Anchorage at 5:30 Monday morning. "I'll be at the airport to pick you up for breakfast," Jim informed the Juneau investigator. It is a one hundred-fifty-mile trip from Soldotna to Anchorage that takes almost three hours. He slept four hours at home to rest up for the journey and was parked at the curb in front of the terminal when Wilcox arrived. The two men drove to a local place, Gwennie's Old Alaska Restaurant for breakfast before driving to trooper headquarters in town.

The local trooper staff had given them a small interview room to conduct their confidential business.

"Here is the file I have prepared for you, Gary. Most if it is supposition, but the evidence and conversations are noted for you to review. The men I suspect to be involved and paying off legislators own about eleven canneries in the state. They are very powerful men. You need to be very careful who you share this information with, because, if my suspicions are correct, this goes all the way to the lieutenant governor. Senator Price assured me the governor is not involved and said he trusts him. I hope that's true because this is going to put some very powerful people in prison. We both need a friend with the power to protect us." Steadman smiled and watched as Wilcox opened the file. "Those three cannery owners all live in Seattle, but they have goons here in Alaska. Be careful. If you need help call me and I'll come to Juneau. Do you have any questions for me?"

Gary was still looking at the file. "I don't think so. It looks to me like the file has all the information available. For what it's worth I have a file containing notes of snitches and friends of mine who have given me names and dates of shady transactions by some of the same people I see listed in the file. I won't rule out calling you if I need backup. I'm too close to retirement to have it taken away from me now. And any one of the names on this list could do that, not only to me, but to you as well. I don't like using the phone for this business, so if I have questions I'll send you a letter. If I need backup I'll call you on the radio or phone."

"I wish I could go down there and help with the investigation, but I have too many other irons in the fire right now. You can work around the capitol without raising suspicions. Don't take any chances and call me if you need anything. Right now, Gary, I have to see the colonel. Stay here and look at the file. When I finish I'll take you back to the airport."

"I appreciate your taking precautions about leaks on this one. I'll try to keep the investigation discreet. Go ahead with your meeting while I look over the file."

Jim Steadman stood to leave knowing he had the right man for this case.

≋• Chapter 31 •≋

Monday morning saw Senator Price's staff in the office continuing to compile data gathered at the four-day session in Kenai. Linda was a wizard at collecting statistics and analyzing the data. The data included more than just the information supplied by the speakers at the hearings, but numbers and types of fishermen in the districts being visited. It included the amount of fish reportedly caught in each district by each of the several user groups. Andy was not included in the staff working on the statistical data being studied, since he had other trooper duties to attend.

Don found it surprising the senator had not committed to a predetermined outcome for these meetings. Price was not using the data to confirm his own goal, but to search for a goal. This fact alone was enough to make Webber admire the legislator. He had found the senator to be fair and objective in judging each speaker. He knew each speaker was biased in favor of his own type of fishing and use of the resource. Don had to admit he was not as impartial about the testimony as he should have been. Sorting the data was mind numbing and dull but a necessary part of the job.

Linda, Don and the senator were gathered around the coffee pot for a morning break. Don was rubbing his temples with the palms of his hands when the senator noticed.

"Tedious work, isn't it, Don?" asked the senator.

Don chuckled a little. "You caught me, Senator. I'm not used to working in an office all day. I'm really interested in what we're doing, but I have to get up and move around from time to time."

The senator smiled. "Linda and I go through this every year. It's still almost five months until the legislature returns to Juneau. Our problem is that we must complete all these hearings and compile the data in order to pre-file the bills we hope to pass this year. It always takes more time and more effort to do the research and compile the data needed than it does to write and submit a bill. This bill will be too important for all involved to make any mistakes.

"We will have fierce opposition on the floor, both from every fishing user group and from Fish and Game who believe they are the world authority on fish management. I believe, like you, they have failed to preserve spawning stocks. Each user group blames the others for the problem when, in fact, they all contribute to the declining fish stocks. Our job here is to redefine our priorities and to see that management goals are met. If we fail we will lose our standing as the number one fish producer in the world. We can go on catching the fish and reducing the spawning stock or we can reduce the fishing pressure from all user groups. This will be painful to many people, but I'm hoping it will save the fishing industry as a whole."

"I understand, Senator, and I agree with what you're trying to accomplish, but I wish I could be sure we will succeed in the task."

"You will find," said Senator Price, "we never know the answer to that question until the final vote on the floor of the legislature. You're a commercial fisherman and I know you are biased in your thinking. That's natural, but I also know you recognize the truth of the problem. I admire you for your hard work on this project knowing it will impact your own career. It is the very reason I want you on my team. Remember, being in on this project will give you a voice in the final solutions we will present to the legislature. You should also prepare yourself for the abuse you will take from many of your commercial friends. It will be a rocky road, my boy."

Don gave a big sigh. "I know you're right, but I also think you are underestimating the resistance you will get from the Department of Fish and Game. They will defend their kingdom to the death. They've stopped the efforts of the Fishermen's Association in the past. They'll use their 'scientific data' to refute your every argument. It is going to be a duel to the death. Those boys are tough."

"Tell me, Don, if we lose can I come to you for a job as deckhand on the *Chilkoot*?" asked the senator with a grin.

"You bet, Senator, and we'll fish until the fish are gone and we'll both look for new work."

"Enough gloomy talk. Let's go back to work." Dalton Price was uneasy about the outcome much like Webber, but as he always said, 'You can't win the lottery if you don't buy a ticket.'

Sergeant Gary Wilcox was in his office planning a strategy for learning about lobbyist wrongdoing and possible bribery. His mind kept going back to the phone calls made to Senator Price by Waylon Goff. He had been careful to disguise any kind of threat, but Gary had seen this tactic in the past. It was going to be difficult to get evidence against the cannery owners because they usually hid behind a corporate screen. All three of the owners said to be involved resided in another state making it difficult to get banking records in a discreet manner. In checking what little data he had, he noted Waylon Goff had recently made a business trip to Seattle. He would begin by checking out the reason and final destination of the trip Lieutenant Governor Goff made at state expense.

Investigations such as this one are usually slow and tiring ordeals, but for Wilcox they were challenging and exciting. Like searching for pieces of a jigsaw puzzle the picture slowly takes shape and once the picture is identified the remaining pieces fall into place easily. The process had taught Gary Wilcox the art of patience. Never get excited and never try to force one of the pieces that didn't want to fit. The station and power of the players in this puzzle would make that virtue even more important. Wilcox had been given the names of three cannery owners and probable conspirators in this case. He found the owners of the corporations owned and operated almost a dozen major canneries in the state. He also noted the gross income for the three corporations was nearly enough to pay off the national debt. It was an amazing fact to see the ledger sheets and calculate the total net profits of the three companies. This sole fact was the probable motivation in this crime, he thought.

Gary ran a one-man office most of the time, but he had one office employee, Mrs. Darlene Dupree. She was in her early sixties and had the personality of a box of soap. She was short and frumpy and lacking a sense of humor. She kept her hair braided and wound in a knot on the back of her head. For her lack of ability to make public contact she had a quality Wilcox admired. She had been an accountant in her earlier life and retired when her husband passed away. He wanted someone to help him maintain some sort of accounting of the data he was to use as evidence in his investigations. As it turned out she was perfect for the job. She had a mind and memory like a computer. She had the ability to ferret out inconsistencies in data better than anyone he had ever met in his career. He put her in charge of searching the records of the corporations to see if there were large, unaccounted-for payouts or unusual amounts of money paid to lobbyists or persons in the state government. He warned her that these payouts would be camouflaged and hidden. This was her area of expertise and she loved her work.

Andy was now fully recovered and splitting his time between his regular trooper duties and his obligation to the senator and the panel of which he was a member. The next scheduled hearing was set for Anchorage convening in a large hall in the Loussac Library. They were set to begin Wednesday morning. The members of the panel were to be billeted in the downtown Captain Cook Hotel on a government rate. Don and Andy had adjoining rooms and the other members were all on the same floor, making it convenient for short after-hours meetings. It also made it simple for Andy to keep track of his security charges.

The senator arranged a dinner meeting Tuesday evening for the panel in preparation for the hearings. Linda gave a short talk on what the previous hearings had accomplished and what they expected during the Anchorage meetings. Once she finished, she asked if there were any questions or suggestions about tomorrow. There were none, but Winston Dugan raised his hand.

"Yes, Winston," said the senator, recognizing Dugan.

"There haven't been any questions directed at me in the last three meetings and I wondered if it was necessary for me to attend."

The senator smiled at the question. "Yes, Winston, I want you there. You are important to the management process of the commercial fishery. You will be asked to give input when the hearings are completed and will need to know how the public feels about the present management policies as well as how to improve these processes. I think it is imperative you attend and be available for any questions the public may have for you."

"Very well, but I have other things I must attend to and this seems to be a waste of my time."

"I'm sorry your feel this way, Winston. If you have complaints I will see you after breakfast and we can discuss it," replied the senator.

"I think we should," agreed Dugan.

With the breakfast meeting ended all the other delegates returned to their rooms, but Senator Price and Winston Dugan remained in the dining room, sitting at one of the tables drinking coffee.

"OK, Winston, what's bugging you?" asked the senator.

"Actually, I think this whole thing is a waste of time. You should keep politics out of the regulation process and leave it to professionals, people trained in this field." Dugan seemed to be protecting his own kingdom.

"Since we're alone I'll say this to you now. You have so mismanaged the fish allocation process it should be a criminal offense. And, if the truth were known, I believe it probably is a criminal offense. You've played favorites to the commercial fishing industry and the management of the canneries at the detriment of salmon stocks for so long it has now put the entire species at risk. You have fought every effort to correct the problem and been applauded by the commercial fish interests. Even you should be able to see that if we don't do something to change the system there will be no fish for you to manage. I want you to sit here in these meetings to hear the frustration being voiced by fishermen on every side of this argument. When we finish you will have a voice in the corrective measures we will propose. Quit being a part of the problem and become part of the solution. I have had to change my opinions on some issues during these hearings and I would hope you would do the same. I want science to rule in this process, not dollar bills and private kingdoms. I'm not asking you to think like me or any other member of this panel. I know you are intelligent and have the ability to solve problems. That's why I wanted you on this panel. Forget your preconceived notions and make an attempt to do something for the fish which, in turn, will benefit your fishermen. No one group will be exempt from the change, but every group will have to change. Help me to make it as painless as possible."

"A very noble speech, Dalton, but hundreds of commercial fishing families will suffer from your actions. I'm not convinced any of this will work."

"Tell me, Winston, just how well do you think the present system is working?" asked Price. "Your present management policies are destroying an entire salmon species. If you continue there will be no wild salmon left for you to manage."

"You can't cite one thing to support your claims," blasted Dugan.

"Oh? I think I can." The senator spoke with a set jaw and stiff back. "When your commercial fish policies ruined the fish stocks on the west side of upper Cook Inlet you closed the fishery. You moved all the set net fishermen to the east side and gave them sites outside the nets already in place, thereby further restricting the spawning fish from reaching the two largest spawning beds on the east side. The area is now referred to as the strawberry patch because of all the net buoy markers to be seen in that area between the Kasilof and Kenai Rivers. I think that is one of the most glaring failures you, personally, have made. This is your chance to correct some of those failures."

Winston was shaking his head. "You know nothing about fish management or science. I'm going to stay with this panel and possibly help show some sense of reason at the hearings. I totally disagree with your motives and conclusions. In the end I may be the voice of reason at these hearings. We had better go if we are to have a meeting today." Winston stormed from the room in anger.

≋ **Chapter 32** ≋

Senator Dalton Price banged the gavel to open the meeting at exactly nine a.m. The first order of business was to have Linda read the statement of objectives and instructions to the gallery. The gallery itself was filled to capacity with the outer hall crowded with onlookers milling around to see if they could find a chair somewhere.

Linda Barton called the first name on the long list of scheduled speakers. It was a well-known chef representing his hotel chain. The crux of his statement was his concern the changes to be made in the fishing regulations would impact the prices of the fresh fish he purchased each day. His reputation was based on availability of fresh caught wild Alaska salmon. The chef added his hotel chain advertised the restaurant in food and travel magazines with worldwide circulation making his business a worldwide tourism promoter for the state of Alaska. He expressed fear the change in regulations would lead to dramatic price increases that would take him and his hotel out of the world market thereby impacting the tourism industry in the state. He invited the entire panel to an evening dinner at his restaurant as a guest of the hotel.

Senator Price responded saying he and the panel would love to have dinner at his establishment, but could not accept the gratuity, thanking him for the offer. The ethics of the proposal dictated he decline the offer publicly.

When he finished Linda called the next speaker, a Chamber of Commerce representative who also spoke of the ramifications of price increases for wild caught Alaska salmon. He noted the amount of Canadian and Peruvian farmed salmon was available year around, though the fish lacked the quality of wild salmon. In the end those fish were still salmon and tasted like salmon and only aficionados would detect the difference in the texture of the meat. He urged the senator to ask the state to reconsider fish farming as an alternative to the loss of fish.

182

The senator gave a quick explanation of the state position on farmed fish, explaining the value of wild caught fish. He also stated there were six billion pounds of fish being exported from Alaska, much of it caught on the high seas where the state had little or no influence. Those fisheries were regulated by the federal government, most of it without success. Federal enforcement agencies placed observers on the ocean-going fishing vessels, but much of the catch is transferred at sea outside U.S. jurisdiction and beyond enforcement. This inefficiency is one of the reasons the State of Alaska does not want federal enforcement within the state boundaries such as in Cook Inlet.

The arguments continued with speakers from every user group having a say in the matter. By evening adjournment all members of the panel were exhausted. Linda had compiled reams of notes to be gathered and analyzed upon their return to Homer. Don as well as the other members had also made pages of notes on which they would have to follow up at the end of the hearings. Winston Dugan was the only member who refused to take notes. He had not said a word during the meeting and showed little interest in the proceedings at any time during the day. Dugan was in his room watching TV late in the evening when his telephone rang. "Winston Dugan," he answered.

"Winston, how is it going?" asked Waylon Goff, one of his bosses.

"To be honest, I don't like it and I wish I could leave. If this continues and Price gets his way I am going to lose control of Commercial Fish." It was a frustrated Dugan answering.

There was a long pause before Goff replied. "I'm on your side, Winston. I may have a way to make it worth your while to press your issues and preferences in these hearings in Anchorage."

"What do you mean 'make it worth my while?'" asked Dugan.

"I have control of a fund separate from the government pool out of which I may be able to compensate you with a financial bonus if you can get vocal with your views and challenge Price's agenda. I believe the same as you, that the status quo is much better for everyone than the one being explored by the senator and his panel of hand-picked yes men. Are you interested?" Goff waited for an answer.

"Possibly, but I must tell you that I have already had one conversation with the senator about this. He's a very powerful man and I don't want to lose my position with Fish and Game over these hearings."

"I, too, am a powerful man in this state and I understand your problem. Do you suppose you would be interested in the Commissioner of Fish and Game position?" inquired Goff.

There was another pause before an answer. "I've never thought about it, but I think I could do as good a job as the present man. He has no backbone and won't back up his area supervisors. Is that an actual possibility?"

"Oh, I think, with your help at the hearings, it is a very real possibility. You might want to work toward that end and make a little extra cash to boot." Goff was becoming bolder with his offer to Dugan.

"Let me think about it tonight and if I agree I'll try to change some minds at the meeting tomorrow."

"I'll be watching my computer for information about the hearings and how they are trending." Goff was feeling like he had won the day. "I'll call you tomorrow evening at about this same time."

The following morning Winston avoided the senator at breakfast. When the meeting convened the senator gave his daily instructions to the speakers and opened the meeting. The first scheduled speaker was an upper Cook Inlet drift boat fisherman.

"My name is Dudley Christopher, I fish the F/V *Stardust*. I'm a drifter in the Inlet. My total annual catch has dropped every year for the past six years. This year I had boat repairs causing me to end the year with a net loss of income. I can't feed my family with red ink. If I'm reading the direction of these meetings correctly you will further reduce the number of fish I will be allowed to take. There comes a time when I have to say '*Whoa*,' that's enough to give. I am here to protest any regulation changes that will reduce my catch numbers. I'm sorry, Senator, but I can't go along with this new idea of management."

The speaker paused in his argument, giving Winston Dugan the opportunity to speak.

"Senator Price, I would like to answer this man's objection, if you may allow?"

Dalton knew he was taking a chance, but decided to allow Winston to speak. "Winston Dugan, Director of Commercial Fish Division, will respond to this request."

Winston turned on his microphone. "Mr. Christopher, I appreciate your position. The senator has taken it upon himself to revamp the commercial fishing rules that have been in place since the mid-1950s. As a Fish and Game biologist I have spent my entire career protecting the fish in Alaska waters. I fully understand the plight of the commercial fisherman probably better than anyone in this room. The decline of returning fish cannot be laid at the feet of the commercial fisherman. Since the 1970s sport fishing has grown at an astounding rate. Thousands of fishing lines are put into Kenai Peninsula rivers each year. A personal use fishery has developed attracting tens of thousands of fishermen with hand held nets to the mouth of the Kenai River as well as the Kasilof River. Commercial fishing rules were put into place long before these new pressures on fish stocks came into being.

"To say the decline of returning fish is due to commercial fishing is a fallacy. The tourism industry advertises worldwide to attract fishermen from every corner of the world to come here for a fishing adventure. This has had a very adverse effect on the king salmon returning to our rivers. This pressure has affected both the numbers and size of the returning kings. Sockeye salmon have suffered the same fate. Since the advent of the personal use dip net fishery the numbers of adult fish returning to the spawning beds has nosedived. This was never the case prior to this new fishery, but today the commercial fisherman must pay the price for allowing an unnecessary fishery to exist. I agree with you Mr. Christopher, it is not the commercial fishermen who should bear neither the guilt nor the consequences of these latecomers. Thank you for listening to me. I feel your pain, Mr. Christopher, and I will do what I can to correct this attack on your way of life."

"Are there any other comments?" asked a shocked and appalled Senator Dalton Price.

Speaker after speaker came to the table, each from a different user group, some wanting change in the system and others, like Mr. Christopher, opposed to any changes at all unless it came from another user group. Throughout the day the mood of the panel became darker, but the senator moved on hoping something would happen to improve the day. It didn't.

It was shortly after noon in Juneau when Gary Wilcox returned to the office from lunch. His right hand person/secretary/assistant, Darlene Dupree, was waiting for him.

"I've been waiting for you, Sergeant," said the woman with greying hair.

"Is there a problem, Darlene?"

"No, but I think I've uncovered something interesting in the phone records. You remember you asked me to see if there was any link between Waylon Goff and any of the cannery companies?"

"Yes; did you actually find something?" asked Wilcox.

"Perhaps, of course, I have no way to determine the content of the call, but there were several calls, both to and from Mr. Goff and the number at the office of Mr. Sam Nelson in Seattle. One call was the day prior to his trip to Seattle." She passed the information with a little excitement in her voice.

"Great job, Darlene, the dots are beginning to connect."

"I have another bit of news that may be as mysterious. The records sent to me by the phone companies were up to the minute and Mr. Goff had made a call to one of Senator Price's panel members. Not to the senator, mind you, but to a member of his panel. Last evening, one of the last calls made by Mr. Goff was to Winston Dugan. He's the Fish and Game rep on the senator's panel. I was surprised when that name turned up."

"I don't know how you do it, Darlene," said Wilcox, who was shaking his head.

"I was truly shocked when that name came up. I thought the computer had made a mistake, but it verified the time and length of the call. It was actually completed to a room in the Captain Cook Hotel where the panel members are staying this week. I don't know which room number."

"You are a wonder, Darlene. Keep working on it. I'm going to call Jim Steadman to let him know. Good work, gal."

Gary Wilcox sat at his desk attempting to sort out what events would account for these men to call each other. It wouldn't make any sense under normal circumstance, but if you put evil motives with it, it could mean something. He dialed Jim Steadman.

"Hello, Gary," said Steadman, reading his caller ID.

"Are you having a good day?" asked the Juneau investigator.

"One of those wonderfully boring, data filled days," said Steadman, laughing. "How about you?"

"I don't know what it means, but my assistant, Darlene, found a couple of things in the phone records that may confirm your suspicions about the lieutenant governor. She found phone calls to cannery owner Sam Nelson on the day before he went to Seattle. She's still checking the records. The other thing she found was a phone call made yesterday to Winston Dugan, a member of the senator's panel. I don't know how, but I thought it may tie into your list of suspicions."

"Wow," said Steadman. "I just had word that Winston went rogue at the hearing in Anchorage today. He went on a rant in an attempt to derail the credibility of the senator and his panel. The word I got was that the senator was furious, but let him speak and Winston went on to, basically, say the panel had already made up its mind to dismantle the commercial fish industry. I haven't seen a transcript but I had a call from Andy Biggs confirming the rant. You know, Andy is on the panel, too."

"It sounds like we stumbled onto something to confirm your original suspicions," said Gary. "I'll call again if we find anything else. Good luck, old man."

Chapter 33

Early the following morning Sam Nelson was in his office drinking a cup of coffee. He stood at the rear of his office which contained a large glass wall looking out over Lake Union. The office building was situated such that this window viewed the lake over the top of the boat storage units below him and up the lake a short distance from the entrance to the lock system. Across the lake he could get glimpses of traffic on State Road 99 above the lake and on the far side. It was a sunny morning with little wind to disturb the surface of the lake. This had always been a calming view for Sam and today was no different. Alaska is on a different time zone from Seattle giving Nelson an hour to enjoy this relaxing panorama. At ten minutes until the top of the hour Sam dialed Goff's cell phone number.

"Good morning, Sam," answered the lieutenant governor.

"And good morning to you, Waylon. When we last talked you said you were to make contact with someone new. I was checking to see how that went for you."

"I have good news, Sam. I spoke to my man and made him an offer. I didn't know, after we spoke, if he would take the offer or not, but I have word he took it. He's a member of the senator's panel and they are holding meetings in Anchorage this week. In response to one of the speakers my man unloaded on the senator and the panel. He said the senator was out to get all commercial fishermen and the hearings were a sham to make it look like it was unbiased when, in fact, they weren't. He carries a lot of weight with the commercial fishermen because he's in charge of the state's Commercial Fisheries Division. I heard the senator was livid."

"Good Lord, Waylon! That is a stroke of luck. Do you think the senator will fire him from the panel?" asked Nelson.

"I have no idea what he'll do, but it certainly turned the momentum toward our way of thinking. I'm waiting to hear if Winston Dugan is seated at the hearing table when the meeting begins this morning."

"Call me as soon as you learn anything at all. This is a fight we can't afford to lose."

"Sure thing, Sam. It's still a couple of hours until the meeting starts in Anchorage. As a side note, I've had a couple of calls from friendly legislators inquiring as to what pre-filed bills the senator is planning. Of course, I have no idea at this point. There is plenty of time for that. It is still over four months until the legislature convenes. I'm keeping an eye on things, and luckily, the governor hasn't noticed what we're doing." Goff was feeling pleased with the progress toward his promises he had made in this fight.

At the same time Goff was on the telephone with Nelson, Senator Price entered the dining room for breakfast. He sat alone at a small table near the rear of the room. The waitress bought him coffee and left a menu. He was consumed with thoughts on what to do about Dugan, staring at the menu but not really seeing it, when a voice interrupted his thoughts. It was Don Webber.

"Good morning Senator. May I join you?" he asked.

"Of course, Don. In fact I'm glad to have the company this morning. Please, have a seat."

"You seemed deep in thought and didn't know if I should bother you, sir. I just wanted to see if you had decided how to deal with Winston and his outburst at the meeting yesterday."

"I haven't made up my mind. He knows better. If I remove him from the team there will be outcry from the commercial fishing sector as well as from Fish and Game, both claiming bias. I'm just undecided." He stared at the menu again. "Have you eaten?" he asked.

"Not yet, but I don't want to disturb you if you need time to think."

"Sit still, Don, and have breakfast with me. I would like to hear your opinion. You have been at this with me from the start. What do you think I should do?" asked Price.

The waitress brought coffee for Webber along with another menu.

When she had left Don sipped the hot coffee and looked the senator in the eye. "This is your decision to make, sir, but if it were me, I would let Winston continue on the panel. He is only one voice and he's angry because he thinks you are attempting to take away or reduce his authority. People don't like to have their kingdoms threatened. I think it will do more good to ignore his outburst at yesterday's meeting and go on as if nothing had taken place. I have one further suggestion, sir. Kodiak is all about fishing, but in-shore salmon fishing is a very small portion of the industry out there. I think we could end these meetings with the one we are now holding and invite anyone in the Kodiak area to respond by mail to your office. It's only a suggestion, Senator."

"I thank you for your input, Don. For what it's worth I have been considering the same possibility. I'm glad you came to breakfast. Let's order." It seemed the senator had made up his mind.

When the panel gathered in the meeting room their mood was dark. Little was said as the committee took their seats at the table. The gallery was talkative and cheerful as they waited for the gavel to fall with the usual mumble of subdued conversation and occasional laughter around the room. Senator Price studied the faces of his panel especially that of Winston Dugan. He had decided to say nothing to him or about him as he prepared to open the meeting.

Again, there was a diverse list of speakers slated to take the microphone. The senator banged the gavel at precisely the top of the hour. Linda read the rules to those gathered in front of the panel and finally called the first speaker to the table. The day wore on speaker after speaker taking his turn with little reaction from the head table. Winston seemed angry and said nothing the entire day. When the final speaker had finished in the late afternoon the senator thanked everyone for attending and for their input.

When the room was empty he turned to the panel and thanked each of them for participating in the exercise. "You have each added a different dimension to the discussions and I give you all my thanks. I have decided to cancel the final set of meetings in Kodiak and allow them in that fishery to respond by mail. I have done this because of the few fishermen affected by state laws and regulations. Most of the Kodiak fleet fishes under U.S. maritime regulations. I will give them an end date to respond to this panel, but will not use your time to personally take testimony.

"I would like each of you to give me a written statement about your feelings in regard to the series of discussions and to give me your insights into how you would like me to proceed with the changes in our fishing laws and regulations. I have just over four months to write this new bill and submit it for discussion in the new legislative session. I will consider every suggestion. Again, I thank each of you for your participation. I declare this meeting adjourned."

Each of the panel members came by to shake hands with Senator Price and to thank him for being patient. There was one exception and that was Winston Dugan who stood and walked out of the meeting room without speaking to any of the panel members.

Andy and Don had come to the meeting in the same vehicle and planned to drive back to Homer this evening. Both men were tired and happy the ordeal was finished, but both knew they would be busy helping the senator work on the final draft of the proceedings and give input into the changes in the final senate bill.

It was late when Waylon Goff finished his conversation with Winston Dugan and called his benefactor in Seattle. "Well Sam, I think we made some headway. I just finished talking with Dugan and he gave me a rundown on the Anchorage meetings. We have one thing in our favor. Price decided to call off the meetings scheduled for Kodiak. I think the speech made by our man in yesterday's meeting had a great deal to do with that decision. All we can do now is wait to see what kind of legislation he proposes to the new legislature."

"All that sounds good, Waylon, but you know as well as I we cannot become complacent. There is too much at stake here for us to let down our guard. You will have to stay on top of this and keep me informed. We cannot afford to lose this fight. Even minimal changes could cost us millions of dollars. That's earnings I cannot afford to lose. Thanks for the call. Stay on top of this and let me know what legislation is proposed as soon as it's available. Good night." Sam Nelson was still worried in spite of Waylon Goff's optimism.

Monday morning Gary Wilcox was in his office early only to find his right-hand staffer on the job. Her desk and the floor around it were covered with computer printouts of phone records, bank records, mileage reports and a myriad of other lists of data. Gary put a white paper bag on top of the paperwork littering her desk.

"Good morning, Darlene," he greeted her. "I brought you a foo foo coffee and Danish as a bonus for your diligence."

"You are so thoughtful and generous," she said with feigned disgust.

Gary laughed and asked, "What time did you come in this morning?"

"Oh, I've been here about two hours. I've found some interesting things, too, like Goff called Nelson again last night. And some interesting folks have made some large bank deposits in the last couple of days. Some of them aren't on our list of suspects, but they are connected to the end objective."

"You amaze me, Darlene. Are you always suspicious of everyone or are you just grumpy with everyone?"

"I've learned everyone is a crook. I haven't checked on you yet, but I'll bet you're a crook, too."

"I'm glad to know you measure everyone with the same stick," joked Gary. "What have you found?"

"I realize these sums deposited could be from legitimate sources, but they caught my eye because they involve legislators or lobbyists and government officials like Winston Dugan, for example. He made a large deposit yesterday to his savings account in an Anchorage branch of his bank."

"Do you mean our Winston Dugan?" asked Gary.

"The very same," she said as she leaned back in her desk chair and removed the lid from her fancy coffee.

"Are any other members of the senator's committee making unusual deposits?" he asked.

"None I've found," she said as she took a bite of Danish.

"Finish your coffee and roll and we'll try to put together a chain of evidence. We may have a bribery scheme in play here if we can connect deposits with possible payments by Goff. What's the next step for you, gal?" asked the investigator.

"I have been crosschecking the phone records with deposits made by officials connected with the investigation. There are other things, too, that could be under the counter payments. In one case there are travel tickets and resort reservations paid by a lobbyist, but in the name of a legislator. I'm still following up on that one."

"I'll call Jim Steadman and fill him in. I think we will have a very full day of connecting the dots, thanks to your psychic abilities. I'll be back in a few minutes, after I call Jim." Gary was excited by the news, though he didn't yet have names to put to the deeds.

Wilcox and Steadman were on the phone for nearly an hour before he returned to confer with Darlene. They began the process of matching phone numbers and names as well as bank accounts. It was always difficult to follow the shadowy trail of illicit cash but with hours of diligence and persistence it could usually be done. This was one of those times. It took time to build the web leading from Sam Nelson and his corporation to

Lieutenant Governor Waylon Goff to local lobbyists, legislators, and other government figures like Winston Dugan. In this electronic age of business there are never any faces only numbers, but they are as identifiable as a mug shot. By the end of the day Gary Wilcox and Darlene Dupree had mapped a circumstantial case against several local lobbyists, Winston Dugan, and the lieutenant governor. Gary knew he would be required to get the go-ahead from his commander before proceeding further. After all, a trooper sergeant can't just bring the lieutenant governor in for questioning without ruffling some feathers in the governor's mansion.

The model they had managed to put together involved many prominent Alaska citizens which Wilcox knew he had the authority to bring in for questioning, but it also led to Sam Nelson who operated several canneries in Alaska, but resided in Seattle, Washington, outside of Trooper Wilcox's jurisdiction, making the process more complicated. He and Steadman would first have to meet with the colonel if they were to talk with Nelson.

≋• Chapter 34 •≋

The trooper colonel called Jim Steadman into his office and had his receptionist arrange a three-way conference call with Gary Wilcox and the governor. A time was set by the governor and the conference began.

"I am in my office with Sergeant Steadman and we have Sergeant Gary Wilcox on the line in his office in Juneau. I'm sorry we had to bother you, but a sensitive situation has arisen, one in which you need to be advised. It concerns state government, sir."

"All right, Colonel, let's get to it."

"I'll let Sergeant Wilcox explain the situation. He's the other investigator in this case. Go ahead, Gary."

"I'm sorry, Governor, but there just isn't a nice way to put this. We have uncovered what appears to be an influence peddling and bribery case with threats made to Senator Dalton Price. It involves your lieutenant governor, Waylon Goff. We have found phone and banking records possibly linking him with a group of cannery owners attempting to influence the outcome of the hearings the senator is holding to determine changes in the salmon fishing laws within the state. The phone calls confirm conversations between Waylon Goff and Sam Nelson who resides in Seattle. An employee of Mr. Nelson's has been arrested twice in connection with the hearings. Banking records have confirmed large cash payments to several lobbyists and Alaska legislators. The deposits are in cash and we cannot confirm the payments that came from Nelson, but the timing is suspicious. Goff made a trip to Seattle in recent days and the payments began shortly after he returned. We don't have enough real evidence to arrest any of the suspects, but one of the suspects is a very powerful man and linked to you by election, prompting us to make this call. I want you to understand we have found no evidence of your involvement, but decided you needed to know where this investigation is headed." Wilcox stopped talking to give the governor a chance to absorb these details.

"How sure are you that Waylon is directly involved?" asked the governor after a short pause.

"There is no hard evidence, sir, but the trail leads through him and to make this work it had to come from someone of power and influence in the state government. We had to make sure you were not involved and that's why the delay in calling you. Sorry, sir, we had to be sure." Wilcox was hoping the governor was a tolerant man.

"I understand, Sergeant. I find it difficult to believe my old and trusted friend is involved, but I can see how you would suspect him. Is there anything you want from me at this time?" asked the governor.

"No, sir, we just wanted to advise you that we are investigating someone in your office. Unless you order me to stop I'll continue the investigation."

"No, I want to see the investigation completed. I will attempt to be careful about what information is passed on to Waylon Goff. Rumors travel slightly faster than the speed of light in this environment, so I'll try to keep knowledge of this conversation to a minimum. I would appreciate it if the colonel would keep me personally advised as to the progress of this investigation. I thank you for your vote of confidence and I'll be watching this as it develops. Is there anything else?"

"Not from me, sir," said Gary.

"I think we've told you nearly all we know at this time, sir. I'll give you updates when we have them," added the colonel.

When the governor had hung up his phone the colonel advised Wilcox to continue with his investigation, being mindful of how this will look when it hits the newspapers. "We must keep this quiet as long as we can," said the colonel. "I want you to make this your priority and move as quickly as possible, Gary. It sounds as if the governor is on our side and I want to keep it that way."

"Do you need anything on your end?" asked Steadman.

"Not at this time, Jim, but if I do I'll call you. Right now I suppose I should go out front and help Darlene." Gary hung up the phone and leaned back in his chair, wondering if he should have told Jim Steadman to contact Senator Price to pass along the new information and news of the governor being advised.

In Seattle, cannery owner Ioshi Morita was on the telephone speaking in Japanese language to a man in Japan he knew well, a Japanese business associate. "I don't like the way things are moving, Kogi. Sam Nelson is doing things that are unnecessary and dangerous."

"What do you mean by that?" asked Kogi Yakamoto.

"He has enlisted a high-ranking politician to be his front man in the effort to stop a senator from creating new legislation to control our commercial fishing industry. I don't trust this man. He is weak and has no discipline. He works for only the money," explained Ioshi.

"I understand, but what do you want me to do?"

"At this point, nothing. I fear the Alaska State Troopers will begin an investigation and our involvement will become known."

"What would you have me do?" asked Kogi.

"At this point, nothing, but I intend to offer Sam a good price for all his holdings in Alaska. If he accepts, I may need a short term loan to cover the sale until after the next salmon season. The man is becoming much too bold with his bribery plans which jeopardizes all of us." Ioshi Morita was, indeed, a troubled man.

"What of your other business partner, Mr. Goodloe?" asked Kogi.

"I have not spoken to him about this, but the time to do so is approaching. He, too, is troubled with the dealings of Mr. Nelson and shares my fears."

"I will see to it you have the money available when and if you need it. You are a good man with good business sense, Ioshi. I admire you. We here in Japan need the fish you ship to us. I remember your father when we were in school, before the war. We were classmates and friends. He protected me in those days. Today I am responsible for many of my countrymen and I try to emulate the values your father taught me. How is he doing, by the way?"

"He is still true to his beliefs and strong in his old world faith, but his body is becoming frail. He misses my mother greatly." Ioshi spoke with a sad voice.

"I fear we are all suffering the same fate, Ioshi. One cannot outrun the clock. Give him my best. I think of him often. I ask you to please keep me informed as to what is taking place with you." With that short statement he hung up the phone.

Ioshi was pleased he had secured financing to make it possible for him to eliminate Sam Nelson's interference with the peaceful resolution of the current situation. He was born and raised in the United States, but raised and believed in the ways of his father's faith and loved his father's home country. Kogi Yakomoto was a powerful man in Japan, the head of one of Japan's most powerful orders of the Yakuza.

Prior to World War II both he and Kogi had joined the order to which he still commanded while his father, wounded in the war, moved to the U.S. with his new wife to start anew in America. He had done well in business, making him and his family very wealthy. Ioshi was now reaping the benefits of his father's good fortune as well as his friendship with one of Japan's most powerful men.

Ioshi pressed the numbers on his desk phone to call Sam Nelson at his Lake Union offices. Nelson answered on the second ring.

"Hello, Ioshi. What can I do for you today?" asked Sam, noting the caller ID on his digital phone.

"Hello, Sam. I was calling to learn if there was any news about our situation in Alaska. Have you heard anything new?"

"Only that the senator had cancelled the final meeting in the hearings he is holding. I'm hoping this is good news for us. Why do you ask?"

"You may have guessed I feel differently than you about how all this is proceeding. Eric is willing to go along with your plan, but I am having doubts. I suspect the methods you are employing are illegal and underhanded. I don't believe this is the proper way to attack this problem. I would like to make you an offer that would be profitable for you and, at the same time, relieve you of any responsibility in this issue." Morita was attempting to be cautious, but at the same time anxious to get the offer on the table.

"I will not abandon my plan, Ioshi. At this point I believe it is moving along quite well. What offer could you make me that would change my mind?" asked a curious Sam Nelson.

"You own two canneries in southeast Alaska one in Kenai and two in Bristol Bay. I am interested in making you an offer to include the canneries, all your permits and fishing vessels you lease to operators. This would include all facilities and licenses you own in Alaska. If you would give me a total value on these properties I would be willing to make you an offer for the package. Are you interested?"

Nelson was stunned. "You want to buy my entire Alaska holdings?" he asked.

"That is correct. I would expect an honest evaluation and I would need a little time to verify your evaluation. But I am willing to buy those holdings at a reasonable price while allowing you to make a reasonable profit. This would relieve you of the need to continue any further down the path you are now treading and take away the need for you to take any unconventional chances with your companies. Are you at all interested?"

"I'm going to have to think about it, Ioshi. This is a complete surprise to me. How long will this offer stand? I would need some time to consider it."

"The offer will stand for two weeks to the end of the month. If you accept, I can offer you full payment by the end of October thereby taking the uncertainty out of next season for you."

"I will certainly consider it. Thank you for the call and the offer." Nelson carefully set his phone back in the cradle and leaned back in his office chair, smiling.

He turned his chair around to view the panorama of Lake Union and to consider the possibilities of the offer he had just received. 'Why would he make this offer at this time?' he wondered. And 'Did he make the same offer to Goodloe?' Questions, questions, questions. He must look for answers. He turned back to his desk and reached for his phone to call Eric Goodloe.

"Eric Goodloe, here, how may I help you?"

"Eric, it's Sam, Sam Nelson."

"Hello Sam, good to hear from you. What's on your mind?"

"I was wondering, have you had a call from Ioshi recently?"

He thought a second, "No, not in several days. Why?"

"Just curious. He called me this morning and chatted. He sounded uneasy about how I was handling the Senator Price affair. Are you having any second thoughts about it?" asked Nelson.

"No, I've been quite happy to let you take care of that," claimed Goodloe. "Why? Did Ioshi seem unhappy with the way it was going?"

"Not really, but he made me curious about his reasons for calling me and I wanted to be sure you were still on board." Nelson didn't want to divulge the real reason he was calling. "Sorry to have bothered you, Eric. I'm going to call my man in Alaska and see how we are doing there. I'll call you later."

His next call was to Waylon Goff. "Hello, Waylon," he spoke when the lieutenant governor answered. "How are things going up there?"

"Very well, Sam, thank you for asking. I have two more legislators on our team as of this morning. It's been expensive, but I think we have the votes at this time to defeat anything the Homer Senator may propose."

"That's good news, Waylon. I was just curious, and I suppose a little uneasy about how it was progressing." Nelson was satisfied Goff had nothing to do with the call from Morita. "Keep up the good work. I'll call again in a few days."

Now Nelson had one more call to make: Lester Goode. "Hello, Lester, Sam Nelson here. I was calling to see if you had heard anything from Gus Bjornson?"

"Not a word, Sam. He went back to Cordova is all I know. I was glad to see him leave, quite honestly. You need to get rid of that one, Sam. He's trouble."

"I agree, Lester. I'm planning to do just that. Is there anything going on up there I should know about?"

"I haven't heard of anything except they cancelled the hearings scheduled for Kodiak. They advertised it to be a write in testimony hearing. Send a letter to the senator and voice your opinion. I think the senator was afraid he was going to run into trouble like he had in King Salmon. What's next, Sam?" asked Lawyer Goode.

"I don't know yet. I talked to my man in Juneau and he thinks we have the votes to stop Price. I hope he's right. I'm just following up on some details that have worried me and Gus came to mind. I'll let you know if anything changes. Good to talk to you, Lester."

Nelson again turned his chair to see the lake. His conversation with Ioshi Morita still troubled him, but he had not been able to find any reason or change for him to worry about. Perplexed and uneasy he decided he would leave the office and go to his club to relax and have a drink. It would ease his worries.

⋙ Chapter 35 ⋘

As an investigator Gary Wilcox commanded a secure office in the Juneau state trooper complex. He actually had two offices, one for himself and one for his assistant, Darlene. She had been hired originally for her typing and computer skills, but Gary realized early on that she possessed skills no one had seen. She had the ability to sort numbers and compile facts relating to them. This skill had been the reason Gary Wilcox was such a successful investigator. When Sergeant Wilcox entered the office he noted the mess looked the same as it had when he left the night before.

"Good morning, Darlene," he said, moving some of the papers aside to have room to set the latte he had brought for her. "Have you been here all night?"

She swiveled her desk chair around to face her desk and reached for the cup of fancy coffee. "Nope," she said as she tested the heat of the coffee. "But I did come in early. I had the phone company send me yesterday's list of phone calls made to and from Mr. Goff's two personal phones and I have been sorting through that mess. He made several calls to legislators from his cell phone. I think the list of names is very interesting. He also had a call from Sam Nelson's office in Seattle. It was a short call, but interesting anyway. I wish I could listen in on some of those calls. But I suppose the FCC would get upset about that." She held her coffee cup in one hand while she reached over the desk to retrieve a stack of yellow legal pads from the far side. "Here are some of the things I found," she said as she handed him the notepads. "I listed them in groups: caller, receiver, length of call, and location of the calls."

"I wish I could do what you do with these numbers, Darlene. You are a wizard." Gary was scanning the lists and they were indeed interesting.

"When I was young and in school I wasn't called a wizard, I was called a witch," she responded.

Gary turned to leave the office carrying the stack of notepads. "Finish your coffee and come to my office. We'll see if we can make any sense of these calls." He nearly laughed aloud when he turned to see her sprawled like a rag doll in her office chair as he left her small office.

At his own desk he picked up the phone to dial Jim Steadman. After their initial greetings Gary gave him a verbal account of the findings in the telephone call logs, and explained Darlene had found new calls in today's list. "I think we should begin to put some pressure on these folks and see if we can get one of them to admit to something. We don't really have any hard evidence and I don't see much chance of getting any without making one of our suspects nervous and spilling the beans. I can call Waylon Goff and ask him to come to my office for an interview. I can tie him to Sam Nelson and to about four legislators by the phone lists. There are, I think, four lobbyists he is contacting also. I was thinking if I made him nervous he might call some of those numbers again to let them know we might be onto them. What do you think about that idea, Jim?"

Steadman thought a moment before answering. "Do any of the suspected legislators live in this part of the state?"

"Yes, as a matter of fact, Representative Leslie Eaton from Palmer and Representative Harry Mead from Wasilla. You know? If you contacted them and I met with Goff we might just spook someone into a panic and make a mistake.

"That's what I was thinking, too, Gary. When would you like to do this little dog and pony show?"

"How about now?" asked Wilcox, "I can call Goff and ask him to stop by my office, at his convenience, of course."

"You are a crafty devil, Gary. I'll call and make appointments with the two you mentioned. If we can get them calling each other they might just call the money man in Seattle for advice. I'll have to drive to the valley for the interviews, so it will be late this afternoon before I can call you with any results."

"Good," said Investigator Wilcox, "I'll give Waylon Goff a call right now. Call me when you get back to your office."

It seemed like a simple plan that, in reality, was only a fishing trip. He was reaching for the phone again when Darlene came into his office.

"Have a seat Darlene. I'm about to ask Waylon Goff to stop by the office for a little chat." She sat as Gary dialed the office of the lieutenant governor of the State of Alaska.

The secretary answered and said she would forward the call to his office. There was a long pause before Goff answered. "Sergeant Wilcox, good to hear from you. What can I do for you?" he asked in a cheerful tone.

"Yes sir, we haven't talked for quite a while. I'm working on a case right now and I would like you to come by my office for a few minutes, if you have the time. It involves some of our legislators and I need to get your opinion about what to do. Can you stop by here later this morning? I just have a couple of items I want your input about before I proceed."

"Certainly, Gary, I can be there shortly before lunch. Will that be satisfactory?" inquired Goff.

"That will be perfect. I'll let the receptionist in the front office know I'm expecting you. Thank you, sir." Gary was smiling when he hung up the phone. "Clean this place up, Darlene. The lieutenant governor is coming to visit."

"Get someone else to clean up. I'm too busy." She faked a grumpy attitude. "I do have to make you a list of the new calls and contacts from today's list and it sounds like I have to complete it before noon."

"I don't know what I'd do without you," he said in sweet tone, mocking her anger.

At eleven o'clock the receptionist in the front office called to say he had a visitor. Gary walked to the front and escorted Waylon Goff to his office. As the men entered Darlene followed with a stack of yellow sheets from the notepads.

"These are the notes you asked for, Sergeant," she said pleasantly, handing him the notes and leaving the room. Gary closed the door for privacy.

"It's good to see you again, Mr. Goff. We haven't worked together in quite a while." He spoke as he walked around the desk to take a seat.

"Yes, I think the last time was that charity theft you investigated. I was charged with the task of terminating that young aide. But what is it you need to know today?" asked Waylon.

"I don't want this to get out of my office, sir, but I'm investigating a possible bribery case in which four legislators may be involved. Because these are public figures I must ask you to keep our conversation between us until the investigation is completed. Are you comfortable with that?" asked the investigator.

"Of course, Sergeant, I'll be discreet. What information do you have?" he asked.

"I have information that four legislators may be taking payoff money to stop some proposed legislation during the next legislative session in

January. Senator Dalton Price is writing several bills that would change fishing quotas for each of several types of fisheries across the state. There is a great deal of resistance to the new measures and even one personal threat against the senator. I really don't know what the legislation entails, but it is getting a lot of attention. We have reason to believe at least four legislators have taken payments to stop this legislation from getting passed." Gary was being as ambiguous as possible.

Waylon Goff had a worried look on his face. "Are you free to tell me who these four legislators are? This is, after all, my area of responsibility. I should be allowed to know their names."

"I agree, sir, but until we have definite proof of a felony bribery case, I don't feel right in naming the individuals. I can tell you we suspect an out-of-state cannery official with an import/export license of furnishing the cash. I may need your help with the warrants when it comes time to arrest this person. My counterpart in Anchorage is in the valley as we speak in an attempt to interview two of those suspects. The reason I asked you here is I wanted to know if you had heard any rumors about these bribery cases?"

"Good Lord, no. This is shocking news. The legislature doesn't meet until January, but I have contact with many of the legislators the entire year. No one has said anything to me regarding bribery or influencing legislators. You would have been the first one I would call. Shocking, just shocking. What can I do to help you, Gary?" asked the lieutenant governor.

Gary Wilcox knew he had struck a nerve. "First of all, I remind you this is between us. We can't let anyone know we suspect someone. Second, I would appreciate it if you kept your ears open and let me know if any rumors surface. Like I said previously, I may need your help to secure warrants if we intend to arrest a Washington state resident. I thank you for stopping by, sir. You've been a big help."

Goff stood to leave after the short dismissal. "I'm glad you called me, Gary. I'll do anything I can to help. Please keep me advised of your progress in this matter."

"Thank you again, sir. I'll show you out to the front entry. You've been a great help," said Wilcox as he stepped from behind his desk to open the office door. Back in the office he called for Darlene.

"What's up Boss?" she asked.

"This little charade may have paid off and I owe it all to you. I think I should take you to lunch to celebrate. Do you want a free lunch?" he asked.

"You know me, Sarge. I'll go anywhere for food," she replied.

It was late afternoon when Jim Steadman called.

"How did it go?" Gary asked.

"I was lucky and saw them both an hour apart. They never admitted to anything, but they were both pretty nervous when I told them what we suspected. I'm certain Leslie Eaton called Harry Mead as soon as I left his office. Mead was waiting for me in Wasilla and tried to be clever, but he made one big mistake. He admitted to making some large bank deposits from some land he had sold, but he couldn't tell me which parcel he sold. I told him I could look it up in court records and that made him even more nervous. I'll bet the phone lines are burning up right now. How was your interview with Goff?"

"I think I made him nervous, too. I'm with you. I'll bet the little clique is burning up the wires right now. It will be interesting to see if he called Nelson after our meeting."

"If this is all tied together the way you suspect I'll bet there are phone calls to his cell phone from both Palmer and Wasilla. All we can do now is to wait for results." Jim was chuckling as he hung up the phone.

Don Webber had worked closely with Dalton Price during his time at the office. Don liked the senator and respected his dedication to the task at hand. The letters were beginning to come in from fishermen in Kodiak in response to the cancelled meeting there. Most of the letters, as Dalton had predicted, were from commercial fishermen, though there were some from sport fishermen and some from out of state anglers. Like the speakers at the other hearings each user group wanted the others to pay the price of failing fish stocks, but not their own user group. The one group speaking loudly in their letters was a new group; the high seas fishermen. A few were Alaska bases owners, but most were skippers of foreign boats with federal permits to fish these arctic waters. They, as a united group, denied any responsibility to declining numbers of fish returning to spawn. Their argument was ludicrous stating they had nothing to do with spawning fish. They only fished the high seas catching only fish feeding in the open ocean. Don thought the argument was laughable, but the senator considered each letter and opinion with respect. A skill Don had not yet acquired.

He was happy to have this extra time for making wedding plans with Lucy. Dinners and weekend getaways were a bonus of this job with somewhat normal working hours. Don was beginning to like it.

⇒• Chapter 36 •⇐

Leslie Eaton had called Harry Mead to warn him of a visit from Jim Steadman, urging him to use caution in his conversations with the trooper. "He's a talented investigator, so don't try to be cute with him," he warned.

After the short call to Mead he dialed Lieutenant Governor Waylon Goff's cell phone. Goff had just returned to his office after lunch and his visit with Wilcox. "The trooper was here, Waylon. I don't know how, but they know about the money you paid me. You have to do something. I can't have my name connected to anything scandalous. You said all I had to do was vote against the bills Price was proposing. Now I have troopers coming to my office and accusing me of taking bribes. He knew about the money, Waylon. How did he find out about the money?" Eaton was indeed panicked.

"Calm down, Les. He was only guessing. I was in the trooper investigator's office myself this morning. He asked me to help with a bribery case he is working. He wouldn't give me any names, but if he had proof he would have. I think they're fishing. I don't know what started the investigation, but I do know they would be arresting someone if there was proof. I'm still in control of this situation. The local trooper investigator, after all, asked me to help track down any rumors of bribery. If there was a shred of proof all of us would be marching to the jailhouse in chains. Stay calm and admit nothing. And especially never mention my name, even if you are arrested. As long as I'm the lieutenant governor I am in a position to make a deal for you." Goff hoped those two would never mention him in interviews with troopers, even if they returned for another conversation. He must keep them silent at all costs. "If they come back, I want you to demand a lawyer present. Got that?"

"Yes, Waylon, you're right. I can demand a lawyer and push back the trooper," said Representative Eaton.

Goff sat at his desk for a long time, thinking, but finally got up and went to the door to speak to his secretary. "Mildred, I have some things I must get done. I don't want to be disturbed this afternoon. If anyone asks I'm not in the office."

"Of course, sir," she said as she watched him return to his office and close the door behind him. It seemed out of character for the man who always preferred attention and visitors, but he was the boss after all.

Back inside his office Goff sat in his chair behind the huge oak desk looking out onto the harbor below his office windows. He wondered if he had assessed his visit to Gary Wilcox's office too lightly. There didn't seem to be any reason for the investigator to suspect him, and if he did, why would the trooper ask for his help in tracking rumors of a felony crime? He pondered the problem for nearly an hour with no answers, finally deciding to call Sam Nelson to discuss it with the only one he could trust.

"Hello, Waylon," he answered.

"We may have a problem, Sam. A trooper I know asked me to stop by his office today. He informed me there are rumors of some legislators taking bribes to stop Senator Price's legislation regarding commercial fishing. The bills haven't been filed yet and the vote won't come for another four or five months. He didn't tell me where the information came from, but at the same time another trooper in Palmer met with one of the men I paid. That is too much of a coincidence for me to swallow. The investigator from Anchorage spoke to two of the men we paid to vote our way. I don't know where the leak is, but we have one. It wasn't from me and I must assume it wasn't from you. That seems to leave only one of the two men he spoke with up in the valley. I'm not comfortable with troopers snooping around. Have you heard anything at your end?" Goff spoke rapidly and with a worried voice.

"Calm down, Waylon. This is not the time to panic. The trooper who spoke to you, did he accuse you of any wrongdoing?"

"No, he didn't. In fact he asked me to help him track down rumors of bribery. I told him I would do my best." Waylon Goff was very uneasy now.

"It's my guess that someone reported a rumor to the troopers and they are attempting to track it down. I don't think they have any evidence what-so-ever. Don't lose your cool, Waylon. We're on the final track to stop this farce and prevent Dalton Price from changing the rules. We have to stay on target. Don't let those boys up north spill anything or make any deals with the troopers. Pay them more money if needed, but keep them from admitting anything. My associates here are getting nervous also. I think it's just the pressure of waiting that's getting to them. I want you to call me if you hear anything new. You must keep them quiet."

"I'll do my best, Sam. I have thought about it and can't come up with a reason they would suspect either of us. I've told those two in the valley to keep their mouths shut and to ask for a lawyer if the trooper returns. We may need a little more cash to help with the attorneys. I'll call you if there is anything to report." Waylon Goff wasn't at all satisfied with the way this conversation was going.

"Use caution with our communications. We can't afford to be connected in any way with investigators looking in our direction. Call me if you hear anything new."

Now Nelson was becoming alarmed. It suddenly struck him! Could this be connected with the offer Ioshi had made? If so, how? Was it possible his plan to defeat Price was coming apart? Was Ioshi responsible for the information the troopers in Alaska were asking about? There was too much at stake here for him to take anything for granted. He was going to have to meet with Ioshi Morita again to determine if the leak Waylon Goff referred to was one of his trusted business associates, and, if it is, what should he do about it?

Sam Nelson needed time to consider all these questions and decide what course to follow. His original plan was working and it was one he would continue to follow, but he still he had no answers for the new questions asked today. He thought it was a good day to go to his club for a drink and to ponder the questions from the leather chair in the lounge. It was quiet and private there. He could think and not be disturbed.

The following morning Gary Wilcox brought Darlene a fresh, hot latte when he entered the office. Again, her office looked like a tornado had passed through. Phone records were scattered all about on her desk, the floor and in small piles on two chairs. She was busy making notes on a yellow legal pad placed directly on top of one of the stacks of phone records.

"Good morning, Darlene," said Gary. "Are you busy?" He handed her the cup of hot liquid.

"Why must you come in here and bother me when I'm busy? I had an ex-husband that did that and I shot him." Darlene had never married, but glared over the top of the sweet latte.

Gary chuckled at her remark. "Have you found anything in this morning's phone reports?" he asked.

"Everybody called everybody," Darlene laughed and nodded.

"Who called who?"

Darlene put down her coffee and picked up a yellow tablet, "Leslie Eaton called Goff, Eaton called Mead, Goff called Nelson. I don't have Nelson's phone records yet, but we definitely have a trail to follow."

"Did Goff use his office phone or his cell phone?" asked Wilcox.

"All the calls were made on the private cell phones of the men. Do you think they are all taking bets on the Dodgers chances of winning the pennant this year?" she quipped.

"Make me a copy of the list of times and add names to the numbers for me. I'm going to call Jim Steadman to give him the information. He seems to have stirred the pot with his trip to the valley." Gary turned to go into his office.

He was dialing the telephone when she came in and dropped the list on his desk and exited without speaking. As the phone was ringing in Steadman's office he picked up the list.

"Investigator Jim Steadman," the voice answered.

"Jim, it's Gary. It looks like you got some folks excited up there in the valley. The calls went full circle and beyond. Mead and Eaton called each other and then Goff called them. When they finished Goff called Sam Nelson in Seattle. I know we have only circumstantial evidence, but do you think we could get an indictment on this?"

Steadman thought for a moment, "I doubt it. These men are heavy hitters with a lot of money and good lawyers. I think we'll need more than phone records to convince a judge."

"I was afraid you'd say that. If we are on the right track there should be some activity among the players very soon. Do you think we should give Senator Price a briefing on the situation?"

"It might not be a bad idea. They tried to use strong arm measures at the hearings, so it may not be a bad idea to give him a heads-up, just in case," said Steadman. "I'll call him this morning and if he's going to be in his office I'll fly my Cessna to Homer and meet with him."

"I was thinking, Jim. We seemed to have disturbed the peace with our meetings yesterday. What do you say we, you and I, go down to Seattle and pay a visit to Sam Nelson? Perhaps we can shake his tree as well."

"Do you want to talk with Nelson or do you just want to go to Ivar's Fish Bar? Remember the last time we ate there you embarrassed me by eating so much chowder."

Gary laughed, "You were only angry because it was your turn to buy. I'll give you a chance to get even." Now both men were laughing.

"I'll run the idea past the colonel. If he approves I'll make reservations for the trip."

It was almost noon when Jim landed at the Homer airport in his private Cessna 206. He had alerted Andy to meet him there. Andy drove his patrol car onto the parking apron and stopped alongside the plane. He sat inside while Steadman tied the airplane down.

"Hello, Andy," said Jim as he approached the patrol car. How are you feeling these days?"

"I'm all healed up and ready to fight. Speaking of fight, I hear you and Gary are starting one in Juneau. At least that's what the senator told me."

"That's why I'm here, Andy. I think we're making someone in Juneau nervous and I came to warn the senator. By the way, you might remind the senator to be careful about where he speaks about this. It could get him hurt."

"I have already done that, Jim. By the way, have you met Don Webber, the senator's new aide? He's a sharp guy. You'll like him. I'll introduce you when we get to the office."

Steadman closed the door and buckled his seatbelt as Andy started the engine on the state car. He drove directly to the legislative offices where the senator was waiting. Linda ushered the two to the conference room where Senator Price and Don Webber were waiting. She offered them coffee before taking a seat at the table where introductions were completed. Andy had been right. He did like Webber.

When the investigator finished briefing the group on his investigation there was a short pause until the senator asked, "You're saying there is a conspiracy to sabotage these hearings as well as rig the vote on a bill I haven't submitted yet? Who would go to all this trouble?"

"It looks to us as though someone, someone with a lot of money at stake, is working very hard to derail you, your hearings, and your senate bill. Gary Wilcox and I are working together on this case and we think it's instigated by a group of cannery owners. These men are corporate owners of several canneries around the State of Alaska. You have scared the daylights out of them, Senator. I personally believe they are dangerous and you and your staff should be very cautious. I don't mean to frighten you, but they did send men to disrupt two of your hearings. There is no telling how far they will go to stop you." He turned to Andy, "Keep an eye out for them Andy; you know how dangerous they are."

"That's why I'm here, Jim," commented the local trooper.

"Well I guess if you have no questions I'll leave it in your hands here. Andy, if you suspect anything at all I want you to call me. I came to give you folks a report on the investigation and to warn you. Our investigation is ongoing and we now have suspects. I hope we can close this case before anyone is hurt. Any other questions?" he asked.

There were none and Andy drove Steadman back to the Homer Airport. "Keep an eye on them, Andy," he said as he stepped out of the patrol car.

"Will do," was his reply. He watched the pilot take the tie down ropes from the wings and climb into the pilot seat, wave a hand, and start the engine. The Cessna taxied to the runway and took off, leaving Andy to wonder how real this threat actually was.

Back in Anchorage, Steadman drove his car to the trooper building to stop at the colonel's office. Surely the colonel would know by now if his and Gary's trip to Seattle had been approved. It had, but with some limitations which the colonel took the time to explain.

"Remember," said the colonel, "this is to gather information and evidence, not to arrest a suspect. You are out of your jurisdiction down there."

⋙ Chapter 37 ⋘

The redeye flight from Anchorage arrived in Seattle shortly after five in the morning. Arrangements had been made for a rental car with a GPS map system enabling them to easily find the office of Sam Nelson. It was early when they left the Seattle/Tacoma International Airport which gave the two officers time to stop for breakfast. They had killed more than two hours since landing but it was still early. Steadman did an excellent job of following the GPS directions to an exit on old State Highway 99 near the Aurora Street Bridge where they drove the back streets to Lake Union. It had been many years since Jim Steadman had been in this part of Seattle; not since his college days.

"I used to come down here a lot when I was in college," he said as they drove past the huge boat storage buildings. "Yacht owners like to keep their boats here and go out through the locks to the salt water. The fresh water doesn't eat up your boat or electrical equipment like mooring in salt water. There are a lot of big, fancy boats on this lake."

"I didn't know you went to school here. Are you still a Huskies fan?" asked Gary.

"Of course," replied Jim. "Hold on Gary, I think that's his building. The brown building on the right." Steadman stopped at the curb in front of the three-story structure.

"The sign says OPEN," said Gary.

"Shall we go inside and say good morning?" asked Jim as he pulled the key from the lock.

Inside they followed the signs to an office on the second floor. The outer office was empty, but a door in the rear of the little office was open. A voice from the inside called, "May I help you?"

The two troopers stepped to the open door to say hello and to see a middle-aged man seated at the desk in front of a large window overlooking the lake. "Yes sir. We're looking for Mr. Sam Nelson."

"I'm Nelson. Sorry my receptionist isn't in yet. Come in and have a seat."

The two strangers went in and sat in comfortable chairs in front of the large desk. "How do you do. I'm Sergeant Jim Steadman and my partner is Sergeant Gary Wilcox. We are Alaska State Troopers and would like to speak with you about a case we are investigating."

Sam Nelson showed almost no reaction, but stopped writing and sat up straight in his chair. "Of course," said Sam. "What can I do for you? I haven't been to Alaska since early spring when I went to Cordova to inspect one of my canneries."

"I'm sorry we can't discuss the case in detail with you, but in the course of the investigation we came across one of your employees, a Mr. Gustav Bjornson. I believe he's one of your skippers operating a fishing vessel out of Cordova," offered Gary.

"I know the name. He operates one of my lease boats out of the Cordova cannery. I don't know him personally. Has he done something illegal?"

"We aren't sure except he was involved in two disturbances at hearings being conducted by Senator Dalton Price. The hearings had to do with changes in operating procedures for the fishing industry. It seemed unusual because one hearing was in Valdez and the other in King Salmon, two rather remote fishing towns. In each case he caused a commotion interrupting the proceedings."

"I've heard about the hearings. I own several canneries in Alaska and these new laws, as they were explained to me, would badly affect my operations there."

Jim Steadman had the next comment, "Mr. Nelson, we came to ask you if you know or have dealings with Representative Leslie Eaton of Palmer or Representative Harry Mead of Wasilla?"

Nelson thought a moment, "No, I can't recall the names, but of course I can have my receptionist look in the files when she comes into the office. What do these men have to do with Senator Price's hearings, if I may ask?"

"Actually, nothing, but their names came up in the same investigation. We're here to confirm or eliminate names from our list," said Steadman. "Do you do business with any officials in the Alaska legislature or government?"

"Not directly, only through licensing and inspections for the canneries, and those are handled by my managers." Sam Nelson paused again, "This must be a serious case or crime if you came all the way down to Seattle to talk with me. Am I a suspect of something?" he asked.

"Again, we can't discuss the case sir, but I will say we have no evidence you are involved in wrong-doing of any kind. Jim and I are just doing a thorough investigation into a reported situation in Alaska." Wilcox paused a moment, "By the way, do you happen to know Waylon Goff?"

For an instant there was a look of panic in the eyes of Sam Nelson. Both Wilcox and Steadman had seen it, just a flinch like when a dentist hits a nerve with his drill.

Nelson rubbed his chin, "Hmm, I think I've heard the name, but I don't believe I've ever met him. Who is he?"

"He's one of our bosses. He's the Alaska State lieutenant governor. Sort of the operations director for the governor," stated Wilcox.

"Good Lord, is he involved in something?" asked Nelson.

"Like I said before, we're just confirming or eliminating suspects," claimed Steadman. "By the way, just for my own curiosity, you say you've heard about Senator Price's proposed legislation. Do you think it will affect your business in Alaska?"

"I can't say. I don't have enough information yet. If the rumors are true it will cost us a lot of money and increase operational costs dramatically, but again, we can't make plans on rumors, only facts."

Nelson looked up at the open office door. "Ah, my secretary just came in. I can have her look up those names if you like?"

"That won't be necessary, sir. I think you have answered all our questions for the moment. I thank you for the time. It's been a pleasure meeting you." Steadman reached across the desk to shake the hand of Sam Nelson."

"The pleasure was mine. Feel free to come in anytime." Sam began to relax knowing the two were leaving his office.

In the car and in private, Wilcox gave a quick laugh while buckling his seatbelt. "Did you see the look in his eyes when we asked about Waylon Goff?"

"Make a note of the time we left the office and check it with the time he makes his next phone call to Goff. I'll bet its milliseconds, said Steadman, now chuckling too.

"Our flight back is the redeye tonight. I think you should buy me some chowder and clams at Ivar's Fish Bar on the wharf," said Gary.

"Only if you promise not embarrass me this time," Jim replied.

It took almost an hour to drive through town and down to the water front. The temperature had warmed up and they decided to get the order and sit out on the street to eat. It was always a treat to watch the ferry traffic coming and going while they ate lunch.

"How much of his story did you believe, Gary?" asked Jim as they ate.

"Not much," he replied. "His phone records prove him a liar on almost every point. We know he has been talking directly with Goff, and Goff came to Seattle, we think, to meet with Nelson. Goff has had direct contact with those four legislators and with that many more lobbyists. And remember Nelson had direct contact with Bjornson on at least one occasion. We came down here to put pressure on this bunch to try to get them to make a mistake, and I'm betting they will do exactly that. I'm also betting Darlene finds a lot of other contacts after this trip. When we get home I'm going directly to the office. I'm getting off the plane in Juneau on this milk run back to Alaska."

"The flight from Juneau to Anchorage won't be the same without you. Want some more chowder?"

In his office Sam Nelson followed the visitors to the outer office and to say good morning to his receptionist, closing his office door when he reentered. At his desk he used his cell phone to call Goff.

"I just had a visit from a couple of Alaska State Troopers," reported Sam. "I don't know what you have done to make them suspicious, but they claimed to know your connection with two state representatives. Somehow you've been careless and they're on to you. I can't have that trail leading back to me. Find out what they know and fix it." Nelson didn't give Waylon Goff a chance to argue, but hung up the phone.

His next call was to Ioshi Morita. "Hello, Ioshi," he greeted. "I have been giving your offer some thought and was wondering if you would be free to come by my office this morning to chat about it?"

"I would be pleased to meet with you, Sam, but I have other business this morning. Could we make it this afternoon?" asked Morita.

"Of course, what time would be convenient for you?"

"I can be there by four, if that is good for you."

"I'll be waiting, Ioshi." Upon hanging up the phone he returned to the front office to speak with his secretary/receptionist.

"Can I help you?" she asked as he approached her desk.

"Yes, I need for you to get into the corporation files and bring the assessment files to me. I need to know exactly what our total holdings are worth. I also want you to get our accountant, Bosworth, on the phone for me."

"I'll call Mr. Bosworth right away, but the other files will take some time to gather. How soon will you need them?" she asked.

"I need them for some research for a meeting this afternoon. You won't have to search the files; I can do that myself. Bosworth will do the final search, if it comes to that." Nelson thanked her and returned to his office.

He sat in his big leather office chair staring out onto Lake Union wondering what other details needed tending to cover his tracks connecting him with Waylon Goff and Senator Dalton Price. Then it struck him. Something one of the troopers had mentioned. He called the offices of Lester Goode.

"Good morning, Sam," answered the lawyer.

"Good morning Lester, do you have time to talk?"

"Always for you, Sam. What's going on?"

"I'm having some troubling contacts with the Alaska State Troopers. They came to my office this morning and mentioned Gus Bjornson. He has become a liability. I want you to contact him and make him an offer to disappear. I was thinking to offer him the boat he leases from me and a Peruvian tuna fishing permit. We can give him enough money to finance the trip down there, but I don't want to go much deeper than that. Can you help me with that?"

"Of course, Sam. He must have become a terrible liability to spend that much to get rid of him," commented Goode.

"He has. They've connected him with me and to actions he took at Senator Price's hearings. I told them he was only an employee. I don't want him available to refute that statement. This whole situation is becoming far more expensive than I had ever anticipated. I want to tie up these loose ends before they cost even more." There was anxiety in Nelson's voice.

"I understand, Sam. I think I had better have him come to my office for this talk. I'll get back to you with the results. It will take a few days on this one. I'll get back to you after I talk with him."

"Thanks, Les. I may have more work for you after my meeting this afternoon." Nelson spent the early afternoon worrying, hoping he was now in front of the curve and not behind it. He wanted to go to his club, but decided that should wait until after his meeting with Ioshi.

His secretary finally came into his office with a huge stack of folders and files and placed them on the conference table. "Would there be anything else, sir?" she asked.

"Yes. Did Bosworth say what time he would arrive?" he asked.

"Yes, he said he would be right down and should be here momentarily."

"Show him in when he gets here, and see that no one disturbs us. This may take most of the afternoon."

"Yes sir," she said and went back to her desk.

A few minutes later Bosworth (no one seemed to know his first name) entered to take a seat in front of Nelson's huge desk.

"What can I do for you, Sam?" he asked.

"I've had an offer to sell the company. I want to know what I own and what I should ask for the entire corporation, including this office. My copies of all the paperwork are there on the table. You have duplicates of all this as well as tallies of operating expenses and peripheral costs. Can you give me a horseback figure, including a reasonable profit for myself, by three o'clock today?"

Bosworth whistled in reply. "That's a tall order Mr. Nelson. I can use your files to calculate a total, but it will only be approximate. It will take several weeks to give you an exact figure."

"Good, I need a figure I can work with. A man is meeting with me to make an offer at four and I need to know if he is in the ballpark with his offer. You had better get busy. You can use my office. There is a calculator on that table over there." He pointed to a side table with a computer, a printer and other electronic devices. "Tell my secretary if you need anything. I'll be back in about an hour." On his way out of the office he stopped and instructed the secretary to give him anything he needed. He was going to lunch.

⇒• Chapter 38 •⇐

I n Homer this same morning Don Webber, Linda Barton, and Senator Dalton Price were busy in the office composing a draft bill to submit as a pre-filed senate bill. Don marveled at the amount of research that went into this phase of the legislation. Every figure must be verified, every criminal case must be verified, every statistic must be verified, and on and on it went. Don's part in all of this was to verify all the facts and crosscheck the sources of information for accuracy. When he was in the office he was so consumed with his work he forgot about the time. Only when he was finished for the day did he allow himself to think about Lucy and their wedding planning. As the senator's aide he had a great deal of responsibility accepting calls directed at the senator. He heard the complaints and accepted the kudos for the senator. Most of the requests for assistance he forwarded to Linda for action. His efforts were rewarded with a pay raise for a job well done. Don liked working with both Linda and the senator. This position had been offered to him as permanent and now he was considering the offer, with time off during the summer for fishing.

The job also required him to read all correspondence related to the new legislation. Most of the negative letters came from commercial fishermen, a few from river guides, and a few from personal use users. The only governmental department to reply was Fish and Game. Nearly one hundred letters from biologists working for the department were recorded. Few of them gave constructive criticism, but scolded the senator and his staff for passing the blame for this dilemma on to the fish department and its administrators. Most letters declared the regulators only did what they had to do to protect fish stocks ignoring the fact that none of what had been done has saved the fish but sacrificed them for the benefit of fishermen and cannery owners.

To look at the problem as individuals it would seem they had a good argument, but when the overall picture was viewed all groups were at fault.

There was no single group, public or private, to blame. It was a cumulative result by all users and regulators. The problem had been skillfully ignored since the elimination of fish traps in the mid-fifties. Today the problem had become acute, demanding action. This was the reason Senator Price had decided to undertake the task of rewriting the laws and regulations meant to protect the resource, something that had been ignored for far too long.

Don had done his best to be objective in his new position knowing commercial fishermen would expect him to favor them. For as much as he enjoyed his new career it was always good to go home at the end of the day. Being able to see Lucy each evening was a true pleasure.

In his Lake Union office Sam Nelson had worked all afternoon with Bosworth, the accountant. The two men had used assessment values as a base to arrive at a sale price for all assets in Nelson's corporation. Bosworth had used the office computer to list all known properties and assets listed under the corporate name. Sam scanned the many pages and looked at the final total, deciding he could use this sheet as a negotiating base.

"That's the best I can do with the time we have, Sam. I don't know what you're up to, but if you want me to stay and back your play, I'll be happy to do that."

"If this deal goes through I'll need you to do the final paperwork. You did outstanding work here today. My meeting is scheduled for a half hour from now and I want this to be private, for now. Tell my girl out front how much I owe you for today and she can pay you in cash." Nelson spoke while still reading the printouts he held in his hands. "I'll call you if I need anything more. Thanks, Bosworth."

He was still looking at the figures when the receptionist opened the office door to admit Ioshi Morita. Sam was still seated at the conference table and stood to greet his visitor.

"Have a seat, Ioshi. Would you like some coffee or tea?"

"No thank you, Sam. I have just come from a luncheon meeting and couldn't eat or drink anything else. I see you have been busy."

"Yes, I've had my accountant here most of the day in an effort to put a value on the corporation. I think I have all the assets and liabilities listed here for you to review. A final tally may be slightly different than the figure listed here. Of course, you realize the figures you are looking at are base figures and do not reflect the total value of the company." Sam rubbed his chin thoughtfully. "I'm curious, Ioshi, why the sudden interest in buying me out?"

"I wondered if you were going to ask," he said smiling, an unusual thing for the oriental to do. "I have decided to take my company in a slightly different direction from the path you are pursuing. Rather than create a conflict within our operating agreement with each other and with Eric Goodloe I thought it more profitable to make you an offer for your corporation. I would benefit from the increase in processing facilities and its permits and you would no longer need to take chances with the State of Alaska. If we can come to an agreement on price I am prepared to cash you out completely. My agreement will not forbid you from entering the fishing market again if you care to do so."

"You are very generous and I commend you for your openness. I'll give you some time to review the printouts you see on the table. When you finish we can begin our negotiations." Sam was excited about the offer and curious to hear the opening bid. "If you want to take these figures with you and review them, feel free to do so."

"Thank you, Sam, but I have researched your company and its holdings. The figure I see here is very close to the one I was given. I am prepared to offer you this figure plus twenty five percent for 'Blue Sky.' I think this is a generous offer and I hope you are prepared to accept it. If you do, I will have the papers drawn and arrange for a cash transfer to your bank. We should be able to complete the sale in two weeks."

Nelson was dumbfounded by the offer. It was far more than he had expected and even more than he was going to ask. "I will think you offer over, but it seems fair. I didn't realize you had the ability to make such a deal. May I call you with my answer, say tomorrow?"

"Of course, and may I have a copy of your figures to compare with my own?" asked Morita.

"Certainly," said Sam calling his secretary to make copies of the sheets for his guest.

Ioshi accepted the folder filled with the copies and said goodbye to Nelson. The buyer showed no emotion about the deal making Sam wonder if he had left cash on the table or if he had truly made a good deal. He would go to the club and think about it.

Over the next week there was a flurry of activity in the ongoing investigation for both investigators. The number of telephone calls among the lieutenant governor and his political contacts became daily calls while his conversations with Sam Nelson nearly halted. Near the end of the week and late in the day there was a phone call directed to Jim Steadman. It was from Harry Mead, representative from Wasilla.

"Trooper Steadman. Do you remember me, Harry Mead?"

"Yes sir, I remember you. What can I do for you?"

"I'm in Anchorage and I would like to meet with you. Is that possible?"

"Of course, Mr. Mead. When do you want to meet? I can see you if you want to come to my office at trooper headquarters."

"No, not there. I want to talk to you privately, incognito, so to speak."

Steadman thought about it for a few seconds, "Where did you have in mind?" he asked.

"I have a hangar at Merrill Field. We could meet there, but please don't come in a trooper car. I don't want anyone to know I'm talking to you. Do you understand?"

"Yes, I believe I do, sir. What time did you want to meet and where is your hangar?" Mead gave Jim the hangar location and explained he would be there in half an hour.

Steadman had been set up in the past and sat at his desk considering this possibility. He decided this was a case of a witness becoming frightened by the possibility of going to prison and being disgraced. He called the colonel on the in-house phone to advise him of his intentions to meet with the representative.

"Be careful, Jim," was the advice from the boss trooper.

He took an unmarked car to the airfield and located the hangar. Parking in front of the main door he stepped out of his car and knocked. Mead had seen him through the window in the door and opened it before the trooper could knock.

"Come inside, quickly," he said. With the trooper inside Mead looked out the window for several seconds to be certain there were no spies watching. The entry area doubled as a small office. "Have a seat," said Harry.

Jim sat in a metal office chair and noticed Harry Mead was sweating profusely. "What's on your mind?" Jim asked in a calm tone.

"I want to make a deal," began Mead.

"What sort of a deal?"

Mead hung his head. "I lied to you when you came to my office in Wasilla. I know some things I'm willing to tell you, but I don't want to go to jail for doing so."

"What sort of things?" asked Jim, casually.

"About bribery and vote fixing," said the legislator.

"If you are personally involved I can't make you any promises, but I can speak with the District Attorney and advise him of your cooperation. My investigation leads me to believe you are a participant and may be indicted anyway. My advice is to come clean and possibly get a break from the prosecution. Have you talked with a lawyer about this?"

"No, but I know my rights. I just don't want to get in any deeper than I am now." Harry looked at the desk top, avoiding eye contact with the investigator.

Is it all right for me to record this statement?" asked Steadman.

Mead nodded and Jim took a small recorder from his pocket and placed it on the desk. He spoke into the recorder making note of the date, time, and speakers on the tape.

"OK, sir, why don't you just tell me what you know?"

"First of all, I want you to know I never had any intention of breaking any laws. At first I was offered some small favors by Waylon Goff and I took them. Then there were requests for me to help swing a vote. It was in my favor to do it and I got a cash bonus for the work. Inch by inch I was pulled into some not-so-favorable votes. I'm not proud of my actions and I wanted to get out, but Waylon used my past record to make me comply. Most of these votes had to do with the commercial fishing industry and giving an advantage to the canneries. Any vote that took catch limits away from the commercials I voted against. As you know, all fishing regulations are reviewed by the legislature. I helped see to it the commercial industry did not suffer losses during low fish returns. I was paid for my votes. There are others doing the same thing and I can give you their names. Most votes are close, but we had enough power to swing the outcome our way. That was the way we were instructed to vote." Harry paused.

"Are you willing to give me the names of the other legislators involved and paid by Waylon Goff?" asked the investigator.

"Yes," answered Mead in a quiet voice.

The interview continued for nearly an hour, much of it verified with a folder containing names, dates, times and incidents in which he and the others were involved. Near the end of the interview Jim asked, "Why are you making a statement at this time?"

"I can see another vote-fixing instance coming up. Senator Dalton Price has been attempting to reform the regulations and allocations for years. It looks like he's going to get a bill on the floor this year. I don't want to be involved in defeating this bill. I'm in favor of the changes and ashamed of my previous involvement. I just want to try to make it right. Money has been the motive for all of this. I don't know who Goff represents, but we're losing our resource to greedy factions who think nothing of taking the profits and forsaking the good men and women who depend on the fishing industry as a way of life." Harry Mead was the picture of a defeated and repentant man.

"I thank you for doing this. I know how hard it must have been for you. I'll talk with the DA and recommend leniency for you. I must advise you to resign from the legislature and contact a good attorney to defend you in a case we are certain to bring to court. I'll do my best to obtain warrants for the names you are giving me in an effort to keep you safe. I will, most likely, need to speak with you again soon. Thank you again, sir."

Jim called Gary Wilcox as he drove back to the office.

Chapter 39

Steadman explained to Wilcox what had transpired in the past hour. "I'm on the way back to the trooper post now to see the colonel. If he gives the word I'll get a warrant for Waylon Goff and you may have the pleasure of taking him to jail. I'm sure the boss will call the governor to advise him of the situation."

"Wow! The dominos fell quickly when they began to fall. Call me as soon as you finish with the colonel." Gary was excited about the prospects ahead but cautious. He had seen cases come apart in the past.

Back at the office Steadman went directly to the office of the commander and asked to see him. The colonel listened intently to the account and asked at the end what direction he wanted to take. Jim said, "I think I should go to the DA and have warrants issued for all the men on this list. If you approve of that action I think it would be best if you called the governor to warn him of the impending arrest of his lieutenant governor."

The colonel thought a moment, obviously troubled with the direction this case had taken. "This is how I want you to work it, Jim. You go to the DA's office and explain it to him. The two of you go to the judge and have the warrants issued. When they're signed and in your hands I want you to call me. I'll call the governor and have him send Goff to Gary Wilcox's office where he can officially take Goff into custody. I don't want to embarrass the governor any more than we can help it. This is going to be a public circus when it hits the newspapers and I want to make certain only the guilty are hung out to dry. I want our part in this done as quietly as possible."

"I understand, sir. But our work isn't done yet. Unless we can get Goff to say he was hired by Sam Nelson, we have no case against him. Nelson was clever about that. We have to convince Waylon Goff to give us evidence that will implicate the money man. I also think once we arrest Goff you should meet with Senator Price and explain the entire mess to him face to face. He and his legislation are the first victims in this plot."

"I agree," said the colonel. "Get down to the DA's office. I'll call him to let him know this is important and he needs to see you now."

Two hours later there were five signed warrants issued and signed by the judge. All five names were government officials. All five were charged with accepting bribes and several other associated crimes. In accordance with the commander's wishes Steadman returned to the colonel's office.

The trooper commander read the warrants and nodded. "Stick around, Jim. I want you here when I call the governor. I'll ask him to send Goff to Gary's office to get him away from the capitol building and out of the public eye."

Steadman nodded and waited while his boss called the governor and explained the plan. The governor was disappointed, but agreed to the action. The next call by the colonel was to Gary Wilcox to inform him he should expect a visit from Waylon Goff and he should have a second trooper on hand when Goff arrived. "I want all this done in private if at all possible," said the colonel. "I'm faxing you copies of the warrant right now. Be ready for him."

"Yes, sir," was the only reply.

Next the colonel called the captain in charge of the Fairbanks post. "Justin, this is the colonel calling. I have an urgent matter for your attention and immediate action." He explained the need for a coordinated effort in arresting the four legislators on the list. "I'm faxing you copies of the arrest warrant for Senator Leslie Eaton. I'm waiting for a call from Wilcox in Juneau. When I get it I'll call you."

"Yes, sir," was the only reply.

All was set to begin when the call came in from Gary Wilcox saying he had Waylon Goff in his office.

The colonel's next call was to the trooper on duty in Bethel. The instructions were the same after he learned Representative Lewis Beaver was at home in Bethel. It was a short wait, less than an hour during which time Jim Steadman had driven to Palmer to meet with a trooper sergeant there with his copy of the arrest warrant for Leslie Eaton.

In Juneau Gary waited in his office with another trooper until the arrival of the lieutenant governor. The secretary showed the official into the office and left, closing the door behind her. Gary was behind his desk while the other trooper stood near a file cabinet, waiting.

"Sergeant Wilcox, how are you? The governor said you needed to see me right away. Is there some problem?" asked Goff.

Gary picked the warrant from the desktop. "Sir, I have here a warrant for your arrest," he said, handing him the papers. "I hope you will comply with the arrest procedure without any trouble. Once you are booked at the jail you will be allowed to call your attorney."

The second officer had stepped up behind Goff, waiting.

"I don't understand, Gary. Why am I being arrested?" asked Goff.

"There is a list of charges beginning with bribery and malfeasance and other charges. A list is provided on the warrant. There may be other charges when the investigation is completed."

Goff found himself in an impossible and unforeseen situation. He had little to say. "May I call my lawyer from here in your office, Gary? For the privacy, you understand."

Wilcox nodded to the other officer to allow the call before applying handcuffs to the prisoner and handed the lieutenant governor the telephone on his desk. After finishing the call Goff stepped back and placed his hands behind his back. "OK, I guess I'm ready," he said.

"Take him into the outer office," Wilcox told the other trooper. "I have to call the colonel before we go." It was only a short drive from Gary's office to the jail facility where the prisoner was to be booked. Once the remand sheet was signed the lawmen went back to Gary's office.

In both Fairbanks and Palmer pairs of troopers contacted local legislators with the same result, startling, yet, peaceful arrests. The arrest in Bethel was a little different and had to await the finish of a presentation at the high school by the legislator. The local trooper and a city policeman confronted Lewis Beaver as he exited the school and asked him to come with them in a four-wheel drive patrol vehicle. Once inside the car they announced his arrest and took him across town to the state jail facility.

On his way back to Anchorage Steadman stopped in the hangar at Merrill Field to pick up Harry Mead and deliver him to the Anchorage jail for booking. It was all rather anti-climactic and without drama, but it didn't take the press long to learn of the arrests and clamber for information from each of the jails as well as the office of the governor. The circus had begun.

The following morning the Seattle newspapers had the story; "*ALASKA LIEUTENANT GOVERNOR ARRESTED.*" Sam Nelson was in shock when he finished the article. His first action was a call to Lester Goode. "What's going on up there, Les?" he demanded.

"I honestly don't know, Sam. I only know what I read in the newspapers."

"I want you to find out what you can and get back to me right away. I have a big sale in the works and I don't want this fouling it up. I need information right away."

The news article also caught the attention of Ioshi Morita. He immediately called Sam. "Have you seen the papers?" he asked.

"Yes," said Nelson," this is quite troubling."

"Does this have to do with your business dealings in Alaska?" inquired Ioshi.

"I don't know yet, but I have people looking into it as we speak."

"I think it would be in both our interests to speed up the transaction we spoke of. It would do neither of us any good if it came out that this governmental turmoil is connected to you or your company. I would like to complete our arrangement as soon as possible. It would separate the company from the publicity and, perhaps, you from the publicity as well."

"Good idea, Ioshi. I'll contact my agents and lawyers as well as my accountant if you can have the contracts ready for signing. I want to complete the deal as soon as we can." Sam was worried he might be implicated in the bribery scandal and had no wish to be in an Alaska prison with Waylon Goff and the others. With the sale of the cannery corporation he could easily vanish from the known world.

Meanwhile the governor of the State of Alaska was busy working on a public announcement dealing with the arrest of the lieutenant governor and four state legislators. This message was set to be delivered tonight at six.

A local criminal lawyer had come to the jail to see Waylon Goff. He never passed judgement on the prisoner, but began by asking what his reasons were for bribing fellow officials. At first Goff was reluctant to answer his inquiries until the lawyer, Jason Pittman, became impatient.

"Mr. Goff, you called me to come and defend you against these charges. I won't do that unless you level with me. I must know the extent of the evidence against you. You can tell me you did it or you can deny it, but you must tell me everything or I will not represent you. Your choice."

"I'm sorry, Mr. Pittman. This is so embarrassing. I have just had my entire career ruined and my reputation destroyed. I know some will say I did it to myself, but I have worked hard for the State of Alaska. The things I did were for the benefit of the state. I was paid for my actions, but I never took anything from the state." Goff stared at his shoes as he spoke.

"It won't matter to a jury about your reasons, only that you manipulated votes in the legislature. It was your job to prevent that from happening not to use it for your own purposes. My advice is for you to call the trooper investigators and tell them who paid you, and you and I will try to make a deal with the prosecution to shorten your sentence. I must warn you the troopers would never have arrested the lieutenant governor of the state without very convincing evidence. Now, what do you want me to do? Defend you or leave you to find another attorney?"

"I want you to stay. I don't know what evidence the troopers are holding, but if one of my group gave them information it will be damning." Goff still refused to make eye contact.

"You haven't said who paid you or for what reason, but if you think he'll help you now you had better think again. It's my experience he will never show himself. You're going to be on your own. The only leverage you have is knowing who he is and what reason he had for these acts. I encourage you to help the investigators finish their job and get him. This is your defense we're talking about and you must make the decision."

"I made a promise to this man and he paid me for my efforts. I don't feel right about betraying him now," said Goff.

The lawyer shook his head in disbelief, "Your contract with him to promote an illegal act is not binding, but your contract with the voters of this state is. Remember every member of the jury will be a voter. Your only chance to escape severe sentencing is cooperating with the investigation. I seldom make that recommendation, but you have no good options. The choice is yours. The information was strong enough against you that a judge issued a warrant for your arrest. That information came from somewhere. We can plead not guilty and go to court and I will defend you to the best of my ability. We can enter a guilty plea and leave it in the hands of the judge, or we can go to the DA and investigators in an attempt to make a deal. In my mind the last option is the only one that will benefit you."

The silence in the small room was predictably long. Finally Goff asked, "How much time do you think I'll get?"

"A lot less than you will if you don't make a deal." Jason Pittman was an experienced defense attorney being honest with this potential client.

"I don't know what to say. How much time do I have to think about it?"

"Mr. Goff, the decision is yours. I will represent you at the arraignment tomorrow morning. You have until court time tomorrow. If you decide you will not take my advice by then I will resign this case after the hearing. I'll see you in the morning." He left the jail and his client to think about his options.

⮑ Chapter 40 ⮐

I t was late that same evening when Gus Bjornson walked into the office of the cannery manager in Cordova. He had seen the cannery manager's truck parked in front of the office. The office door was unlocked but when Gus entered there was no one in the outer office.

"Hello, is there anyone here?" he called out.

"I'm back here," replied a voice from the back office.

Gus walked into the manager's office to find Wilford Seaton seated at his desk. "Mr. Seaton, I'm Gustav Bjornson. Mr. Nelson said if I came in here you would have some papers for me."

Seaton stood and offered his hand. "Pleased to meet you, sir. Yes, Mr. Nelson asked me to prepare a file for you." He stepped from behind his desk and walked to a tall file cabinet in the corner. Reaching inside he brought out a thick folder and carried it back to his desk. "Have a seat Gus. Mr. Nelson said your name was Gus."

"Ya, that is my name. He said I should come to the office and sign some papers."

"I had them prepared for you to sign." He opened the thick folder. "This is an agreement stating he is transferring ownership of the boat you usually lease for fishing. The shop has worked on the boat and it is in tip top shape. Even put in some new electronics and overhauled the engine. It will pass inspection at any port in the world as she sits."

"Yes, that is what we agreed," said Gus.

Seaton put the paper on the desk for him to sign and pulled the title to the boat and all the maritime registrations and titles from the file. Next was an envelope containing a check in the amount of $50,000.00 to the name of Gustav Bjornson. "This check is for the amount stated in the agreement you must sign." Finally, he pointed to a large leather chart case sitting beside his desk. "That case contains all the manuals for the equipment on the vessel.

Inside is also a manual instructing you how to use the electronic navigation equipment. You have charts and navigation points anywhere in the world. I have pre-registered your itinerary enabling you to make a direct course to the country of Peru. You will have to check in with customs at any port you enter for fuel or other reasons. Mr. Nelson urges you to proceed at once and as directly as possible. The boat is fueled up and ready for your departure. You fished the boat this year and are familiar with its operation. If all is as you agreed you need to sign the last page of the agreement."

"I agree," said Gus, finding the last page of the document which he promptly signed. I am leaving as soon as I load my stuff on board. I bought food and I'll check to be sure there is drinking water on board. I plan to stop in Portland to pick up a deckhand."

"Here is your copy of all the papers, sir. Have a pleasant journey."

"I'm leaving my old truck on the dock. The title is in the jockey box. You can have it for being so nice." With that short goodbye he picked up the chart case and his thick copy of the folder and departed the office. At the dock he inspected the boat to find it as Seaton had said. Loading his personal belongings he stepped onto the deck, untied the mooring lines, and slowly motored away from the cannery dock in Cordova, Alaska for the last time. Days later a trooper came to the cannery to look for Gus, but was told he was gone from Alaska.

The morning following his arrest Waylon Goff was preparing for his transport to the Juneau courthouse when he was told he had a visit from his attorney. He was relieved when he heard the news, fearing Jason Pittman would not come back. He was taken to the attorney visiting room once more.

Pittman was seated inside, waiting. "What have you decided to do?" he asked.

"There is nothing else I can do, I'm going to cooperate with the investigators," said the prisoner in an orange jump suit.

"Good, in court you will plead guilty and I will have the judge set bail. We will pay the bail and they will bring you back here to be released from custody. I will pick you up at the front door and we will go to my office where we will discuss my fee and exactly what you will tell the trooper investigator. In court you will say nothing unless the judge asks you directly. Understood?" Pittman was giving concise instructions based on years as a defense attorney.

"Yes, I understand," Goff said weakly.

"OK then, let's get you out of here. I'll see you at the courthouse."

The front of the courthouse was crowded with reporters and onlookers who had heard the report of Goff's arrest, but the prisoners were delivered to a private entrance at the rear of the courthouse. There were two other prisoners with hearings, both on drunk driving offenses, both pleaded not guilty and a court date was set. Goff was the last to be heard. The judge, whom Goff knew personally, went through his litany and finally asked how he would plead.

"Guilty, your honor," replied Goff as he was instructed by Pittman.

The judge set a sentencing date and notified the prisoner he would not be the judge sentencing him since they were acquainted. He named the judge and asked if there was anything else.

Jason Pittman stood, "Yes, your honor. I ask you set bail for my client. He is a public figure in a public position. He owns property here in Juneau and is not a likely flight risk. There is nowhere he can go without being recognized."

The judge thought a moment and spoke to the District Attorney, "Any objections?" he asked the DA

"None, your honor," was the reply.

"Bail set at $20,000, cash only. Pay the clerk." With that short statement he stood and left the courtroom.

Pittman turned to his client, "I'll pay the bail and come to the jail to get you released."

A few hours later the two men sat in Pittman's office. "Now, this is how it works, I will call the investigator; his name is Gary Wilcox, a Trooper Sergeant. I know him and he's a good man. You can trust him to do what he says he will do. Don't play games with him. Tell him the truth and tell him what you know. Don't guess at things. It will be uncomfortable, but I'll be here during the interrogation. If you have a question of me just ask. If he asks anything I think is not appropriate I'll say something."

Waylon Goff reluctantly agreed to the terms and Pittman called Wilcox.

When Gary arrived at Pittman's office he carried a large briefcase with the tools of his trade packed inside. One of those items was a state of the art recorder. Introductions were made and everyone shook hands. When everyone was seated at the table Gary turned on the recorder and read the names of all present into the microphone.

"I know this is a difficult time for you, Mr. Goff. I will try to make it as easy and as short as possible. We covered all the formalities in the introduction on the tape. First of all I want to know if you have a prepared statement you wish to read for the recorder?"

"Mr. Pittman and I have a prepared statement which you can read later. You already know the general facts of the case. I do want to say that I was elected by the people of the State of Alaska and I failed in my responsibilities. For that I apologize to the citizens of this state. I hope I make up for some of those mistakes with this statement."

Gary Wilcox asked him to give a summary of his actions. Waylon Goff paused only long enough to compose himself and began to recite all the legislative bills he had influenced. The list included bill numbers and dates as well as the names of the legislators he paid to vote on each bill. His narration included the motive which was for the control of the fishing industry to remain in the hands and dictation of the cannery corporate owners. The monies used to pay for votes came directly from those cannery bosses. He supplied the names of Sam Nelson, Eric Goode and Ioshi Morita and stated his belief the latter two were reluctant participants and that Nelson was the brains of the scheme. His statement lasted more than an hour causing Gary to stop him at one point and change the cartridge in the recorder. Jason Pittman had said nothing during the entire statement. At the end of his statement Goff leaned back in his chair and gave a sigh of relief. "I believe I have covered everything," he said.

Gary had only a few questions on minor points in the statement finally saying, "Thank you gentlemen. I think that covers about everything for now. I'll advise the District Attorney of your statement and advise him you have cooperated fully. I thank you for your very complete statement." He turned off the recorder and put it back into his briefcase.

Jason Pittman finally stood to speak. "Sergeant Wilcox, I thank you for being patient with my client. This is not easy for him. He has lost his position in government and his reputation in the public. The newspapers are going to be after him to make statements which I will advise him not to do. He committed these acts willingly knowing the consequences and has pleaded guilty in court. The only thing left is for the judge to sentence him. I want to keep his public humiliation to a minimum, if possible."

"I understand, counselor. I urge you to call me if you feel your client is suffering harassment of any kind. I'll have this statement typed up and I'll call you and your client to come to my office to sign it. Meanwhile we will pursue further warrants for the names you have mentioned in the statement. If there are no more questions I'll leave you alone. Thank you very much." With that Gary picked up his briefcase and returned to his office.

In his office he handed the recorder to Darlene Dupree, his only office staff, for typing. "Call the colonel for me, Darlene. I think I need to go to Anchorage to meet with him and Jim." That evening he boarded a flight for Anchorage where Jim Steadman met him at the airport at near midnight. The meeting with the colonel was scheduled for eight hours from now.

In the headquarters office a discussion ensued to determine which suspects were to be issued warrants. It was decided the only name that could be connected to Goff and his statement was Sam Nelson whom he stated was the only one he had contacted personally.

Because the warrant was to be issued for a resident of another state the DA would call the Alaska governor who, in turn would call the governor of the state of Washington. Washington State Police would arrest Nelson, and Jim and Gary would go to Seattle to bring the man to Alaska for trial. It was complicated, but the system worked well. The calls were made and the warrants issued. Nelson was arrested in the late afternoon while sitting in the lounge of his club near Lake Union.

Steadman and Wilcox traveled to Seattle by commercial airline to bring the corporate CEO to Alaska to stand trial for an entire page of charges.

While in jail in Seattle Nelson had called Lester Goode to meet with him when he was booked into jail in Anchorage where the troopers said he was to be remanded.

The formalities had been completed and Goode was allowed to visit his client. Surprisingly, Nelson was more concerned about the impending sale of his corporation than he was about his upcoming arraignment and trial.

In the attorney visiting room Sam Nelson gave Lester Goode a sheet of paper with a long number written on it. "This is a bank account number for my new account in Switzerland. I want you to contact Ioshi Morita and be sure all the terms of our agreement are met and when the money is paid I want it sent to this bank account. I have enough money to take care of you in my Seattle accounts. I want bailed out of here, NOW!" he ordered.

The court system was not as impressed with Nelson's list of properties as they were with Lester's credentials as his attorney, and it was three days before he was allowed a very steep bail. His next court date was set and he was ordered not to leave the State of Alaska.

Lester Goode traveled to Seattle to meet with Ioshi Morita and to complete the sale of the business for Sam Nelson. The money was sent from a bank in Japan to the Swiss bank and the account of a numbered patron.

⇒• Chapter 41 •⇐

After hearing the news of the arrest of Waylon Goff and the four legislators as well as the arrest and extradition of Sam Nelson, Senator Dalton Price was elated. The tensions he had suffered were now abated. He called a meeting of his office staff to relay the news and let them know he was now going to draft a final bill to submit to the January legislature. October was fading and winter would soon take over the landscape. He would need nearly all the remaining time to formulate a bill with accompanying regulations that, he hoped, would save the spawning fish stocks in all Alaska waters and rivers.

The meeting was short and celebratory with coffee and rolls. "And," said Senator Price, "Nelson's lawyer said he was going to give the state the names of his accomplices and specific times and dates where he had his cannery managers pressure and pay Fish and Game managers to keep fishing periods open to allow the canneries to keep operating and maintain seasonal workers. This word comes directly from the governor. I'm hoping this information will greatly enhance our chances of getting this legislation approved in both houses of the legislature."

In Anchorage Lester Goode had been in the courtroom to help his client enter his plea of guilty and meet with the District Attorney to make a deal for his client: shortened sentence for giving the state the names of his confederates in the bribery cases as well as who and how the cannery cartel had manipulated fishing period management policies. Once the deal was struck it was determined Nelson should remain in jail until trial because he was deemed a flight risk. He had a lot of money and influence and the ability to travel to any destination in the world.

Once the legal matters were set Lester Goode, working for Sam Nelson, flew to Seattle to meet with Ioshi Morita in order to finalize the sale of the canneries in Alaska to him and his small corporation and direct the payment to a Swiss Bank account. The amount of the cash to be transferred to the numbered account was a staggering $250 million dollars. All went as agreed and the papers were signed by Lester as the representative for Sam Nelson.

It was the cash transfer in which Lester had made one small alteration. The numbered account registered to Sam Nelson was not the numbered account given to Ioshi, but a substituted number registered to one Lester Goode. It took two more days for the final transfer and all the court registration of the property transfers. Once everything was signed and the cash transferred, Lester left the new office of Ioshi Morita, located in a small office building once owned by Sam Nelson, near Lake Union.

Lester drove directly to Seattle/Tacoma International Airport where he boarded a flight, not to Alaska, but to Los Angeles, California. In Los Angeles Lester Goode vanished from the face the earth. He met with a man who furnished him with a new passport and identification cards which he used to attain tickets on a flight to Atlanta, Georgia, where he, once again changed his identity and vanished.

When Sam Nelson could no longer contact Lester he contacted another local law firm to represent him in court and with the District Attorney. Sam had known he was about to go to jail, but counted on Lester to get him a much reduced sentencing. The new lawyer did his best, but in the end Sam had given the state the names, dates and all information about those who accepted his bribes. In turn the state reduced his sentence to fifteen years with fines totaling $250,000.

Sam ordered the fine and the law firm paid out of his personal accounts in the Seattle First National Bank. He reasoned he would not have to serve the entire sentence with good time and his option for parole. What he didn't know was the Swiss Bank account, he had counted on as his retirement nest egg, was empty. A fact it would be many years before he learned.

During the Thanksgiving holidays there was a wedding in Homer. Don and Lucy were married with their honeymoon in Hawaii. Don was now a valued member on the staff of Senator Dalton Price. His main project was verifying information for the new fishing regulations to accompany the bill to be submitted prior to the January opening of the legislative season.

After the honeymoon Don moved into Lucy's house with her, since her place was larger than his small cabin. He and Lucy were both busy with business, Lucy with her insurance company and he with the upcoming legislative season. He had become accustomed to office life but was apprehensive about his duties in Juneau.

The senator along with his two staff members traveled to Juneau in time for the opening of the legislature. Senator Price was hopeful he had written a bill that would save the dwindling salmon stocks. Don and Linda did the leg work around the office while the senator twisted arms for votes on the upcoming measure he proposed. It was going to be close. There were four new members in the legislature, one new senator from Fairbanks and three new members of the House of Representatives. These had been appointed to fill the remaining terms of the politicians who were now in prison for abusing their positions in the Alaska State Legislature.

On the day of the vote Dalton was uncertain how it would turn out. "Keep your fingers crossed," he had told Don. The vote was taken and the measure they had spent so much time and effort drafting failed by two votes.

In the senator's office the three, Dalton Price, Linda Barton and Don Webber held a somber meeting.

"All those hearings, all the expense, all the effort, all of it for nothing," moaned the senator. "I thank both of you for sticking by me during all this. I don't think I've ever been this disappointed. I think we would have won but for the influence of the Department of Fish and Game telling the representatives how much science had gone into managing the resource and that they needed more money and more personnel in order to do a better job. Disappointing to say the least."

"I don't know how you can do this year after year Senator. We held those hearings and listened to fishermen from every user group complain and offer suggestions and yet, in the end we will be doing the same failed things we've done for the past fifty years. When will it all end?" asked Don.

"When there are no fish to be caught and no profit to be made. When there are no more votes to be bought and when there are no more kingdoms to be protected, just as it has been for the past fifty years. I tried my best and failed. I failed to gain more taxes for depleting resources. I failed to control fishing periods. I failed to limit the numbers of fishermen in every user group. I failed to wrest control of the fish from Fish and Game, who has managed the resource to near extinction. The public wants change and yet those of us in charge of making change have failed them and the fish. It's heartbreaking, but we have to try again next year, just like we have done in years past. There are so many good hearted and hardworking people who will be saddened by today's vote. I hate to say it, but this action will create more Willie Hicksons and others who resent us for not accomplishing our goals and meeting our responsibilities." Senator Dalton gave his address from behind his large desk. It was plain he felt real pain from the defeat.

"I know how hard you have worked and how badly you feel, Senator, but you did what you could and I'll go back to sea in the spring in order to make a living by fishing, continued Don. I know you did everything within your power to get this done, but we lost. I'm hoping next season will be a better fishing season, but I have my doubts and for all the reasons you worked so hard to correct. I thank you for trying, sir. I hope you will allow me to be on your staff next year to take up the fight once again. If we give up there will be no voice for the fish. I want to be known for fighting alongside you to be that voice."

And once again the cycle begins. "It's like *deja vu* all over again," in the words of Yogi Berra.